To C

CW00548318

I LET YOU FALL

Best wishes,

SARA DOWNING

QUILLA BOOKS

Copyright © 2022 by Sara Downing.

All Rights Reserved.

No part of this publication may be reproduced, distributed, or transmitted in any form or by any means, including photocopying, recording, or other electronic or mechanical methods, or by any information storage and retrieval system without the prior written permission of the publisher, except in the case of very brief quotations embodied in critical reviews and certain other noncomercial uses permitted by copyright law.

ISBN:
978-1-63161-185-8

Sign up for Sara Downing's newsletter at
saradowningwriter.co.uk/newsletter

QUILLA
BOOKS

Published by Quilla Books
An Imprint of TCK Publishing
www.TCKpublishing.com

Get discounts and special deals on our best selling books at
www.TCKpublishing.com/bookdeals

Check out additional discounts for bulk orders at
www.TCKpublishing.com/bulk-book-orders

For my dad.

Prologue

Six Weeks After the Accident

It's joyful weather, a day for looking up rather than down, for seeing the blue of the sky, latticed with vapour trails, not the grime of the dusty pavements. As the doors open, she blinks her way into the brightness.

Outside at last. Space. Freedom.

The sounds of the city are all the more vivid for her separation from them—a breeze swishing the tips of the trees, horns blaring and a siren whining somewhere far off, the multi-lingual babble of passers-by. This is the real London, not the version she is used to seeing from upstairs, muffled into silence by double-glazed glass, snapshotted into a single scene and bordered by a window frame. She takes a moment to gaze around, as though seeing everything for the first time.

She descends the steps, nervously finding her footing, unsteady in the crowds that for so long she has only observed from on high. With her nose pressed to the window, she would write their stories in her head, create imaginary lives for them to while away the hours. How different it is to be among them now, creating a narrative for herself at last.

An open-topped bus crawls past. Tourists leap to their feet to snap at anything and everything, shutters clicking as they capture the Tudor turrets of Lambeth Palace on one side, the distant Houses of Parliament on the other.

What will they see of her in their photos, she wonders. A misplaced shadow on the pavement? An unexplained shape, like a fingerprint smudge on a lens? It cannot be anything more substantial, she is sure.

A party of school children nears the crossing ahead, neatly two-by-two and dressed in mini high-vis jackets. Her heart melts at their innocence and their constant chatter. Two teachers lead, clutching the hands of the first pair. The group concertinas like a huge, fidgety caterpillar as they wait to be led across the road.

She hears the motorbike before she sees it, at first a low purr on the far side of Lambeth Bridge, louder as it continues at speed across the Thames, then a thundering roar against the idling hum of slower-moving vehicles.

The children are crossing now. A teacher with a smile almost as wide as her open arms beckons them across the lane. The bike takes the corner into the roundabout, leaning low to one side. The biker's knee almost grazes the ground and as the traffic lights flick to red, there is no time for him to react.

In that split second a feeling of certainty settles upon her.

This is it.

Her moment.

Her reason for being here today, outside the safety of her room.

She rushes onto the crossing and throws herself between the children and the bike. She sees a flicker of fear in the teacher's eyes before she closes her own and prays to a God she has never truly believed in.

She hears the rider's muffled groan beneath his helmet as he realises what is about to happen. There is a screech of rubber on asphalt, and she feels the impact deep in her core.

And after, the noise becomes silence.

PART 1

MAKING SENSE

1

The Day of the Accident

The mechanical *click* of a ventilator marked the seconds and minutes since the battle was won.

As the medical team yanked at blood-spattered gloves, Eve shuddered at the squawk of latex on skin. Through the small hours of the morning, she had watched them operate on this woman, drill into her skull in the race to save her, her head a mess of blood and bone. Between the dressings and an oxygen mask, only a small area of the woman's face was now visible. Her skin was so pallid, so dead looking; how was it possible that she could still be alive?

'Well done, everyone,' said the older of the two surgeons, stretching his arms to the ceiling. 'This was a tough one. We were lucky. Go home and get some rest. Lucy, would you mind speaking to the parents first?'

Eve had been surprised to find herself there, unqualified as she was for any role in an operating theatre. But she had witnessed this woman's fight for life, seen her blood spilled, so walking away wasn't an option. Nathan would be wondering where she was, and Buster mewing over an empty bowl, but they would have to wait.

'So, what happens now?' said Eve.

A nurse leant over the patient, checking the machinery, the wires, and tubes which fed into the woman. 'You've been through it, haven't you?' she said, sighing. She turned away and began to sort through a pile of paperwork on the counter behind her.

'How long will she be like this?' asked Eve.

They were interrupted by a face at the window, and a porter pushed open the door. As the nurse turned to greet him, Eve was struck by the man's height, and by his wide smile and twinkling eyes. All for this nurse's benefit, she was sure.

'Glad to see you,' said the nurse. 'Lots to move.'

'Where's she off to then, Niamh?' said the porter, kicking the brake lever on the trolley and turning it around. He grabbed the smaller trolley, which housed the equipment, with his other hand. A canister of what Eve assumed to be oxygen sat on a rail underneath.

'Do you think I should come, too?' asked Eve.

'ICU, obviously,' said the nurse, patting together her papers. She signed a form on a blue clipboard and placed it at the foot of the bed. 'You'll need these. They're ready for you down there.'

The porter turned back to look at the nurse. 'You OK?' he asked.

'Yeah,' she replied. 'This was a bad one.'

'Anything I can do? Gin and a shoulder? I'm off duty after this.' He shuffled awkwardly from one enormous foot to the other.

The nurse smiled. 'Nice try, Farrell, but not tonight, thank you.' She stood back and looked up at him. 'Same age as me, she is. Got me thinking, that's all. When you leave for work in the morning you just kind of take it for granted that you'll make it home in one piece in the evening, don't you? But something like this . . . well . . . but for the grace of God, there go I.'

She crossed herself and cast her eyes to the heavens.

Farrell shivered. 'You've got me all of a wobble, too,' he said, puffing out a breath and patting his chest.

'So,' said the nurse, 'shall we go?'

The door swung on its hinges and Eve ran to catch up with the procession pushing along the bloody and battered woman. The nurse helped Farrell manoeuvre the trolley into the lift.

'Tell them I'll be down to see her in the morning,' she said. 'I just hope she makes it till then.'

Alone in the lift with the porter and the patient, Eve reached out to press the lift button before realising that she didn't know which floor they were heading for.

'You'd better do it,' she said, retreating to the corner.

As the lift doors opened again a buzz of medical staff swooped, whisking the trolley through to a small private room. The dim night-lights did little to mask the gravity of the high-tech equipment surrounding them.

Eve followed them inside and stood by the wall, watching the team attach yet more machinery. There was a disturbing beeping sound, which halted when someone flicked a switch, to be replaced by a gentler ticking as the machines settled down to their collective duty of keeping the patient alive.

Still Eve wondered who the woman was. And why did they need Eve here?

No one had told her she shouldn't be there, and no one tried to shoo her out of the way. Thinking back over the past few hours, no one had really taken any notice of her at all. It was a miracle that they had saved this poor woman, but what did it mean for Eve?

Now seemed like a good time to go. It wasn't as if she could do anything to help, but she was so tired, so bone-achingly exhausted that she wasn't sure she had the energy to move.

Perhaps she'd stay a little longer. Sit down here and get some rest.

When she woke up later, she'd find out exactly what was going on.

2

One Day After the Accident

When the door swung open, Eve jolted awake.

She pulled herself to her feet, expecting stiffness from a night spent on the floor, but it was surprisingly absent.

A nurse bustled in, blonde hair in a tight bun, tiny waist still visible beneath her shapeless scrubs. She pinched the woman's wrist with slender fingers, her gaze fixed on a distant point as she marked the beats. She wrapped a blood pressure cuff around the woman's arm, then checked the monitors before entering her findings onto the vast chart at the foot of the bed.

'I suppose we'd better get you ready for your visitors, for what it's worth,' the nurse said. She tugged a blue plastic apron from a dispenser on the wall, slipped it over her head and wrapped the ties around her waist, then plucked a pair of disposable gloves from a box. Eve put her fingers in her ears, not wanting to hear that awful squawk again.

Gently the nurse tucked a stray lock of hair back from the patient's face, revealing a swathe of shaven scalp. The stark memory of bone beneath flesh flooded back; Eve blinked in an attempt to steady her swimming vision.

Above the dressings the woman's remaining locks splayed across the pristine pillow, a tawny fan around her head. Sunshine on snow. Minus the blood from last night, there was some familiarity to the woman's features, Eve thought, a line to her jaw that reminded Eve of her sister. Her insides clenched.

Eve looked away as the nurse completed her duties. This poor woman didn't need an audience.

'There, you're all nice and clean now, my lovely,' said the nurse. 'Let's hope you don't give your family too much of a scare today.' As she consigned her soiled apron and gloves to the relevant bins, the nurse's smile faltered, as though a cloud had passed over her face. She held the door wide and beckoned to someone in the corridor.

'I'll be off then,' said Eve. 'You need some time with your visitors.' The arrival of visitors ought to be a private moment. This woman's family—her husband, parents, children maybe—would be distraught and Eve didn't want to get in the way.

But then she stopped in her tracks. Her stomach jolted.

Eve's parents entered the room. Why were they here? What would compel them to visit some stranger in a London hospital, miles from their home? On a Saturday morning, of all things, when they normally did their shopping. It had always been a battle to extricate her parents from their weekly routine, no matter how enticing the proposition.

Mary, Eve's mother, turned to look at her husband, her face ashen, age and frailty etched into deep lines.

'Oh, Douglas,' she said, as he joined her. 'It really is her, isn't it?'

Douglas put his arm around his wife, who gingerly picked up the sleeping woman's hand, cupping it in her own.

'She's so cold. Look at her, all these tubes, my poor love. Oh, my goodness.' Lowering herself into a chair by the side of the bed, she seemed to collapse inwards, as though someone had sucked out her skeleton and left the rest of her body to fend limply for itself.

Eve moved towards her mother, but Mary leant away, tears coursing down her cheeks.

'It really is her, isn't it?' she repeated between sobs.

Bile rose to Eve's throat, her chest tightening. But where her heart ought to be pounding, there was calm.

No heartbeat.

'I'd hoped we'd come in this morning,' cried Mary, 'and it would all be some terrible mistake, and it wouldn't be our little girl lying in this bed. And then she'd call us and tell us they'd got it wrong, and that she was fine. It was just a case of mistaken identity or something. After all, it could be anyone underneath all that . . . stuff, couldn't it?'

There had to be a rational explanation for this, but Eve's head reeled as one ludicrous idea after another flashed through her mind:

The woman in the bed was a long-lost relation Eve had never met; her mother had a child from a previous relationship, whom she'd kept secret all these years. A half-sister for Eve, maybe? Her parents had kept secrets from her for her entire life.

But Eve knew none of this was true. Dread crawled into her core like a worm. She bent double, clutching at a chair for support. And then something howled. Something primeval, the noise of an animal suffering. No one reacted. No one else had heard it. Of course they hadn't, because it had come from her. From deep within.

From inside the woman no one knew was there.

Moving towards the bed, Eve crouched down to read the name on the chart, to confirm what she already knew.

'Eve Chapman,' she read aloud, but she was the only one who could hear.

Buried

Everything hurt. She tried to curl into a small ball, cocoon herself from the outside world, shield her body from the pain, but she couldn't move. Arms were rigid at her sides, legs made of lead. And the darkness, like no darkness she had ever witnessed before. Darkness like the cold whisper of death.

What had they done to her? Buried her alive? She was in a coffin. Beneath the dank earth. Condemned to rot away. She would never get out. She was going to die here. It would be slow and painful. No one would know what had happened to her. That she was trapped. Couldn't get out. Blood pumping too fast. Heart pounding.

Dying slowly.

Then voices. People were there. Very close by. They were coming for her. Coming to get her. Dig her out of this hole. Prise open the coffin.

'Help me. I'm alive. I'm in here. Get me out of this place. Please.' Her plea was small and insignificant. It didn't sound like her voice at all. Because her mouth wasn't moving. The only voice she had was inside her own head. No one could hear her.

The talking stopped and there was a dull whoosh. A door closing?

'No, come back! Don't leave me! Please don't go.'

When she stopped shouting in her head, she heard it. Someone was humming. A song she recognised from the radio. How could anyone hum at a time like this? But at least someone was still here. That would mean they would get her out and she'd be fine. If she could hear people, then it couldn't be a coffin. A room, perhaps? A prison cell? Dark, so dark. Terrible, terrifying darkness.

And then a pressure on her hand, in the delicate place

between bones and tendons. She'd felt it before, at the beginning. A squeezing and a rush. A warmth through her veins, heady and strong, like the first sip of gin on a Friday night.

Stay calm, she thought. Breathe. Everything will be fine.

She would think only happy thoughts from now on. Look, here she was at the seaside. There was Nathan. She raised her hand to wave—'Hey, Nathan!' And Hattie, too, her sister. Her friends were all there. Her family. It was a party, everyone was smiling, running in and out of the waves, screaming as the cold water hit their toes, but then running back in and doing it again. Everyone she loved was there and they were all smiling at her.

Good times . . .

And then sleep.

3

One Day After the Accident

Eve sensed someone was watching her.

She raised her head from her knees to see a face at the window. The man's hands cupped the glass, bright blue eyes darting between her and the woman on the bed, then resting on Eve. In her discomfort she smiled, but he didn't return the gesture.

He moved away and Eve jumped up. She watched as he slouched down the corridor, broad shoulders hunched forwards, hands in pockets. She reached to push open the door but stopped short. It was a compelling feeling, of something pinning her there, as helpless as a skewered butterfly. If it really was her body on that bed, then it was no longer as simple as turning around and walking away, was it?

With a rising sense of abandonment, she leaned against the wall and slid downwards once more, pulling her knees to her chest and resting her head. She was tired. So very tired.

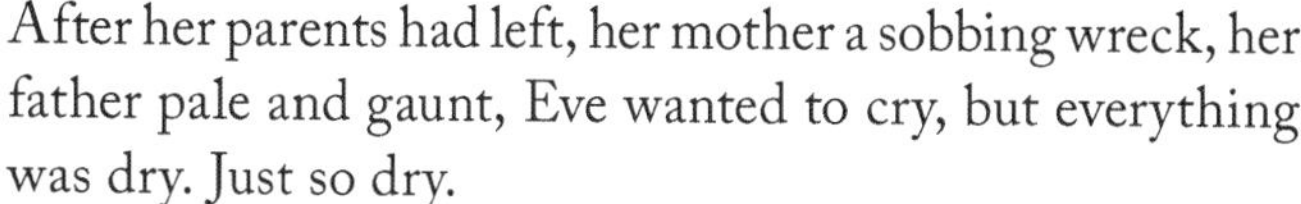

After her parents had left, her mother a sobbing wreck, her father pale and gaunt, Eve wanted to cry, but everything was dry. Just so dry.

Then her sister, Hattie, arrived with fat tears leaking from her eyes. Eve found it unbearable not to be able to offer comfort of any kind, and was relieved when Hattie left.

And finally, after five long hours, the door opened again and there stood Nathan. She thought she felt her heart ping in her chest, but knew it couldn't be real, separated from her as it now was, beating away inside that useless body of hers.

It wasn't until she saw the loose bow tie around Nathan's neck that Eve remembered where she should have been the previous evening. She had been looking forward to the ball for so long—longer than Nathan, most likely. If things were the other way round, she wouldn't have gone without him. Nor would she have turned up here, hours later, with the nonchalant air of someone who had been drinking champagne all night.

Hurt, betrayal, disbelief, sadness. Eve didn't know which felt worse.

'You have the cheek to turn up now, like this,' she said, the words sticking on her lips. 'How could you, Nathan!'

A kind of breathlessness seized her unbreathing frame. She charged towards him, arms clenched across her chest like battering rams. She barrelled into him with all her might, but Nathan didn't move, didn't react at all. Why would he? She was useless, powerless. The part of her with any physical strength was prostrate on the bed. The part of her with the thinking power had no physical strength at all.

'You should have been here sooner!' she yelled. 'Mum and Dad came, and Hattie, too. But where were you? Quaffing champagne and nibbling canapés probably.

God forbid anything should upset your perfect little world.'

As quickly as the fury had risen, it abated, and once again Eve slumped to the floor. She watched Nathan as he circled the bed, peering at the wires that disappeared down the front of her gown, tracking their path from her side to the many machines. Then he squinted at the monitors, all of which pumped out data she knew he wouldn't understand. He followed the line of the IV in her hand to the drip, then another tube from her nose to the cylinders of liquid food. He bent low over the bed, examining the dressings on her head, reaching out to touch them, before changing his mind and recoiling.

'You're hoping it's not me, aren't you?' she said. After all, she hadn't even recognised herself to begin with. 'You're hoping this is all some terrible mistake and you can go home, leaving this poor wretched soul for someone else to deal with. Let it become another family's problem, eh?'

'I'm so sorry, Eve,' said Nathan, collapsing onto the chair by the bed and taking Eve's free hand in his. 'I should have been here sooner.' He wiped at a tear with the back of his hand.

'Yeah, too right you should.'

'I don't know if you can hear me, but there was an incident. At the gallery. Some terrorist thing and they put us all in lockdown. The whole evening was a complete write-off.' His voice was soft, almost inaudible through his tears.

'That's a bit of an elaborate story, Nathan, just to get out of coming to see me,' said Eve. She couldn't understand why she felt so bitter towards him, but she could feel herself softening, even as the harsh words left her mouth. Why would he make up something like that?

'We weren't allowed to leave the building. When you didn't arrive, I kept checking my phone to see what was happening, but there was no message from you. I was so worried, Eve, but when I knew they weren't going to let us out for a while, I was glad you weren't there. And then I got the message from your dad, and I asked to leave but they wouldn't let me.'

He put his head in his hands and sobbed.

'I'm so sorry, my darling girl. So bloody sorry I wasn't here with you.'

Eve wished she could take back the hurtful words she had thrown at him. Of course he would have come sooner. This was Nathan, the man she loved.

'And now you're like this. They say it's serious,' he said, stifling another sob. 'I'll never forgive myself for not being here.'

'Oh, Nathan, I wish you could hear me. It's going to be all right,' she said to him, putting a hand he couldn't feel on his shoulder. 'It has to be.'

If only he could at least *sense* her presence somehow. If only she could make him understand that she wasn't in that body, but by some strange turn of events she somehow stood beside him, around him. A broken, displaced spirit, desperate to reach out to those she loved and tell them that everything was going to be all right.

Nathan rose and crossed the room. Eve went to him and slipped her arm around his waist, resting her head against his shoulder. It was comforting for her, even though there was no substance to the touch. When she looked up at him, his skin was pallid, tears streaming down his face.

'Please get better, my darling girl,' said Nathan. 'I don't know what I'll do if you don't.' Then, as though scared of waking her, he tiptoed from the room, his head bowed.

It was too much, too painful.

All Eve could do was close her eyes, and sleep.

'Hello,' said the man standing beside Eve, jolting her awake.

She craned her neck to look up at him, blinking back the tiredness that dragged at her eyelids. Embarrassed to be caught sleeping, she hauled herself to her feet to find she only reached his shoulders. His eyes were a luminous blue and his blond hair slightly too long, curling up gently over the collar of his white shirt. She was struck by how pristine, how perfect he looked, although there was a vagueness to his outline which she couldn't explain.

Eve cleared the sleep from her throat.

'I saw you earlier,' she said. 'You were out in the corridor. How come you can see me? Like this, I mean.' She waved her hands to indicate her new body, this unfamiliar form which she now inhabited.

'That's right,' said the man, with a voice which was surprisingly deep. 'I'm sorry I walked off. I was hoping it wasn't going to happen to you, but it did.'

'So you really *can* see me? *This* me? How is it that . . . why is it only you that . . . Oh, I don't understand.' Her hands went to her hair as she paced around the room. 'Who *are* you even? Do you work here or something?'

'I'm Luca,' said the man. 'And no. Not really. But kind of, I suppose.'

Eve frowned.

'So why is it only you that can see me? None of my family can. Nor my boyfriend. I thought he might at least be able to sense me in the room, but no. He couldn't see me. Couldn't hear me. Couldn't feel me at all. All everyone can see is that body on the bed. Everyone except you.'

Eve felt a tear begin its trail down her cheek and went to brush it away, but her hand touched thin air. A dry sob caught in her throat as she continued, 'We were meant to have gone to this ball and I thought he had gone without me, and I was so cross with him. But of course, he wouldn't do something like that. I wanted to tell him everything was going to be OK, but I couldn't.' She looked up at Luca. 'I'm sorry. I've only just met you and I'm sure you're not interested in any of this.' Her voice faded to a rasping whisper and her shoulders drooped.

Luca placed a hand on Eve's shoulder. Her skin tingled.

'It's fine, Eve,' he said. 'You can tell me anything you like.'

'How did I get like this? What's it all for?' asked Eve.

'You need to be patient for now,' said Luca. 'It takes time to fully understand it. Just take each day as it comes and try not to overload your mind with too much too soon. Focus your energy on that body over there. On getting it better.'

'So how do you know who I am, anyway?' said Eve.

'It's on that big chart at the foot of your bed. Along with numerous other things that I'm afraid I don't understand. Easy, really.' Luca folded his arms and grinned.

'Oh. Yes. Of course.' He had no right to mock her; she didn't even know the man. She leaned forward and squinted at him, one finger raised, as though to prod him. 'So, does that mean . . . Does that mean you're . . . Are you like me? I mean, are you . . . Is your real body in a coma, too? Is that why you can see me and no one else can?'

'I'm afraid so,' said Luca.

'Oh, God,' said Eve, panic settling in now. 'Please don't tell me that there is a whole load of us, floating about in the corridors, waiting to get back inside our bodies? This is all too much. Jesus Christ, it's like I'm starring in my own personal episode of *The Walking Dead*. I must be dreaming. This is a bloody nightmare. At some point I'm going to wake up, aren't I? Pinch me, Luca. Can you pinch me, please?'

Luca laughed, and Eve frowned. She didn't know how to process the information he was giving her, limited though it was. Everything she had once thought of as normal had disappeared during this most bizarre of days. Nothing made sense anymore.

'I'm afraid it's not quite as straightforward as that,' said Luca.

'No, it wouldn't be, would it?'

'You really just need to focus on yourself right now,' he said.

'I know. You've said that already.'

'Well, it's true. I can help you.'

'What are you, some kind of therapist? Why do you want to help me? I'm no one to you.'

Luca's face was hard to read. What *was* in this for him? Why *was* he getting involved? She didn't need him interfering; it made her uncomfortable. She had to get away. Maybe the fresh air outside would wake her up, and this really would turn out to be some kind of disturbing dream.

Eve bolted for the door and tried to open it, not realising there was no need.

'Eve, wait,' called Luca, but she was already on the other side of the door, surprised at how she had arrived there with no effort at all. As though she had simply glided through it. She glared through the porthole at Luca, then turned her back on him and marched down the corridor.

She made it just a few metres to the nurses' station . . . and then the pain set in. It was like a knife in her side, sharp and slicing. She cried out, and Luca was immediately beside her.

'Oh my God, it hurts so much,' she groaned, stumbling to a chair. 'How can I hurt so much, when I can't feel anything else?'

'It's a different kind of pain. You're not ready to go this far from your body yet. Like I said, you have to give it time. Build up your strength.'

Eve looked up at him. She knew he was trying to help. She knew she should be more pleasant to him, but it was so hard. Every inch of her wanted to shout and scream that this was all wrong, that the woman in the hospital bed wasn't her, that she shouldn't be here, that she needed to get back to her life.

'It will come,' said Luca. 'In time your strength will grow, and then you will be able to come out here into the corridor. You will be able to go even further, to do things that will surprise you. Just not yet.'

'How much time? How long do I have to stay like this?' she asked, her shoulders slumped. 'And anyway, what things? What on earth can I do in a body that doesn't really exist?'

'You do exist, Eve, just not in the form that you're used to.'

Eve sighed. She glanced around her at the real world happening right in front of them, totally unaffected by their presence. A sign over the nurses' station read *HUSH PLEASE* in enormous red font. There was nothing hushed about anything on this ward, she thought, as a porter bustled past, singing 'When You're Young and In Love' and pushing an elderly woman on a squeaky trolley.

An alarm screeched. A pair of doctors in scrubs sprang into action, heading for one of the side rooms close to Eve's.

Nothing hushed about this place at all.

'How come none of these people saw what I just did?' said Eve. 'That I passed through a door, for goodness' sake? How on earth can you explain that?' Her skin still tingled with the feel of it. It repulsed yet astounded her.

'I can't, Eve. I'm sorry,' said Luca. 'I can't explain the physical stuff. I'm no expert on all this. I've just been like this a bit longer than you.'

'Also,' she interrupted, 'how come I can sit here on this chair, without falling through it? How come I can do that, when I just passed through that door like a fucking ghost?'

'Like I said, I'm no expert,' said Luca. 'I've always assumed it has something to do with your ethereal body remembering what it used to do when it was inside your physical body. Like some kind of instinct, I suppose. A pattern of behaviour.'

He shrugged his broad shoulders. She rolled her eyes at his response and turned away.

'Are you all right now, Eve? Can you get up? I'll take you back to your room.'

'I think so,' she said, creaking to her feet. Suddenly she felt winded, as though all the strength had left her. Luca placed an arm around her to keep her upright.

'What did you mean when you said I'll be able to do things that will surprise me? What can anyone do with a body that's made out of—what *is* it made out of? Air? Ether? Fairy fluff and cotton wool? What *are* we made of, Luca?'

Spotting a small mirror in the waiting area close to her room, she sprang ahead of him, before realising she didn't have the energy to make it there unaided.

'No!' Luca yelled, pulling her back. 'Not yet.'

'Why not?' said Eve. 'I just want to see.'

'No,' he said again. 'No mirrors.'

'Oh, for goodness' sake,' said Eve, her shoulders slumping.

'I know you're frustrated,' Luca said. 'You want answers, and I can't give them to you. But try not to worry about anything for now. Come on, let's get you back.'

He put his arm gently around her waist as he led her to the door.

'I can feel *you*,' said Eve, stopping to look up at him, 'but it's the weirdest thing. Different. Not like proper touch at all, but kind of just . . . I don't know . . . soft. We're trapped here, aren't we? How the hell are we going to get out of here? Christ, this really is a complete nightmare.'

'Shh now, you'll wear yourself out with all these questions,' said Luca. 'Let's just get you back, OK?'

'Why us, though? Why not all those other people lying in their beds in a coma? What's so special about us?'

Luca sighed. 'There's a lot you need to know. But not yet. For now, just remember not to go too far. Promise me that you won't try?'

'OK, but please don't make me go through that bloody door again.'

'Not if you don't want to,' said Luca.

'I really don't.'

Fortunately for Eve, a nurse was just leaving her room and the door was still swinging on its hinges.

'There you go, safely back inside. The conventional way,' said Luca, smiling. 'I have to go now, and you should get some rest. I'll see you soon, Eve.' And before she could reply, he was gone.

She was surprised at the noticeable rush of air as he left the room, and then it was as if he hadn't been there at all.

Imprisoned

'Oh, my darling girl.'

It was Nathan's voice, only muffled, as though he were speaking through a layer of cotton wool. A warm droplet landed on Eve's cheek, evaporating as it reached her ear. Was he crying? Nathan never cried.

'I'm in here, Nathan.' Nothing came out. Her lips wouldn't move. Still her body was rigid on the bed, arms fixed at her sides. 'Please don't go.'

His warm breath roved her face, searching, exploring. Inches away, yet out of reach. Then on her bare arm, the one where the darkness sometimes began. The arm they used for the sleep potion.

'Yes, it is me. Really, it's me,' she said.

It was a hospital, she'd worked that out. She was blind and paralysed. It must have been an accident. How else would she not be able to see, nor move? But why couldn't they hear her? Her head hurt with thinking, but whenever she started on a train of thought, the fog and the rush of darkness would put a stop to it, and she wouldn't get very far. Nothing was as it should be.

He was leaving. Footsteps through the cotton wool. Opening the door.

'Don't go, Nathan! Don't leave me here!'

4

The Day of the Accident

'Miss, I'm not really sure what needs to go here,' Will said.

Despite the fast-approaching deadline for GCSE portfolios, a handful of Eve's students still had a few niggling pieces of work outstanding. Will was one of them. He had stayed behind once the afternoon's lesson had ended and Eve could see he had no intention of leaving just yet.

She knew there were problems at home—a brother who was very ill—and Eve tried to be as supportive as she could. She had offered to run some catch-up sessions after school so that he could complete his work away from the distractions of family life, but hadn't planned on this evening being one of those sessions. She had every intention of leaving on time, but it didn't seem right to brush him off just because she had a pressing social engagement.

'Be there in a minute, Will,' Eve said. She glanced at the clock above her desk as she wiped her hands on her apron, leaving a smear of green paint.

A few weeks earlier, Will told her about George, who was two years younger and had been out of school since the beginning of the autumn term with chronic kidney disease. Eve was honoured that Will had chosen to confide in her, but knew she had to be wary of crossing the boundaries. He ought to be talking to his pastoral tutor. She had suggested as much to him, but she was well aware that a boy talking—to anyone—was better than a boy not talking at all. After a Year 12 student had attempted suicide the previous year, she was conscious of how quickly mental health issues could escalate.

'OK, so here you need to write about how this artist has inspired you in your work,' she said. 'Think about the techniques she uses, and whether you might consider using them yourself. They are looking for your opinions. Express yourself. It only needs to be a paragraph or two.'

'Thanks, Miss,' said Will.

'You know you could go home and do it over the weekend if you want to. There's no rush to stay tonight. There's not a lot else you can do on the practical side till that dries.' She indicated the watercolour he had been working on during the lesson, which still needed a little more work. 'If your parents are expecting you home, then perhaps you should go. It is quite late already.'

Will's face fell.

'What is it?' said Eve.

'I, um, I'd rather stay and do it here, Miss, if that's OK? I know it's Friday night and everything but it's just that I can concentrate better here. Mum and Dad will only go on about how George's treatment went today, and I'm just not sure I really want to hear it.'

Eve stood back to look at him. What a huge weight he carried on his young shoulders.

'He's my brother, and all this sucks, but sometimes I just want to go home and be normal for a bit, you know?'

'Well, then,' said Eve with a deep breath. 'In that case, it's fine for you to stay here and do it in school. I can be here till five, but I will have to kick you out then, I'm afraid, or I'll be in trouble with the caretaker.'

'Thanks, Miss.' Will was immediately brighter.

By 5:15, Eve was heading for the Tube, but remembered that she was supposed to collect her new shoes. The sales assistant had promised her they would be in with a week to spare, but then they weren't. Finally, she had called the previous day to say that they had arrived.

The shop was just off The Strand, so Eve decided to hail a cab. Once in the taxi, she messaged Nathan to let him know that she was running a little late but that everything would be fine. She would be there, at the gallery, in time to meet him and stand by his side as he took his place in the receiving line for a host of distinguished guests. She knew how much this evening meant to him.

Nathan called her straight back.

'Not that boy again,' he said. 'Isn't this becoming a bit of a habit?'

'If you mean Will, then yes, him,' said Eve. 'And no, it's not a habit. He needed a quiet place to work. Things are tough at home.'

'Crikey, you need to be careful, my love.'

'What are you getting at?' said Eve.

'Well, kids that age and teacher crushes, you know the kind of thing. Staying late after school. Special attention. Teacher's favourite. Just be careful.'

'Oh, come on, you know full well there's nothing like that going on.' As she raised her voice, Eve saw the taxi driver's eyes flick up to the rear-view mirror, and when he turned down his radio to listen, she dropped her own volume to an angry whisper. 'The poor kid has way too much on his plate for that. It's important he has someone to sound off to. It's especially important with boys, you know how it is.'

'No, not really,' said Nathan. 'Anyway, I'd better go. Promise me you won't be late?'

Nathan was a senior curator at the National Gallery which, to Eve, seemed very glamorous. They'd met when she'd escorted a party of Year 12s to an event there, and despite the presence of twenty or so seventeen-year-olds, the attraction between them was instant. They'd exchanged numbers, and after a successful first date, followed by second, third, fourth, and fifth dates on consecutive evenings, both knew that something significant was happening.

As they sat in the steamy window of *All Bar One* in Leicester Square during date number three, Nathan had made a pronouncement:

'I've never met anyone quite like you, Eve. You light me up.'

'What do you mean?' Eve had said, resting her chin on her hand as she gazed across the table at him. Their drinks remained untouched.

'This might sound really corny, but I just *know*. Don't you? I have this feeling, deep in here.' He patted his chest.

Eve did know. She had known right from the start that Nathan was a cut above the handful of pleasant enough—but not quite right—men she had dated over the past couple of years.

But would it be wise, this early in their relationship, to tell him that he *lit her up* too, even though she found his turn of phrase quite perfect? They had only been out three times, after all. Anything could happen. She might yet discover something about him that she didn't like, although she doubted it very much.

'I really like you, too,' was all she said in reply. She smiled as she reached for the straw and stirred her cocktail, eyes flicking up and down as a warm glow spread from her neck to her face.

Nathan had been delighted when he'd managed to secure a couple of tickets for the charity ball. Although he was reasonably senior—and about to be even more so, since the possibility of a significant promotion had recently reared its head—the tickets were allotted by ballot, and therefore like gold dust. Not everyone who wanted to go would have the opportunity to attend.

'Get yourself something really special to wear, won't you?' he said to Eve, flapping the tickets under her nose. 'We need to look the part amongst all those celebs.' Eve couldn't wait; the school staff barbecue was about as glamorous as her own work events normally got.

But here, in the back of the taxi, Eve just couldn't erase poor Will's face from her mind. It went with the job, she supposed.

They made it as far as Charing Cross Station before the abysmal Friday night traffic brought the taxi to a standstill.

'Think you'll be better off on foot, love,' said the driver.

'That's fine, thank you,' said Eve. 'Just drop me here.' Time saved now meant she might not be too much later than planned getting home. She wanted everything to be perfect for the evening ahead; she had been looking forward to it for so long, and it meant so much to Nathan.

Thankfully there was no queue in the shop and Emily, the sales assistant, had the shoes waiting for Eve behind the counter.

'Do you think you should try them on?' Emily asked.

'Well . . . I . . . I suppose I should, just in case,' said Eve, taking a seat.

'They look a bit snug,' said Emily, as Eve forced her feet into the shoes. 'Are you sure you still want them?'

'Yes, yes, it's just the heat, I'm sure,' said Eve. 'I've been rushing around a bit. They'll be fine later when I've cooled down.' She paraded in front of the mirror, trying to ignore the pinching in her toes. 'They are rather lovely, though, aren't they?'

'Beautiful,' said Emily. 'Is tonight the big night? Maybe you should wear them home, break them in a little? They're such good quality leather, they'll soon soften up. Get a cab, though. Don't even think of getting on the Tube in them.'

Eve paid quickly and was out on the street again in a matter of minutes, teetering on her heels as she checked her watch, relieved to see that it was only 5:45. She spotted a taxi with its light on in the distance, but the traffic still wasn't moving. She couldn't wait for it. She'd manage on the Tube. It was only a short walk. She'd take it carefully.

Everything would be fine. She would get back to her little house in plenty of time, preen and polish herself until she shone. Slip into her new dress and those fabulous shoes. And then, she would jump into yet another cab that would whizz her to the waiting arms of her handsome boyfriend for a glamorous and spectacular evening.

It was all going to be so perfect.

At least, it should have been.

5

Two Days After the Accident

Eve's parents and Nathan arrived at the same time, but that was as far as the common ground extended. Her parents cleaved to one side of the room, silent and still, their faces pale and old, while Nathan paced on the other side, deep furrows lining his brow, fingernails tapping on his teeth. However they chose to deal with their pain, Eve couldn't bear to see them all like this.

It occurred to her that, in some twisted way, things were better for her—as she currently was—than they were for her loved ones. She knew that she was all right and they didn't. She knew that there was life beyond that inert body on the bed. Things must look bleak, though, if all you could see *was* that body.

'Please don't give up on me,' she said, even though she knew they would hear nothing. 'I'm going to be OK, I think. It's fine here. I'm doing fine.'

She hoped they didn't believe she was dying. She didn't think she was, but she couldn't be entirely sure. What she did feel was hard to explain, it was like . . .

Her thoughts were interrupted by the arrival of the surgeon.

'Mr and Mrs Chapman? Mr Kellerman?' said the surgeon as she closed the door behind her. Eve's parents were immediately on alert, hollowed eyes in blanched faces darting from side to side as they searched for clues in the surgeon's expression. Nathan halted by the window, his back to them, arms folded. When he turned around, his eyes were glistening.

Eve remembered this surgeon from the operating theatre. At the time, she had seemed the more junior of the two surgeons who'd worked on her, and she was the poor unfortunate who was tasked with talking to the relatives afterwards. Eve hadn't realised at the time that it was her own parents who would be on the receiving end of the news, and she shuddered now as her memories readjusted themselves accordingly.

The surgeon tucked her blond bob behind one ear and took a deep breath.

'I'm Lucy Thompson. I am one of the surgeons who operated on your daughter,' she said, shaking hands with Eve's parents. Nathan's arms remained folded and he turned away. 'What do you understand about what happened to Eve?'

'She fell and hurt her head and now she's in a coma,' said Douglas. 'How bad is it, Dr Thompson?'

'Surely you're *Miss* Thompson, aren't you?' said Nathan, spinning to face the surgeon. 'Not *Doctor*. Don't you all drop that title when you get too important for it?'

'Nathan!' scolded Douglas, glaring at the younger man.

'Sorry, that was very rude of me,' said Nathan. 'Do please go on.'

The surgeon smiled a thin smile and turned towards Eve's parents.

'We haven't been told much yet,' said Mary. 'How long will she be like this?'

'Well, let's start with the positives,' said the surgeon.

Eve didn't think that would take long.

'Your daughter has done incredibly well to get this

far. Her accident caused significant injuries to her head and brain. However, she is showing all the signs of responding as well as we could expect her to.'

Eve's mother emitted a strange, strangled sound and sat down. Her husband placed a hand on her shoulder.

Eve shrunk back into a corner of the room. What if this woman said something that none of them wanted to hear? What if she said that if Eve did make it back, she would be a shadow of her former self, needing to be spoon-fed and have her basest needs dealt with for the rest of her life? If that was the case, then Eve knew she would rather stay as she was than be a burden on those she loved.

Or worse still, would she pronounce that there was no hope, and at some point, the medical experts might decide it would be kinder to switch off the machines and let Eve slip peacefully away?

If they did come one day and pull the plug, would she be stuck like this, trapped for eternity in an existence without a proper body? Was this what being dead would be like? If so, then at least it was far from a state of nothingness, where the deceased existed only in the memories of their loved ones.

In an ill-timed moment of clarity, Eve found herself suddenly more understanding of those who grasped at the theory of an afterlife.

'The tests we have carried out indicate that there has been some brain damage,' said Miss Thompson. 'We don't know at this stage if this will affect Eve's normal functions when . . . if she wakes up.'

'If,' cried her mother. 'If!'

'When will you know?' asked Nathan.

'We might not know for some time yet,' said the surgeon.

'That's hardly a satisfactory answer, is it?'

'Nathan,' snapped Eve's father, 'I know you're upset, but please give the doctor a chance to explain this to us. It's important that we all understand what we're up against here.' Eve had never seen her father look so furious. Her mother rose from her seat to be by his side.

Nathan glared at Douglas and turned to face the window once more. Eve was torn; her mother and father had each other for comfort but Nathan had no one. She approached him and put an arm he couldn't feel around his waist. When she looked up at him, tears were rolling down his cheeks. It twisted at her non-existent insides.

'It's all right, Nathan, I'm fine,' she said, stroking his face and knowing he would neither hear nor feel the comfort she offered.

Eve thought of all the times in her life when it would have been quite useful to be invisible—a fly on the wall, silently observing, no one knowing that she was there. And here she was now, no one could see her, and she so desperately wished they could.

'We're doing all we can,' said Miss Thompson. 'If she continues to respond as well as she has so far, then we have every reason to believe she will come out of this coma.'

Douglas took Mary's hand and led her back to her chair. Eve was relieved; her mother had never been terribly strong in stressful situations. She had always been a worrier, seeing danger where there was none, fretting about consequences which might not even happen. It terrified Eve to imagine what must be going on inside her mother's head, now that the dreadful thing she had been worrying about all her life had actually happened.

Her father always tried to put on a brave face, but

Eve was sure that this was for her mother's benefit, staying strong for her, so that—at least outwardly—one of them was holding things together. He would succumb eventually, though.

Eve remembered when her sister was ill a few years back—a cancer scare that turned out to be a false alarm—how quickly he had fallen apart. But Eve had never seen him looking as pale and tired as he did today, somehow weathered, like a piece of old fabric that had been left out in the elements and was starting to fray around the edges.

'Please don't be so sad. I'll come out of this,' Eve said, resting her hand on her mother's arm. Her mother was wearing one of her little summer cardigans, despite how warm it must be in the hospital. Eve saw that it had started to go bobbly at the elbows from frequent washing. She wished she could pick off those tiny woollen balls now, like she used to when she was a child.

'Oh, this is so frustrating,' Eve said. 'It's not fair that I can't tell you anything. I'm going to be all right.' To her, her voice was a yell, but she knew that not one single dust particle in the room would be disturbed by it. 'I must.'

How did she know it would be all right? Maybe it was wishful thinking. And hope. Because if she didn't have hope, then what else was there?

'So there really is nothing else you can tell us at this stage?' her father said.

'I'm afraid not,' said Miss Thompson. Eve's father reached forward, as though to cling to the surgeon and force her to tell him something more.

'Is there a chance . . . I mean, is there a chance she might not come back to us at all, Doctor?' said Eve's mother, her voice cracking.

'We would all like the same outcome here, Mrs

Chapman. I'm quite hopeful that Eve will come back to us in her own time. Obviously, we will keep you posted with any developments, but if ever you have any questions, please do get in touch.'

'So you've told us all you can about the medical stuff,' said Nathan, 'but you haven't mentioned scarring. It looks like her face was badly damaged.'

Eve's mother spun round, a blazing fire in her eyes that frightened even Eve. 'Really, Nathan, how could you think of such a thing at a time like this?'

'Our priority for the moment is getting Eve medically well,' said Miss Thompson. 'We can deal with other issues later.'

'I'm sorry,' said Nathan. 'Of course it is. I didn't mean it to come out like that.' He glared at Eve's parents.

The surgeon hesitated. 'If you'll excuse me, everyone, I have my round to attend to. I'll be back later,' she said with a brief nod.

As the door closed, there was a groan of anguish from Mary, and Eve watched as her mother crumpled like a tent without any poles.

'Oh God, Douglas, what are we going to do?' she said. He put his arm around her, pulling her close.

'Please try not to worry, Mum,' Eve said, stroking her mother's hair, though not a single strand strayed out of place. 'I'm not dead. Not yet.'

Caged

She wasn't blind; her eyes just wouldn't open. Eyelids made of lead, like the rest of her body.

The darkness wasn't always the same. Sometimes there was a brighter glare beyond her eyelids, as if she were dozing on a sun lounger. Other times, it was the deep peacefulness of sleeping in a room with shutters over the windows. It reminded her of the holiday she and Nathan had in Santorini the summer before. No glaring sun to wake them, just darkness, and they would sleep undisturbed till late morning.

She might now be able to distinguish night from day, but she had no idea how many of those nights and days had passed, because the death-darkness could come and take her at any moment—a shot in the hand or a prickle in her arm—and then she would lose all track of time. Sometimes the death-darkness would come of its own accord, without any help from the others.

The death-darkness was like no other darkness. When she was in its clutches, she had no hearing, no feeling, no thoughts. Just black nothingness, which she could come round from, or disappear into, as though someone had flipped a switch.

They were angry. She'd heard them arguing. They shouldn't do that. It wouldn't help. They should be nice. To each other. She loved them all.

Couldn't think now. Had to sleep.

The death-darkness was approaching, and fast.

6

Four Days After the Accident

'Come on, let's go,' said Luca. 'Today I'm going to teach you how to do something useful.'

Luca had looked in on Eve several times over the previous few days, but on each occasion, she had either been asleep or very drowsy, muttering a few barely coherent words before drifting off again. He'd have liked to talk to her again sooner, but it was vital to her recovery that she got her rest, and he hadn't wanted to intrude on that. He just hoped she didn't think he had abandoned her.

Today as he peered in through the porthole window, he had seen her sitting dejectedly on the floor, head in her hands.

And that boyfriend of hers, rushing off down the corridor as though he had somewhere more important to be.

Prick.

As Nathan left Eve's room his phone rang, and Luca hung back to observe. A nurse glared at Nathan and pointed to the *Please Switch Off Your Phone* sign just above his head. He flashed her a smile and turned to face the wall, continuing his call in a hushed tone, hand close to his mouth.

'Yes, I've just been in,' Nathan said in a low voice. Luca sidled up to him, his chin almost on the other man's shoulder. 'No, no progress yet. Yes, I can get there, don't worry about that. I'll be in. You know how important this is to me. Yes, I'll see you there.'

Luca tried to see who the call was from, but Nathan quickly pressed the red button and put the phone back in his pocket. He looked at his watch, glanced over his shoulder at the window to Eve's room, and strode toward the double doors. Luca watched as they swung closed behind him.

'What do you mean, something useful?' Eve said now, as he pulled her to her feet. 'How can I ever do anything useful in this pathetic state?'

'Come on, you'll see.'

'But I thought I wasn't allowed to go far. I don't want it to hurt again, like it did the last time.'

'Don't worry, we'll stay close by. There's a lot we can do round here.'

'So, where is *your* body then? How far can you go from yours?' snapped Eve. She began to twirl around and around, her arms outstretched.

Luca watched her quizzically.

'I suppose you've been in here so long, you could nip off to the south of France if you wanted to. Grab a cocktail by the pool and a couple of hours' sunbathing without it hurting at all. You've had a lot of practice, hey? Yay. That really fills me with hope of ever getting back to normal again. I'm going to be floating around this hospital for ages, just like you. Drifting about the corridors like some poor, stray ghost, abandoned, without a hope in the world.'

She stopped twirling and looked up at Luca, one eyebrow raised.

'Have you quite finished?' he laughed.

'Yeah, all done,' she said, blowing a stray strand of hair out of her eye. 'I suppose sometimes this weightlessness thing is quite fun.'

Luca cleared his throat. 'Come on.' He turned to her, taking both her hands in his. 'This will be fun, too, trust me. More fun than you could ever imagine having as a disembodied spirit.'

'So, is that the technical term? Disembodied spirit?'

'Who knows. Let's face it, we're making this up as we go along, aren't we? Back in the day we wouldn't have believed we could ever be where we are now. But whether you like it or not, we are here, and we just have to accept it, get on with things, and hope that one day soon we'll get our old lives back.'

'I'm not sure I'm ready to accept it just yet. I mean, all this is killing my family. And Nathan. Did you see the state of him earlier? I don't think I can just put it to the back of my mind and *get on with things*.' She made speech marks with her fingers.

'Well, I'm afraid that there isn't an alternative, so for now you're coming with me. Let me show you something impressive.'

'Are you always this bossy?' asked Eve, a reluctant grin tugging at the corners of her mouth. She insisted they wait for someone to open the door to her room, then Luca led her along the corridor.

'Now, sit down here and watch,' he said.

'Bossy,' repeated Eve.

She sat on the same chair by the nurses' station, the one that had proven the limits of her pain threshold the last time she left her room. She hadn't dared venture out at all since then, for fear that it would hurt too much and she would be defeated yet again. And although she would never have told him so, she hadn't wanted to try without Luca there to look after her.

This time, however, there was no sudden pain.

She had some vague recollections of him coming to see her on several occasions, but each time she had been so groggy that she wasn't able to talk to him properly. Today she felt much better, and she hoped that was a good sign.

Maybe she would be going home soon after all.

Luca left Eve on the chair and wandered back down the corridor, squeezing through the people coming and going, his body, or rather his form, expanding or contracting as it needed to. His eyes were wide as he played to his audience like the star of a silent movie.

'OK, so you can make funny shapes with your body. So what?' said Eve.

'Watch and learn,' said Luca. 'Just watch and learn.' His eyes locked onto hers, and he tugged at his shirt cuffs and wiggled his fingers, like a magician about to begin a trick.

This time Luca moved much more slowly, observing the passers-by, looking for a target. He stopped by a young woman, a visitor, who had just come through the main doors to the ward.

Her eyes were downcast, her face as grey as the anaemic coffee dispensed with an evil splutter by the machine in the corridor. The woman stopped in front of the door to a side room, steeling herself to go further. Still she looked at the floor, unable to lift either her chin or her spirits. As she reached round to drop the phone she was holding into her handbag, Luca rested his hand on her shoulder and gave it a gentle squeeze.

To say that the woman felt Luca's touch in the normal way would be wrong, but clearly she had sensed something. A caress, a featherlight stroke, a breath of air on the back of her neck. As Luca removed his hand the woman touched her own shoulder, her fingers resting there for a couple of seconds. Then she glanced behind, as though expecting to see someone else. When she saw that no one was there, she turned back to face the door, took a deep breath, and fixed a smile on her face before entering the room.

The woman had clearly gained reassurance from Luca's touch, no matter that its source was somehow otherworldly. That one small gesture had given her the courage to go into the room, ready to face up to whatever she would have to deal with in there.

'That's incredible,' said Eve. 'She felt you, didn't she? How did you do that?'

'It's all about focusing your energies. You'll learn to do that, bit by bit. Do you want to have a go?'

'Me? Do you think I could?'

'Of course you can. You have to concentrate really hard, and you might not get it quite right the first few times, but yes, you're perfectly capable of doing it. Give it a go?'

'Sure, but what if I get it wrong, or I completely freak someone out? I don't want to scare anyone.'

'You won't. You won't be that strong yet, and so you'll have to choose your target carefully. But use your gifts wisely and eventually you will be able to do a lot of good. Come with me.'

'You sound like a sage old prophet,' said Eve, stifling a giggle.

'You're welcome,' said Luca.

Luca led Eve further down the central aisle of the ward. There were many small side rooms similar to her own, before the ward opened out onto a larger, rectangular area where several beds were surrounded by flimsy floral curtains. Eve didn't understand the system for private room allocation but was glad she had a space of her own.

'Look,' he said. 'Those people over there. Do you want to try something with them?' He nodded towards a middle-aged couple who were turning away from the bedside of an elderly woman. The patient was propped up on pillows, conscious but very frail. A Tommee Tippee cup sat on the table across her bed. 'Who do you think they are to the woman?'

'Well, they could be her children. Or a child and their partner, I guess,' said Eve.

'Yes. You can see how sad they are, can't you? First, you have to take the time to watch, and listen to what they say, judge the situation, work out what's going on.'

Eve and Luca moved a little closer to them.

'Surely they can't move her now, can they?' the woman said. 'It looks to me like they're giving up on her, shipping her out, like she's too much trouble.'

'No, love, it's not that,' said her partner. 'They just need the bed. She doesn't need intensive care anymore.'

'Oh my God, this is horrible,' said Eve. 'I feel like I'm intruding. We shouldn't be here. It's all so private.'

'Wait a minute. Keep listening. I think you'll be able to help them.'

The woman continued: 'But then she'll just get abandoned in some geriatric ward, left to fend for herself. You saw her, she's not even capable of feeding herself. They won't have the time for her down there. Won't have all the special care she needs.'

'Well, she can't stay here, love. Just because she's your mum doesn't mean they're going to make an exception for her. We'll just have to make sure we keep coming in a lot, and that she's getting well fed and looked after. I'm sure she will be, they've been wonderful with her so far.'

The woman began to cry quietly, glancing back over her shoulder. 'See you tomorrow, Mum.' But the old lady had fallen asleep again, a trickle of saliva snaking from the corner of her mouth.

'This is so sad,' said Eve.

'Try something now,' said Luca. 'See if you can touch her. The daughter. She's the one who needs the support. Give it a go. Look at your hand and concentrate on it. Focus all your strength into it and see what happens.'

Eve put her hand up and looked at it, turning it over, wondering how this slightly translucent appendage could possibly do anything to anyone. She focused hard and, after a few moments, laid it gently on the woman's back. She felt a slight tingle ripple up her arm. The woman stopped in her tracks and Eve recoiled.

'She felt me, didn't she! I can't believe it! It kind of tickles, doesn't it? It's weird. Closest thing I've had to a *proper* feeling, though, since I've been in here.'

'That's good, Eve, really good. But don't stop. She needs more. Put your hand back on her.'

'Are you sure?'

'You'll be fine,' said Luca. 'Try it.'

This time Eve placed her hand carefully on the woman's shoulder. The woman shuddered as though a shiver had run down her spine. Eve imagined it must feel like that strange sense of recognition that you get during a moment of déjà vu.

The woman took a deep breath and drew herself up to her full height, turning to face her husband. With a resigned sigh she said, 'You're right. Mum will be fine.

I know she will. Come on, let's go.' She took his hand and the pair of them walked slowly towards the swinging doors.

'Look at her face,' said Eve. 'She looks surprised, doesn't she? I think she's amazed herself that she came to terms with the decision quite so quickly.'

'Yes, and you supported her. Your small touch gave her the confidence to accept that she actually knew what she should do, and to make her mind up about things. You helped her see the good in this situation and the positive side to what's happening with her mother.'

'All that from one touch? I don't understand, though. I've tried to touch Nathan, and my parents. I stood between them, put my arms over their shoulders and they didn't feel a thing, and nor did I.'

Luca took Eve's hand.

'I'm sorry, Eve,' he said. 'You won't be able to do this with your own loved ones. Don't ask me why, but if we love that person, then we're not able to make them feel us. It just doesn't seem to work with them, and believe me, I've tried. From what I can gather, we're chosen to look after others, not our own. That's just the way it works.'

'What do you mean, chosen?' she yelled. 'How can we be *chosen*? Isn't it just bad luck that we're in limbo like this? How can there be any *choice* in it all, Luca?'

'Please don't shout, Eve,' said Luca. 'I'm just trying to explain. It's not *our* choice. I should have thought that much was obvious.' He shoved his hands into his pockets and walked off.

Eve stood still, watching him. 'I only asked, that's all,' she said. 'I didn't mean to upset you.' Her voice trailed off to a whisper.

Eve walked slowly back to her room and sat down on the floor, staring once more at the inert body on the bed.

It was all hopeless. Utterly hopeless.

She had to get out of here.

7

His hair tipping back precariously, Rob Barclay chewed on a pen and stared at the ceiling.

Ashleigh, his colleague, tapped on the glass door.

'Boss, do you have a minute for an update?' she asked. 'I have coffee and brownies.'

'Hi, Ash. Of course,' said Rob, coming down to earth with a crunch of ball bearings. 'Always good to see you. Especially with brownies.'

Ashleigh was the senior intelligence analyst on Rob's team. She sat down, pulling her long, auburn plait over one shoulder and clearing her throat.

'I need to get a sign-off for the next phase,' Ashleigh began. 'We're sending in a team tomorrow.'

Rob tried to focus as she explained the details of the operation, but his mind was elsewhere. His young son, George, had dialysis that morning, and when time allowed, Rob liked to go along too, or at least pop in for a while to offer his wife and son a bit of moral support. But this week there was just too much going on for him to contemplate it. He had been in the office since 7:30, leaving Sarah to shoo their older son, Will, out the door for the first of his exams, not only on time but in the right frame of mind to do his best. Then she would take George into St Thomas'.

'Hope it goes well, love,' he'd said, calling just as they were leaving the house. 'Sorry I can't be there today.'

'It's fine, I know you're busy,' Sarah had said. Rob could hear the exhaustion in her voice. He might have a stressful day ahead of him, but he didn't envy Sarah the one she was going to have either.

'How's your boy doing, Rob?' Ashleigh asked, noting his distraction.

Rob sighed, picking at a brownie. 'OK at the moment, but it's so tough for him, poor kid.'

'Presume you're stuck with the dialysis for now till a donor comes along?'

'Yep. This could all drag on for ages.'

'That's rough,' said Ashleigh.

'Yeah, not what you'd want for a thirteen-year-old,' said Rob.

'And how's Will coping with it all?'

'It's hard for him, too. Just hope today goes OK. He's got his first GCSE.'

'Well, you're all in our thoughts and prayers,' said Ashleigh. 'Send them my love, won't you? It would be great to catch up with Sarah sometime, when everything has settled down, eh?'

'Yeah, she'd love that,' said Rob, gazing wistfully across the room. The days when things had been normal, when they could make plans for some kind of social life, seemed a very long time ago.

'Just say the word if you want some time off,' said Ashleigh. 'We've got it covered out there.'

'I know, thank you. But I need to be here. Takes my mind off it. Well, sometimes, anyway.'

Rob couldn't afford any lapses in concentration. Mistakes cost lives, and his superiors would come down hard if it became evident that he hadn't done all he could. He had a wonderful team behind him, but responsibility rested at his door.

The agency worked closely with MI5 and the Metropolitan Police, many of whom Rob knew from the years he had spent in the Met before moving into the private sector. He loved his job, but since the recent terrorist attacks in London, it was getting increasingly hard for anyone to justify not being in the office all day, every day. And sometimes, even later. It ate into their private lives more and more, but such was the nature of the work.

The heightened state of alert meant that another attack was probable, and despite the combined best efforts of everyone involved, something or someone would slip through the net at some point. None of them wanted to be the one to make that mistake or fail to follow up on even the smallest lead.

'We're doing all right, Ash, aren't we?' asked Rob. 'You lot work so flipping hard.'

'Yeah, we're good. No terrorist with any sense had better come anywhere near us,' Ashleigh said, laughing. 'We're all working flat-out, but I love it, boss. We're doing our bit. Making the world a safer place. Well, London at least.'

'It's as good a place as any to start,' said Rob. 'I just need to get my little lad better, then I'll be back on top of everything again, just you wait.'

'You're fine,' said Ashleigh. 'Really.'

As Ashleigh closed the door behind her, Rob took a deep breath. He needed to knuckle down now, to concentrate on the day ahead of him. But first, he had a couple of messages to send.

To Will he texted:

Good luck, son. You're my shining star.
Dad xx

To his wife:

Hope all goes well for Georgie. Keep me posted.
Love you xx

Rob Barclay went back to work.

Voices

'Eve, don't go,' the voice said, but still Eve couldn't work out who it was.

His voice hadn't been muffled, like the ones around her now, who sounded as if they were speaking through a layer of cotton wool. It had been the voice of a stranger, though, disconcerting in its unfamiliarity in a familiar place.

Most of the voices in here were familiar. Her parents, Nathan, friends, her sister. Cali, her best friend from work. People she knew and loved. Then there were the medics that came and went, discussing her to each other and with her family. Their voices, too, had become familiar, and she liked to try and imagine what they looked like based on how they sounded. Old voices, young voices, accents, lisps. It was something to pass the time.

'I'll turn her while you wash,' a strong female voice had said that morning. Broad shoulders, Eve imagined. There was a yank and a pull, and her rigid body was in a different position. A damp sponge had gone into places only someone who knew her intimately should go.

It was utterly undignified.

And then there was the running commentary some of them gave, as though she were on display for all the world to see.

'So, who can summarise Miss Chapman's condition so far?' she'd heard a senior medic say. His voice put him in his mid-fifties, Eve thought. Conventional. Shirt and tie, although weren't ties banned in hospitals these days, for health and safety reasons? Not scrubs, though. Definitely not scrubs. She could picture the eager-eyed medical students hanging behind him, their try-hard voices betraying the level of competition.

'Miss Chapman presented with severe trauma to the head

and was operated on to reduce pressure on her brain.' The student's accent was Eastern European, even through the fog. Eve switched off from the diagnosis as the jargon veered into the technical.

Too much detail did little for her spirits.

The voice that morning though, the day the accident had happened, had been more than a whisper, less than an echo.

'Eve, don't go,' it had said, clear and true.

She'd been leaving for work, but as she'd opened the front door, she felt unable to step out into the glorious sunshine. She could only liken the feeling to a firm hand on her arm, physically preventing her, holding her back, but when she looked down there was nothing there.

Whoever the man was, she didn't know him, she was convinced of that. She'd listened for that same voice in here, amongst the fog-ridden chatter around her, but he didn't come. He wasn't one of them.

She didn't know him.

8

Five Days After the Accident

Eve's friend, Cali, arrived, looking resplendent in a strappy summer dress, shoulders tanned, hair scooped up into a messy bun.

'You look a little better today, dear friend,' Cali said, stroking her unconscious friend's hair.

'You always say that,' said Eve, approaching from behind.

She and Eve had joined Dulstone House on the same day, Eve to teach art, Cali maths. Their obvious newness in the staffroom that first morning had drawn them together and they had been firm friends ever since. Eleven years on, and with school politics and bureaucracy on the rise, it felt good to have a partner in crime throughout their teaching careers.

Cali had visited Eve before, but this time had come with Milo, another teacher at the school, with whom she had been in a relationship for a few months. Eve smiled as Milo put a protective hand in the small of her friend's back, steering her toward the chair at the side of the bed. Eve stepped aside.

'Can't wait to have her back at school,' said Cali, looking up at Milo with watery eyes.

'Can't wait to be back,' Eve said to an unhearing Cali. 'Anything to get out of this place. Even an Ofsted inspection would be more exciting than being stuck in here.'

'We should talk to her more,' said Cali. 'They do say talking to coma patients helps them, don't they?' She leaned forward and took Eve's cannula-free hand.

'I bet you can hear me, Eve, can't you?' said Cali.

'Yes, I can,' said Eve. 'I'm not in there though. I'm over here.'

'I wouldn't really know what to say,' Milo said to Cali. 'It's tricky, isn't it? Bit like talking to yourself. I'll leave it to you. You know her better.'

'You can just say anything, it doesn't matter. Tell her what we're up to today. Or tell her how well she's looking. I don't know. It's supposed to be something to do with the sound of your voice, isn't it? I don't think the content really matters.'

'Oh believe me, it does matter,' said Eve. 'Tell me all the gossip, everything that's been going on at school. I want to know it all. I miss you so much. *And* you can tell me how things are going with this lovely man of yours, for starters.'

Eve took full credit for getting Cali and Milo together in the first place, and she reminded her friend of it frequently. Down in the dumps after a string of failed relationships, Cali was about to give up on men, but not before Eve had decided that she thought the two of them were the perfect match. She'd invited them both over for dinner during the Christmas holidays, and amongst a large group of friends, had made sure that they sat side by side. They'd hit it off, as Eve knew they would, and the rest, she liked to say, was history. Eve suspected it was only a matter of time before there was a little announcement of some sort.

'We miss you so much,' said Cali. 'We all do, but me more than anyone. You're going to be back in no time at all, though, aren't you? You're looking so much better now, Eve, really you are.'

'She looks like shit,' said Milo with a shrug. 'Don't tell her lies, Cali, in case she can hear you and it raises her hopes. Look at her hair. Do you think they had to shave some of it off?'

'Well, she did have a massive operation on her head, so they would have had to. Oh God, Milo, what if she does end up brain damaged or something? I can't imagine life at school without Eve. She's my rock.'

'Hey, I thought you were meant to say positive stuff,' said Milo with a smirk.

'Yes, I know. But it's so sad, seeing Eve like this,' said Cali. 'I love her so much.'

'I love you too,' said Eve. She stepped up to Cali and placed an arm around her shoulder, but her friend couldn't feel a thing. Eve wished she could hug her properly, give her some reassurance.

'Anyway, my love,' said Milo, 'time's ticking on. We should get cracking if we're going to make it in time.'

Cali leaned in close to Eve's body and whispered in her ear, 'I'm off to meet his parents. Petrified, but don't tell him that.'

'I won't,' said Eve, smiling. 'Anyway, they'll love you. Who wouldn't?'

After Cali and Milo left, Eve just sat, staring at the wall.

Back in her real life, she had so little time to sit and think, to just stop and *be*. And now, Eve had more time on her hands than anyone could ever need. It could be too much sometimes, and she wished she could escape the raging thoughts that battled in her head, wished she could actually *do* something, rather than just *think* about doing something.

She had gone over the series of events on the day of the accident again and again, trying—and failing—to find a reason why she had ended up here, like this. She was convinced that her being out of body must have been triggered by something—something she had done, or a particular thing that had happened—otherwise everyone who was in a coma would be out of their bodies, wouldn't they? Eve was relieved that they weren't.

Luca was enough company for now, and she was very glad to have him, but she wasn't sure she could cope with the swarming army of lost souls she had first envisaged.

The details of the accident had been coming back to her in dribs and drabs. There was something odd about that whole day, which at the time she had tried to dismiss with rationality. Had the accident not happened, then she was convinced she would have succeeded. It was only now, in retrospect, that she realised how far the day of the accident had veered from its normal path.

Nathan had stayed over at Eve's house the night before and, as much as she loved waking up with him beside her, his presence always threw her morning routine out of sync. They just hadn't had enough practice at sharing their weekday rituals, although that wasn't for lack of trying . . . at least on her part.

'Your house is just too far out for me to get into work on time,' he would say. So, she tended to spend more nights at his place in the centre of town than he did at hers.

But even that had become trickier since Buster, her cat, had come into her life. Eve lived in Morden, right at the end of the Northern Line, and was lucky enough to have her own place, a former workman's tiny cottage with its own miniscule garden. She would be eternally grateful to Granny Evelyn, after whom she had been named, for bequeathing it to her when she died a few years earlier.

She and Nathan had drunk a lot of wine the night before the accident—way too much for a school night—and then she'd slept badly, as she often did after a boozy evening. When her alarm went off and she'd hit the snooze button a second time, she finally dragged herself out of bed.

As she stood under the shower, even the warm cascade couldn't blast away the strange sensation she had woken up with. She couldn't remember having any dreams, but she woke up unnerved, as though she'd had one which had felt a little too real.

Taking a towel from the rail, she'd rubbed at her hair, dressing and returning quickly to the bathroom to put on her makeup. As she picked up her mascara wand and widened her eyes in the mirror, a sudden movement in the corner of the room caught her attention. The wand slipped and stabbed her in the eye.

'Damn,' she said, putting one hand over her eye, which began to leak black tears in protest.

She spun round to see what it was, but other than her own reflection, she was alone in the bathroom. Shrugging, she turned back to the mirror and grabbed a wipe to remove the smudges from her cheek. Her eye was so sore that she couldn't possibly reapply it now.

Deciding to take the mascara with her for later, she reached to put it into her back pocket. As she did, she felt something brush her arm. It was the most delicate of touches, but it made the hairs on the back of her neck prickle. She rubbed her arm furiously, believing it to be some kind of winged insect that must have come in through the open bathroom window. Eve didn't much care for small, fluttery things, particularly moths. She couldn't bear the rustling of tiny wings and the panic these creatures endured when they knew they were trapped. She reached for the catch and snapped the window quickly shut.

'Eve, don't go.'

The man's voice was crystal clear, as though it had come from inside the room. She spun round, dropping her mascara, which rolled away beneath the vanity unit.

'Nathan?' she called, as she knelt down and grappled on the floor for the tube. Hearing footsteps in the bedroom, she pulled herself up and followed in, one eye still closed. 'Did you say something, love?'

The bedroom was empty. Eve jolted to a halt.

'Nathan?' she called again, louder this time.

'Yep, down here,' came the voice from the kitchen. 'What's up?'

'Oh, nothing,' she called. 'It's fine. Must be Buster up to his usual tricks.'

A shiver ran down Eve's spine as she examined her eye in the bedroom mirror, grimacing when she saw how red it still was. Choosing some earrings from her jewellery box, she wandered across to the bedroom window as she fixed them into place. Buster was sitting on the fence of her tiny garden, one back foot in the air, his toes pointed like a furry ballet dancer while he carried out his morning ablutions.

'You daft cat,' she said. 'One of these days you'll fall off that fence.'

As Eve reached for the window catch to pull it closed, a long white feather, as light as gossamer, fluttered to the floor and landed beside her foot. Buster had recently become quite the hunter; she often found stray feathers around the house. But this one was different, far more exquisite. She picked it up and turned it over in the palm of her hand before throwing it into the bin and heading downstairs.

Eve pulled out a chair and sat down beside Nathan, pushing his pile of papers to one side.

'You OK?' he asked.

'Yeah,' said Eve, frowning. 'Bad night's sleep.'

While Nathan crossed his legs and swiped onto the next news article on his iPad, she drank a gulp of the coffee he had poured for her. She thought better of mentioning the voice she had heard and the strange feeling that overcame her in the bathroom. It was probably nothing. She must have still been half-asleep.

'More coffee?' said Nathan, returning to the news.

'No, I'm fine thanks. I'd better get going,' she said, putting her mug into the dishwasher and planting a kiss on Nathan's lips. He seemed to be making no move to pack up his papers and follow suit. 'You coming? I can wait a minute or two if you want to walk to the Tube with me.'

'No, I'm not quite ready yet,' he said. 'Just need to read this lot for later. I'll be another half-hour or so.'

'Oh,' said Eve flatly.

'Sorry, love, I should have said earlier.' He pushed back his chair to look up at her. 'Your eye looks a bit sore.'

'Yeah, I nearly poked it out with my mascara just now. Looks awful, doesn't it?'

'You look beautiful to me,' said Nathan, putting his arm around her waist and pulling her close. 'You always do. Don't worry, it'll be fine by tonight. You excited?'

'I can't wait.'

'It's going to be great. And you'll look gorgeous in

that new dress. But hey, don't go getting on the Tube in it. Book a cab. I can put it on expenses. Now go, or you'll be late for school.'

He slapped her on the bottom as she left the kitchen, and she let out a little squeal.

'Bye, then,' Eve called as she opened the front door, half hoping he would change his mind and come with her.

'Love you,' he called back.

And then she heard the voice again.

'Eve, don't go,' it said, quite clearly. A sudden chill made her spine tingle. She sensed someone's closeness, an intrusion on her personal space, but again she was completely alone.

'What did you say?' she called out, all the while knowing the voice hadn't come from Nathan. By now he was wholly engrossed in his meeting notes.

'I said *I love you*, babe,' he replied.

'Love you, too,' said Eve. 'See you later.'

Just as unexpectedly as it had arrived, the strange feeling was gone, and Eve closed the front door behind her. Her shoes clicked on the cobbled path to the little garden gate, which squeaked in protest as she opened it. But no more voices spoke to her.

Eve was still a bit flustered as she walked to the Tube station, hurrying even though she was only a few minutes later than normal. She could feel the sun's early heat prickling her bare arms.

In all the confusion she had forgotten to make her lunch, so she popped into a café beside the station and ordered a sandwich and her usual skinny latte with an extra shot, regretting having turned down Nathan's earlier offer of a top-up. Sipping it on the way into the station she felt herself beginning to regain some of her normal calm.

It was just your imagination, she said to herself again as she waited on the platform.

The train pulled in and Eve hopped on. She sat down, putting her laptop bag on her knees. Rummaging inside, she realised she had left her Kindle on the kitchen counter. Now with nothing to read, she glanced up at the advertising boards over the heads of the passengers across from her. As she did, she caught the eye of the man sitting opposite her and he smiled—a rare event in London, so she smiled back, tucking her hair behind one ear.

Eve could tell that the man was trying not to be caught staring at her, though he wasn't doing a very good job. She didn't really mind; it was flattering, and he was far from unpleasant to look at, with blond hair which was slightly too long, and piercing blue eyes. She was surprised to find herself a little disappointed when the carriage doors opened at the next stop and standing passengers blocked her view.

When the crowds parted again a few moments later, he was nowhere to be found.

9

'So, what are they all up to in there?' Eve asked, peering through a small window into a dimly lit room. If it weren't for the thrum of voices beyond the door and the occasional peal of laughter, she would have believed the room to be empty.

'Let's go and see, shall we?' said Luca, pulling Eve through the door.

'You have to stop doing that!' Eve glared at him, shuddering. 'I've told you I don't like it.'

'I thought you'd be used to it by now.'

'Well, I'm not, so please don't do it.' She crossed her arms and scowled.

Luca simply smirked. 'Pay attention, Eve.'

'Bossy.'

Plunged into the centre of a semi-circle of medics, their faces lit eerily by a row of monitors, Eve felt like a late arrival to an interview, flustered and intimidated. It took her a few seconds to remember that none of them could see her and Luca.

A large white screen on one wall bore the projection from one of the monitors.

'That's an interesting one,' said one of the medics.

'Are they really looking at what I think they are?' said Eve.

'Yep. The insides of people's heads,' said Luca.

'Brain scans, then?'

'Yep,' said Luca. 'And they all belong to poor folks like you and me.'

'Gosh, are there really so many in here with brain injuries?'

'Loads. Not just injuries like ours, but illness and disease as well. This is the morning meeting of the neurosurgical team, Eve. They assemble here at eight o'clock every day to discuss new admissions and decide what to do for them.'

'You've been in here before then?'

'Yes, a few times. I don't know why, but somehow I find it reassuring to know that we're not the only ones in this state.'

'If there are so many of them, where are they? Why aren't their souls wandering the corridors like we are?' said Eve.

'Shh, listen,' said Luca, pointing to a middle-aged woman who had risen to her feet. 'She's the boss. She's about to start.' Tall and slim, with expensively highlighted hair, Eve thought the woman exuded authority, even before she said a word.

'So,' began the woman. 'Who is presenting today?'

'The junior doctors have to present the cases,' explained Luca.

'Why are you whispering?' said Eve.

'Seems rude to talk over her,' said Luca. Eve couldn't help the glint of amusement in her eye as she glanced sideways at her companion.

'This CTA shows what looks like an aneurysm,' said a young man, his voice rising at the end of the sentence.

'What's a CTA?' asked Eve quietly.

'I thought we were meant to be paying attention,' said Luca. 'Computed tomography angiography. Glad you asked?'

'None the wiser,' said Eve.

'A right middle cerebral artery aneurysm,' continued the young man, his voice rising again.

'A confident start to that proclamation, Doctor Shah,' said the woman. 'Though your cadence implies some doubt.' Eve approached to read the woman's name badge: Madeleine Ormandie, Consultant Neurosurgeon.

'And what will happen if it ruptures?' asked Ms Ormandie.

'Fifteen percent of people will die immediately and another thirty percent will die within the next few weeks,' answered Doctor Shah.

'He's called Anik,' said Eve.

'Stop looking at their name badges and listen,' said Luca.

'You are entirely correct in your suspicions,' said Madeleine.

'Do they always speak like this?' said Eve.

'Oh, always. It's all a game of one-upmanship in this industry. Brain surgeons are the worst. Top of the pile, I suppose. They know their stuff, though. As you'd hope, seeing as they're the ones doing the brain ops. Watch. It can get quite interesting sometimes.'

'So, what should we do? The radiologists say they can't coil it. What do we do next?' said Ms Ormandie.

'We could operate?' said Anik.

'Do *you* think we should operate?' said Madeleine.

'I . . . um . . . I'm not sure.'

'Well, that's the correct answer, because I'm not sure either. It's not cut and dried here. So, what next?'

'Discuss it with the patient? Give her the option?'

'Precisely the right decision.'

'Oh my God,' said Eve. 'You just imagine they'll know what to do in every case, don't you?'

'Sadly, they don't know everything,' said Luca. 'They can't. I've seen this happen a lot, and sometimes they just have to guess, despite all the genius in the room.'

'So . . . dare I ask . . . were you here when they discussed me?'

'No, I wasn't. I didn't see my own either, thank God. Our bodies are alive though, so we can only presume they made the right choices at the time.'

'But they still don't know if we'll recover, do they?'

'It's an imprecise science, Eve, I'm afraid. We just have to put our trust in the fact that they are trying to do their best by us.'

'Makes you think, though, doesn't it?' said Eve.

'Shall we follow the impressive Ms Ormandie when she goes to see the patient? See who the poor unfortunate is?' said Luca.

Eve hesitated before finally agreeing.

Luca and Eve waited for the meeting to conclude and for the consultant to gather her notes. She left for her ward rounds, a bevy of junior doctors in her wake.

'Stay close, Doctor Shah,' Madeleine said, patting her side and calling him to heel. 'You did well today. We'll see Mrs Wakefield and then I have some relatives to talk to. You can shadow me. This will be good practice for you.'

Eve noted the despondent faces of the other junior doctors; today's teacher's pet had been selected.

'Good morning, Mrs Wakefield,' said Madeleine. 'I'm Madeleine Ormandie and I'm a consultant on the neurosurgical ward.'

The patient tried to pull herself up.

'No, it's OK, stay where you are,' said Madeleine,

placing a gentle hand on the woman's shoulder. 'Did you have a good night?'

'Not too bad, I suppose,' said the patient. 'All things considered.'

'She looks so worried, doesn't she?' said Eve.

'Wouldn't you be?' said Luca.

'So, I need to talk to you today about your options,' said Madeleine.

Eve and Luca listened as the patient tried to understand the surgeon's words.

'She needs our help, doesn't she?' said Eve. 'Poor woman doesn't know which way to turn.'

'Try to offer her some comfort,' said Luca.

'Wait, someone's coming,' said Eve.

A man walked slowly up to the bed, pausing when he saw the medical team around his partner.

'This is my husband,' said Mrs Wakefield. 'Jason.'

'Mr Wakefield, do please come and join us,' said Madeleine.

'What's happened?' he said. 'Is everything OK?'

'We're just explaining the various options available to your wife. One of which is surgery.'

'How the hell is she supposed to decide that?' asked Mr Wakefield, his cheeks turning pink. 'We don't understand how it all works. What the risks are.'

'It's OK, Jase,' said the patient, patting her husband's hand. 'They've explained it all to me and I'm going to go ahead with it. There's no other option, really.'

'But what about the risks? Think of the kids, babe, if you end up a vegetable.'

'Mr Wakefield, we will explain it all to you shortly. I don't want to tire your wife out by going through it all again here, but we'll have a little chat later. Is that OK with you?'

'Try something now,' said Luca. 'With the husband. He looks like he needs it more than his wife. You look after him and I'll take her.'

Mr Wakefield stood up and paced the room, running his fingers through his hair. 'Baby, you don't deserve this.' Then he slumped into a chair, hands covering his face.

Eve approached him and gingerly laid her hand on the curve of his back. She focused on her intent and closed her eyes. A tingle ran up through her fingers and into her arm. She moved her hand from side to side.

Luca held the woman's hand. She had gone very quiet, gazing up at the ceiling. Coming to terms with her decision, Eve thought.

'I'm sorry, babe,' said the husband, looking up. 'I know you've chosen this because you want to get better and come back home. It's a huge risk either way, but if this operation works then you'll be back to your normal self, won't you? And if you aren't . . . well . . . I'll support you, you know I will. I'll look after you, however long it takes you to get better.'

Mr Wakefield stood up and wrapped his arms around himself, as though trying to rub his own shoulders.

'He felt me, didn't he?' said Eve.

'They both felt us,' said Luca.

'We helped them.'

'We did, but I think we're done here,' said Luca. 'Let's stick with Madeleine. We have a new case next, and it's a *tell-the-relatives* thing.'

'Oh God,' said Eve. 'I hope it's not all doom and gloom.'

'If it is, then we'll be there to help.'

Ms Ormandie headed into a small side room, whose layout was strangely similar to Eve's, as was the paraphernalia surrounding the patient.

Another man stood up as they entered.

'I'm so sorry to keep you waiting, Mr. Novak,' said Ms Ormandie. 'Please, let's sit down. I'm afraid it's not the best news. Your wife suffered a stroke after the operation. The tumour was in a very difficult position for us to operate on, and even though we did manage to remove most of it, sometimes a stroke can occur afterwards.'

Doctor Shah stood by Ms Ormandie's side. The young doctor's face suddenly turned deathly white, and Eve could see tears pooling in his eyes. She squeezed his arm, hoping it might give him some courage.

'What will happen to her?' asked Mr. Novak.

'I'm sorry to say this, but it is my professional opinion that she will probably pass away,' said Madeleine slowly.

There was a deep and painful silence that lingered like static in the air.

'How long . . .?' whispered Mr. Novak.

'Possibly a few days, or maybe slightly longer. I'm so sorry.'

'You did all you could.'

Madeleine placed her hand on the man's arm, gave him a pinched smile, then she and Anik left the room.

'I'll stay with the husband,' said Luca. 'You go after Anik. First *tell-the-relatives* for him, I'd guess. He'll need you.'

10

One Week After the Accident

The endless monotony of another day began, for Eve and for her parents, who had arrived for another day's vigil.

'Mum, Dad, you really don't have to keep coming so much, you know,' said Eve, aware that nothing would stop them, even if they could hear her. It wasn't a long train ride up from Epsom to Waterloo, and the station was close to the hospital, but it was too far for Eve's mother to walk with her bad back. It must have been costing them a fortune in short but expensive taxi rides. And seeing Eve like this, day after day, had put a huge strain on them.

Their faces drooped with exhaustion.

'Nathan's not here yet then,' said Mary, putting her handbag on the floor with a sigh and taking a seat. 'Wasn't in yesterday either, was he?'

'He was, Mum,' said Eve. 'He came, like he said he would. In the evening.'

Eve wished her mother wouldn't be so hard on Nathan. He was doing his best, and he did have a job to do. She was sure he would come again that evening, on his way home from work. He hadn't visited every day, like they had, but he came when he could.

'In any case, Mum, he doesn't always have to be here when you are,' Eve said. 'They don't really like more than two visitors, although God knows why. It's not like that useless body of mine is going to find it too crowded in here, is it? She doesn't care. She's out of it.'

It saddened Eve that her parents had never really seen eye-to-eye with Nathan. They tried to hide their feelings for Eve's sake, but sometimes they just couldn't help an ill-timed, hurtful comment.

'When's he going to ask you to marry him?' her mother had asked a few weeks earlier. 'Two years now, isn't it, love? At your age, he really ought to be showing a bit more commitment.'

'Mum, you have no right to say that,' Eve had shrieked down the phone. 'I'm not some lovestruck teenager and what we do or don't do is none of your business.'

She knew that, behind the nagging, her mother meant well, but all that mattered to Eve was that she loved Nathan and she felt safe in his love. For some reason, her parents were unable to see that. Just because she didn't have a ring on her finger didn't mean he wasn't committed. He really was.

Eve was beginning to lose track of what day it was, but it wasn't like it really mattered; she had nothing to do and nowhere to be.

No timetable to stick to, no hours to keep. Free as a bird, only she wasn't free. She was stuck there, watching and waiting. Every day that passed made her ever more conscious of the toll her situation was taking on her loved ones.

'So, Mum, Dad, how are you both today?' Eve said. 'I like chatting with you like this, even though you can't hear me. Feels rude, otherwise, after you've taken the trouble to come and see me.'

'How are you today, Eve?' said Mary, taking the comatose Eve's hand. 'She looks a bit better, doesn't she, Douglas?'

Her mother uttered the same words every time, true or not.

'Yes, dear. If you say so,' said Douglas. His response to that question was always the same.

'I'm good,' said Eve. 'Bored, but good. I wish you could see me like this though, know that I'm still thinking, reacting, feeling—well, kind of feeling, at least. And I've got a friend. Well, it's early days, but we get on. Lots in common. He's, er, nice. Bossy, but nice.'

'Oh, Douglas,' said Mary. 'What must it be like for her to be in there like that, all alone? They say coma patients don't feel anything, don't they, even though they always tell us to talk to her, as though it'll make a difference. But what if she can hear us and feel us, imagine that? The thought of being trapped, not being able to communicate . . .'

'It isn't great, Mum, but I'm not actually in there. I'm out here, and I *can* hear you. It does make a difference,' Eve said. 'Please don't ever stop talking to me.'

'What if we'd lost her that night, Douglas? What if we lose her now?' said Mary.

'We're not going to lose her,' said Douglas, though his eyes stared into the distance. 'We just have to be patient. She's young and strong. She'll get through this. You have to stop being so negative, Mary.'

'It's just so hard,' said Mary.

Eve edged closer to her parents and stood between them, one arm around each of them. She could hear her father's short breaths—a lifetime of cigarettes had taken its toll, even though he had given up a decade ago—and her mother's constant swallowing as she tried not to cry. Eve wished they could sense some essence of her in the room, just some tiny part of her around them.

She wished, too, that she could touch them, and that they could actually feel it.

'I'll go and get us a coffee,' said Douglas, itching for respite.

'Make mine a skinny latte with an extra shot please, Dad,' said Eve with a misplaced laugh.

Mary slumped into her chair with a sigh. 'Oh, Eve, my love,' she said, holding Eve's hand.

Eve couldn't remember her mother holding her hand since she was quite small, and yet she had held it so much recently. Her parents had never been terribly tactile with Eve and Hattie, nor with each other, although they cleaved to one another a lot more these days.

Eve wished she could feel her mother's papery skin on her own. Would it feel much different now to when she was a child? Coming out of school, Mary would hold onto her daughters for dear life as they crossed the busy main road and walked along the pavement towards home.

Eve closed her eyes, and she was back there again:

Her long socks drooped around her ankles, knees scuffed, pigtails coming loose. Hattie was hanging from their mother's other hand, skipping on every other step and chatting away ninety to the dozen, monopolising the conversation as she always did. The picture Eve painted in class that day dangled from her other hand; she was desperate to tell her mother how it had earned her a gold star from Mrs Hendrix, the Headmistress, but couldn't get a word in edgeways because of her chatterbox elder sister.

'Eve, my darling girl, I wonder if you can hear me?' Mary said now.

'I can, Mum,' said Eve.

'I wanted to have a chat with you while your dad's out of the room.'

Eve wished tears could spring into her eyes now—real tears—because she could feel them prickling, even though she knew it was only a remembered sensation, a reflex action. But no bitter salty tears came to wash away the pain.

'I love you so much, Eve. Please come back to us, darling girl. I don't know what we'll do if you don't.' Mary looked towards the door, to check she was still alone, before leaning in closer. 'I'm so worried about your Dad. It's breaking his heart, seeing you like this. You were always his favourite, you know.' A huge pent-up sob escaped her throat, and Eve could feel a lump in her own.

Her dad's favourite? Really? Ordinary little Eve, who had gone through life in the shadow of her older, brighter, prettier, career-minded, and—most importantly now, she thought—married, sister. Now she really could do with those tears; her eyes ached to have a good cry and let all the emotion out.

'Oh Mum, I love you, too. I do wish I could tell you that now. If I ever get back—no, when I get back—I'm going to tell you every day that I love you. And Dad, too.' Fake sobs stuck in Eve's throat, grating like sandpaper.

Douglas came back into the room and Mary sat up straighter in her chair, brushing her eyes with the backs of her hands. One more sniff and she was back in control.

'She's definitely in there, Douglas,' Mary said firmly, smiling up at him with damp eyes. 'I could swear I saw her eyelids flicker when I spoke to her. I told her how much we love her . . . and . . . and . . .'

And then it was all too much, and Eve watched as her beloved mother collapsed against her father's shoulder, her body convulsing as she gave in to her tears.

'Let it out, Mum,' said Eve, rubbing her back. 'Let it all out.'

11

'I'm worried about him, Rob,' said Sarah. Once again, their eldest son had arrived home late from school with a muttered 'Hey' before shooting up the stairs to his bedroom and slamming the door behind him.

Sarah stabbed at a packet of tagliatelle with a knife, and the contents exploded onto the floor. 'Damn it,' she said, bending down with a sigh, trying to salvage what she could before Rubix, the family's black Labrador, crunched his way through the lot.

'It's just his way of coping,' said Rob, grabbing the wine from the fridge and topping up their glasses. 'He misses normal life. It's a lot for a sixteen-year-old to handle, that's all.'

'That's *all*?' said Sarah. 'We have a thirteen-year-old who might not make it to his fourteenth birthday, let alone adulthood, a teenager in the midst of GCSEs and all the crap that entails, and all you can say is *that's all*.'

'Come on, love, don't twist everything I say. All I was trying to say, if you'd let me, is that Will's bound to find it hard. We all are, for goodness' sake. We've had this conversation so many times, and the two of us sniping at each other isn't going to help anyone, is it? Will needs us to pull together just as much as George does. How else is he going to cope with the pressure of the next couple of months?'

Sarah turned to face her husband, still holding the knife.

'So, it's all my fault,' she said, jabbing the knife in his direction. 'It's all my fault that we keep arguing like this.

It's all right for you. At least you get to escape out of this house every day and go to work. I'm here with it, all the time. And I'm not saying I don't want to be, but . . .'

Sarah had to take so much time off work following George's diagnosis that she decided to put her own career on hold. Someone had to be home with him and available to take him to the hospital three times a week for his dialysis, and despite how much she knew she would miss life in the workplace, she wanted that person to be her. She would never forgive herself if the worst were to happen—which was a consequence she couldn't bear to think about—and she hadn't been there for Georgie.

'I know, love,' said Rob, taking the knife from Sarah's hand and putting his hands on her shoulders. 'I've said before that I could take some time off, to give you a break. Or work from home for a bit. I will if you want me to. You could get away for a few days.'

'I can't go away. Not till this is all over. I can't leave him, Rob. Some days I just feel so helpless, but I have to be here. I can't bear it. My poor baby.'

Rob watched as his strong, capable wife crumpled, folding in on herself with grief and desperation.

'Shh, shh,' he cooed into her hair, holding her tight. 'We're in this together, remember. We'll get through it.'

'I'm sorry to take it out on you. I try so hard all day to be strong when it's just me and him here. And then I go and blow my top and you're always on the receiving end of it.'

'It's fine. I feel pretty helpless too, you know. You wouldn't believe the number of times I wished I was a surgeon or a kidney specialist these past few months. What kind of dad am I if I can't save my own son?'

'You're an amazing dad,' said Sarah, cupping her

hands over his unshaven cheeks. 'And you do help him. You help us all.' She took a deep breath and sighed. 'I think maybe we're giving ourselves too much of a hard time here.'

'I think we probably are,' agreed Rob. 'One day soon this will all be over. George will get better, and life will go back to normal. Will's going to pass his exams with flying colours, and this will all be behind us.'

'Do you really think so?' said Sarah. 'I wish I shared your positivity. But I can't bear to think of an alternative ending, either.' A huge sob lodged in her throat, causing her to cough.

'Of course he will. He's our little fighter. To be honest, I've never thought of anything else, other than him getting better. I know he's going to. Know it deep down in here.' He patted his chest.

'Oh, I do love you, Rob Barclay,' she said, planting a kiss on his lips. 'I'm sorry I'm such a miserable cow sometimes. Well, most of the time, actually.'

Rob laughed. 'No, you're not. You're really not, my love.'

Mortified

'BP and oxygen steady. Heart rate up slightly. Vital signs are good. We ought to start seeing some signs of improvement soon.'

About seven or eight of them, Eve thought. One senior woman and some younger ones, vying for attention like overeager schoolchildren. She could sense their eyes boring into her, but there was no running away from it. She was like a museum exhibit in a glass case.

'Of course my heart rate is up,' she said to no one but herself. 'It's always up when you lot are in here, because I don't know what you're going to do to me next and I'm scared.' Her heart began to race the moment it became evident that this latest bunch to come into her room were here to inspect her, not to sit by her bedside and tell her all about the life she was missing out on.

Nurses were the worst, because that generally meant medication and the death-darkness again, or worse still, hygiene-related procedures. They might want to give her a wash, or change the catheter and empty the disgusting bag of yellow liquid that she could only imagine must hang by the side of her bed.

Would she ever pee by herself again? In private, behind a locked door? It seemed an unimaginable luxury.

The students departed but a nurse remained behind. Eve's body was turned to one side and there was a rustle of plastic and paper as the sanitary sheet beneath her bottom was yanked out and a new one inserted. It was all so undignified. She was at their mercy.

She had to get out of here.

12

Two Weeks After the Accident

Nathan hadn't been in to visit for a few days, or at least if he had, Eve had slept through it and missed him.

She stood by the window now, looking for his face amongst the people alighting from taxis, getting off buses and coming up the steps to the hospital, willing each of them to be him— although there was very little chance of Nathan ever taking public transport.

It was only a twenty-minute walk from the gallery and a pleasant one, she thought. Down Whitehall and across Westminster Bridge, easy enough to do on his lunch break or after work. But now and again Nathan could be lazy, taking cabs for the shortest of journeys, which often prolonged them considerably. Eve found this occasionally amusing, but usually annoying. The beating heart of London wasn't huge, and she loved to walk whenever she could, always looking up instead of down at her feet. Despite all the time she spent in the capital, she was still in awe of its constantly evolving landscapes. She loved to see these huge new constructions peeling upwards, reaching for the sky in places where she thought there was no more room to build.

One weekend she had gone with Nathan to look round a show-apartment in One Thames City, even though it was slightly out of his price range. Eve had followed the estate agent round in awe, gazing longingly at the view from the full-length curved windows, imagining how wonderful life would be if she lived up there, high above the streets. Even more so if Nathan had suggested they combine their salaries and move in together. That thought had bugged her for a while until practicality had kicked in—Buster would hate it.

A luxury apartment in the sky was no place for a cat.

Today, the little part of London visible to Eve was as busy as any other day, stop-and-go traffic waiting patiently to queue through the roadworks at Park Plaza. The idling engines, the hiss of bus brakes and the occasional screech of a siren were muted through the closed, double-glazed hospital window. None of it could touch her, up here in her little room, but she so wished it could.

Nathan would hate the chaos of it all, jostling his way through the tourists on the Bridge, all vying for the best spot to have their photo taken in front of the Houses of Parliament.

'Why can't they realise some of us have to live and work here,' he had moaned before, when their path was slowed by dawdling sightseers. 'Some of us have places to be.'

'Don't complain, Nathan,' Eve had said, nudging him in the ribs. 'Visitor numbers will be up at the gallery, so just think of your bonus.'

Each time a man in a suit ascended the hospital steps, Eve thought she saw Nathan's broad shoulders, his long-legged stride, but each time it was wishful thinking. He was instantly recognisable in a crowd, just as he had been that very first time she ever laid eyes on him.

From the moment they'd first met she had been intrigued by this dark, enigmatic man, wanting to know everything about him. When he gave a talk to her pupils about symbolism in Renaissance art, she realised she hadn't heard a word of what he had told them. Instead, her gaze was riveted to the movement of his lips as he spoke, the expressive way his eyebrows rose and fell, the twinkle in his dark brown eyes which, most of the time—she soon came to realise—were fixed on her.

Afterwards, on the bus back to school, she pulled the business card he'd given her from her jacket pocket and entered his contact details into her phone straightaway, for fear of losing them. Then she sat staring dreamily out of the window, hoping that her students would be too busy checking in on TikTok to want to talk to her. She knew if Nathan didn't call in the next couple of days, as he had said he would, then she would have to call him. As it was, he phoned her that very evening, and so began their string of consecutive dates.

Now, as their second anniversary approached, she couldn't bear the thought of not being awake to share it with him.

'Where are you, Nathan?' she whispered, leaning her forehead against the windowpane and gazing down at the pavement below. She wished she could feel the coolness of the glass on her skin, wished her warm breath would steam up the window of this stuffy room.

And then suddenly, as though the crowds had parted before him like the Red Sea, there he was, carrying his suit jacket over one shoulder, shirt sleeves rolled up. His brow was furrowed as he glanced upwards. Eve waved furiously, knowing full well he wouldn't be able to see her. She wondered if the excitement she felt at this moment would make her real heart in her real body beat any faster.

'He's coming!' she called over to it. If only she could make it wake up and talk to him. Wouldn't it be wonderful if he was here when she came round?

The wait for him to come up to her room was interminable. In her mind, she pictured him at every point on the way: she saw him pressing the lift button, checking his watch impatiently as he waited for the doors to close, counting his footsteps along an imagined corridor. When he finally came into the room, Eve rushed towards him, closing her eyes so that she could pretend his warm arms were enfolding her.

'Hello, Eve,' said Nathan as he approached the bed. 'How's my beautiful girl today?' She watched as he perched on one side of the bed and leaned over to kiss her cheek. He took her free hand between his own and raised it to his face.

Eve closed her eyes, trying to feel his touch, to remember what he smelt like.

'I'm not too bad, Nathan,' she said. 'I'm better than you think. I'm trying my hardest here.'

'What am I going to do, Eve?' Nathan said. 'I miss you so much. When are you coming back to me?'

Nurse Jasmine, Eve's favourite, came into the room to check Eve's vitals.

'Hello, Mr Kellerman. How's our lovely young lady today?'

'She doesn't look any different, does she? Surely she should be making some progress by now, shouldn't she?' said Nathan.

'It's still early days. Everyone's very pleased with her actually. The wounds are beginning to heal, and everything is stabilising nicely, which is all we can hope for at the moment. In a few days we might be able to start weaning her off some of these tubes here, see how she does fending for herself a bit. Things won't seem quite so bad when she starts to function on her own a little more, believe me.'

'When will you operate on her face? She'll need plastic surgery presumably?'

'Actually no, she shouldn't. She might have a little scarring, but that would be up to her, once she's in a fit state to make decisions like that. And really, the damage to her face is minimal. There are far more pressing issues at the moment. It's very mild scarring that we're looking at, Mr Kellerman, not disfigurement. It's not like she had burns or anything.'

'But will she look the same afterwards?' asked Nathan.

'I'm sure she will, but really you shouldn't be concerning yourself with that at this time,' the nurse said tersely. She finished her checks and stood up to look him full in the face. 'Stay with her this evening, for as long as you can. Tell her about your day. Tell her how much you love her. It all helps with coma patients. They do say that hearing the voices of their loved ones really does help bring them back. She's still the same person inside, don't forget that.'

And with that, she left the room with her nose in the air, the door swinging on its hinges.

'Well,' said Nathan to Eve with a shrug of his shoulders. 'She didn't have to bite my head off, did she? I just want you back to your old gorgeous self, Eve, that's all. I didn't expect a bloody lecture from some stroppy nurse. Anyway, my lovely, it's just a fleeting visit, I'm afraid. I've got a dinner to get to tonight and I need to pop home first and freshen up.'

And with a quick kiss on Eve's cheek he, too, was gone. As she watched him leave, she wished once again that she could cry real tears.

Despair

She could tell it was Nathan, even before he spoke. There was something about his stride, the clack of his shoes on the tiled floor, the small, breathy sounds he made, even without realising it. When he slept, he was so quiet that sometimes Eve would put her hand on his chest, just to check he was still breathing. He always looked so peaceful in his sleep. But awake, he was never completely silent . . .

He was too busy to be silent.

'How's my beautiful girl today?' he said. Eve felt the bed shift on one side. He probably wasn't supposed to sit there, amidst the wires and tubes. She hoped he didn't see the bag, filling slowly day through night. Eve had never used the toilet if Nathan was in the bathroom; he always insisted on a closed door and total privacy. But she had no privacy now. Everything was laid bare for all to see.

Everyone except her.

Through the fog she heard one of the nurses tell him off. 'I must look horrific,' she said to herself, 'if he's so worried about scarring. Oh Nathan, I'm so sorry. Will you ever forgive me for getting myself into such a mess?'

Eve wished she could cry. Her body needed the release of tears, but that was another part of her that wouldn't work in this rigid state. She couldn't bear to think of Nathan breaking his heart out there, upset to see her looking so beaten up, so useless.

'Tell me you love me,' she said. 'Tell me it doesn't matter how awful I look.'

'I just want you back to your old gorgeous self, Eve,' he said, before muttering something about a dinner date. Sometimes she couldn't hear all the words clearly. Maybe it was just as well.

Then there was the briefest of kisses on her cheek, and the door swung closed behind him. Her heart sank and she welcomed the return of the death-darkness.

PART 2

MAKING A DIFFERENCE

13

Two Weeks After the Accident

Eve wondered why Nathan had even bothered to come the previous day.

Maybe he had bowed to the pressure from her parents, but she didn't want him feeling duty-bound. He had to *want* to see her, commit to making a proper job of his visits, like everyone else did—sitting at her bedside, keeping her up to date with news, talking to her as though she could hear them. Which, of course, she could.

Her life—or whatever this was—would be unbearable without her army of supporters.

Not only had the visits from Nathan dwindled, but Eve hadn't seen Luca for a couple of days, either. Not since the day they had followed that amazing brain surgeon woman around. But then she hadn't gone looking for him, either. She didn't know where his room was, anyway. Hadn't ventured that far afield yet.

What if Luca had recovered and left the hospital? It couldn't have happened that quickly, could it? He'd told her his body was really ill; he'd overhead the surgeon talking to his family recently and had believed he would be in a coma for some time yet. But Luca was no medic, what did he know?

Or what if he had taken a turn for the worse and they'd decided that no more could be done for him and they were giving up, turning everything off? No! She couldn't face life in this place without him by her side.

She had woken this morning with a new sense of purpose, determined to try to go a little further from her room on her own. It would be hard, she knew, but what if Luca didn't come back, and it really was just her now? She needed to know how it would feel to be out there, without him, in the vast expanse of the hospital.

So, with her fingers crossed for courage, she slipped out of the door when her parents left at the end of visiting hours. She hadn't wanted to leave while they were there; it seemed rude, somehow. Plus, the procrastination helped calm her nerves.

She stood outside her room, sick with fear, gripping the wall for support and shaking. Had she really become agoraphobic in the short time she had been in the hospital?

Unable to go forwards, she decided to go sideways, shuffling along the wall until she reached the room next to her own. A quick glance through the window showed that it was in an identical but opposite layout, so that the person in the bed would be head-to-head with her body, a wall between.

She cupped her hands to the glass and peered inside.

An elderly man lay amid a multitude of wires and tubes, attended to by a couple of medics. By his side sat a woman of a similar age, presumably his wife. She, in turn, was being comforted by a second elderly man who stood behind her, his hand on her shoulder.

A nurse came flying out of the room and Eve staggered through the swinging doorway. She righted herself quickly, relieved that she hadn't disturbed them with her clumsiness.

'Oh, hello, dear,' said the man who was standing. 'Do come in.' He was small and bent, his voice husky. He placed a finger to his lips and indicated the man on the bed with his eyes. 'Final moments. Just saying goodbye. They're switching off the machines. Won't be long, now.'

'Oh no, I'm so sorry to hear that,' said Eve. 'Is there anything I can do?' Eve walked towards the bed but stopped short and stared at the man, her eyes wide. 'You can see me!' she gasped.

'Yes, dear,' said the man. 'I can. Look at him carefully, this handsome young fellow in the bed.'

Up close, Eve could see the resemblance. 'Is he your brother?'

The old man chuckled. 'You haven't been here long, have you, dear? You're the one next door, aren't you? I was going to pop in, but you do get an awful lot of visitors, lucky girl. And I had so little time left, I wanted to spend it with her.' He squeezed the woman's shoulder, but her saddened gaze remained fixed on the bedridden man. 'My name's Len, by the way. What's yours?'

'I'm Eve, but . . . you mean . . . you mean . . .? I can't believe I've been so stupid. I'm so sorry, I didn't realise . . . well, I thought it was just me and Luca but . . .'

'It's all right, dear,' said Len. 'Come a little closer. Put your hand here, too. She'll be able to feel *you*.'

Eve placed a tentative hand on the woman's shoulder and squeezed gently. The woman sat up straighter in her chair and took a deep breath. 'It's time,' the woman said, looking up at the doctor. 'I'm ready. Will he feel anything?'

The doctor shook her head gently.

'No, I won't,' said Len. 'I'm ready to go, now, Lizzie dear. Don't be afraid.'

'But how can you just let this happen?' said Eve. 'Don't you want to stay and fight?'

Len stood quietly for a moment, watching his wife.

'I've had my time, dear. Eighty-nine glorious years of good health until this. Sixty-five of them married to my beautiful Elizabeth. I'll see her again one day.'

'Goodbye, my darling,' said Elizabeth, kissing her husband's hand. 'Goodbye, my one true love, till we meet again.' Tears glistened in her eyes, but her face was serene, her back straight. Eve thought she must once have been quite exquisitely beautiful.

'Oh no,' said Eve. She thought she could feel tears in her own eyes. 'I've only just met you. Please don't go already.'

Len smiled at Eve and took her hand. As with Luca, she could feel something, a warm glow almost, and she held on tightly to his spirit form as the medics slowly disabled first one machine and then another. At each stage, they paused to check that their patient was in no discomfort before continuing.

When the ventilator stopped its constant *click, click, click*, the room became eerily still and silent.

'How long will it take?' asked Eve, but when she looked at Len, his form had already become more translucent, less defined. But he was still there, smiling at her.

'Len?' she said.

'Look, I'm breathing all by myself now,' he said. 'But it won't be long.'

'God bless you,' said Eve. She had never been religious, but it felt the right thing to say.

He was there, and then suddenly he just wasn't. Above his body a pale shadow lingered, like an early morning mist. Then Eve saw something rise up from the bed, an outline of the man he once was, a silhouette of his human form. The two shapes merged and then they were gone.

All that remained of Len was the body on the bed.

'You're back now,' said Eve. 'Goodbye, Len.'

'He's gone,' said one of the nurses, placing a gentle hand on Elizabeth's shoulder. 'I'm so very sorry for your loss. Would you like to sit with him for a while?'

The old woman nodded and smiled up at the nurse. 'Yes, please,' she said. 'Just for a few more moments.'

'Take as long as you like. We'll be outside when you're ready.'

'Thank you, my darling, for the most wonderful life,' said Elizabeth, resting her hand over Len's cooling one. 'I know you've gone to a good place now.'

'Oh Elizabeth,' sighed Eve as she placed her arm around the woman once more. 'What a wonderful love story yours is.'

'I'll see you soon, darling,' Elizabeth said as she stood to leave, that serene smile still lingering as her eyes glistened with tears.

And with one last glance at her husband, she turned to face the rest of her life.

Later, Eve's thoughts returned to Luca. Surely what happened to Len couldn't have happened to him. The thought filled her with panic.

She sat, huddled on the floor, hugging her knees to her chest for comfort.

'Come back, Luca, I need you,' she said. 'Oh, what's the point? You won't be able to hear me, will you, if you really have gone?' She lay her head on her folded arms and closed her eyes.

'Oh, so you need me all of a sudden, do you?' she heard from the doorway.

'Jesus, Luca,' said Eve. 'Don't do that! You frightened me half to death.' She leapt to her feet to find him leaning casually against the door frame, legs crossed and arms folded, his blue eyes twinkling. 'How long have you been standing there?'

'Long enough to hear you blathering on,' he said. 'But also long enough to hear you say you needed me, so that was good timing. I'm glad to hear you've missed me, and now here I am.'

Eve hesitated. 'Er, that wasn't what I was saying at all. What I was saying was . . . was . . . oh, sod it, I did miss you. It gets lonely round here, doesn't it? But . . . where have you been? I thought you might have . . . you know . . . gone.'

'Oh, Eve. No, I'm still here.' He put his hand over hers. 'Will be for a while yet, I fear. And yeah, it can be a lonely place. Other than the constant stream of doctors and nurses barging into your room unannounced, that is. And the armies of well-wishers standing round your bed and bawling their eyes out.'

'How do you cope with it all?' she asked. 'I hate all the sadness at my expense. It sets me off every time my parents or Nathan come in. And then yesterday, some of my friends came to visit. Oh God, you should have seen them. There were so many tears you'd think I'd died already. It was hell. And I just sat here on the floor, watching them. Sometimes I wish they wouldn't come. It just makes everyone so sad. I wish I could tell them to stay away until I'm a bit better. Until I'm *back*.'

'Has Nathan been in again?'

'Yeah, a couple of times, but he never stays long.'

'He should be here for you. Be a bit more supportive.'

'He's finding it hard,' said Eve, rounding on him. 'Everyone has their own way of dealing with things. He comes when he can. He's busy at work at the moment. The summertime is always complete madness, with all the tourists.'

'But you're more important than that gallery.'

'How do you know where he works?'

'Oh, I think you mentioned it the other day,' said Luca, looking away. 'Yeah, I'm pretty sure you did. Anyway, fancy taking off for a while? See how far you can get now?'

'Just give me a minute. I want to tell you something first. Something that happened to me earlier.'

'You did a good thing, Eve. I'm very proud of you,' said Luca afterwards. 'What a shame Len wasn't around for a bit longer, though. I'd have liked to meet him, too.'

'He was lovely. I stayed with Elizabeth for a while after. Poor lady. I can't imagine what it must be like to lose someone you've spent pretty much your entire life with.'

'She'll take comfort from her memories,' said Luca. 'And the serenity she felt in that room will go with her.'

'I hope you're right,' said Eve.

'Always,' said Luca with a wink.

'Before this morning,' said Eve, 'I had doubts. I wasn't really sure if we were actually helping these people at all, or if it was just us trying to justify our existence. But I really felt I *had* to comfort Elizabeth. Len knew it would help her, as well. She couldn't feel him, obviously. And then it got me thinking about all those times you get a shiver up the spine, or a moment of self-doubt, and then suddenly you're able to pull yourself together and get on with things. Do you think that's what's happening then? Someone like us is trying to help? It's a lot to get my head round, to be honest.'

'I suppose we'll never know, will we?' said Luca. 'Anyway, shall we get out of here for a bit?'

'I'll try. I'm pretty shattered after the Len thing, though, so not sure how far I'll get.'

'Well, now you have me here to look after you.' He took her hand and they passed easily down the corridor which had so terrified Eve earlier, and through the double doors at the end.

'Will I be all right, going this far?' asked Eve nervously, glancing over her shoulder to the safety of her own room.

'Your strength is growing all the time. But let me know if you find it too much and we'll stop.'

'Can we stop here, please? I need a rest,' said Eve.

They had reached a large waiting area just behind the main entrance of the hospital. After the quietness of her room, Eve was overwhelmed by the pace and the noise of the place and sat down to take it all in. Delivery men in overalls pushed trolleys stacked with boxes. A nurse ran by, fastening her hair into a bun as she hurried to her shift. An elderly woman struggled to push her husband in his wheelchair. Patients, visitors, the bereaved, the old, the young, expectant mothers, proud new fathers. If she sat here for long enough, someone from every walk of life would come by—and not one of them had an inkling they were being observed.

'Here is good. Not too busy,' said Luca.

'Not busy?' scoffed Eve. 'Are you joking?'

'You should see A&E. We'll save that for another day. It's another thing entirely. There's plenty here to be going on with for now. Hang on, let's watch these two.' He indicated a man holding the hand of a young boy of around six or seven.

'I think we should go and find the chapel and say a prayer for Mummy,' said the man. The boy looked up at his father with huge brown eyes.

'Will God make Mummy better?' he said.

'Oh, bless him,' said Eve.

'Shh,' said Luca.

'They can't hear us, can they?'

'No, but you need to listen.'

'I think it just might help her,' said the father. 'Now, where do we have to go?' He turned to look up and down the corridor.

'They look so sad,' said Eve. 'I wonder what's wrong with the wife. Oh, Luca, this is heart-breaking. I hope it's nothing too serious, but then I suppose we'll never know, will we?'

'No one comes to a hospital on a pleasure trip, do they? But you can help. Look, they're going the wrong way.'

'But how? I can't exactly turn them around, can I? Tell me what I need to do.'

'Don't panic, Eve. Think logically. The chapel is over there, just behind them. You need to *make* them turn, not physically *turn* them around.'

'But I don't know how. You do it, otherwise we're going to lose them.'

'Nope, this one is yours. Think, Eve. Work it out.'

Eve let out a huge sigh, ready to admit defeat. Then she noticed that the sign for the chapel was almost directly over the man's head, suspended from the ceiling on a couple of chains.

'Ah, I get it,' she said. 'I need to move that *sign*, don't I? But how?'

'I'll explain it to you after, but for now, just do it.'

She concentrated hard, harder than ever, then leapt into the air and smacked the palm of her hand down. It passed straight through the sign which hung there still, unmoving.

'Oh, God, look at my hand,' she said to Luca. 'It's disappearing.'

'It's fine. It's just the energy you used. Look, it's already coming back.'

Eve watched as the form returned to her fingers. It was like having pins and needles, she thought, only instead of the feeling coming back, the shape was gradually returning instead.

'Come on, quickly,' said Luca. 'Try again.'

'I can't,' said Eve. 'You'd better do it, or we're going to lose them.'

'Nope. You're doing it. Concentrate, Eve. Focus.'

She thought she had been concentrating, but this time she tried even harder. She banished all thought from her mind, other than the intense feeling that she wanted to make that sign move, no matter how impossible she thought it was.

She jumped into the air with a yell and swung her hand. This time, the sign creaked on its chains, clattering as though hit by a sudden gust of wind.

'I did it, I did it!'

'You did, and look at them.' The movement of the sign had caught the man's attention.

'Ah yes, here we are,' he said. 'Come on then, son, in we go.' He held the door open for the boy.

'See? It works if you try hard enough,' said Luca.

'But look at my hand now.' This time it was almost transparent.

'Don't worry,' said Luca. 'It'll come back.'

'So, you were going to explain how it works?' said Eve, watching her fingers return as she wriggled them.

'Well, I'm no scientist, obviously, and all of this is as indecipherable to me as it is to you, but just think about it. You manage to sit on a chair, don't you, without falling through it. And you stand on the floor, without disappearing into it. So somehow your new form must be resistant to matter. You can do those things without even thinking about them because that's what you've always done. You thought you couldn't hit that sign, but it was just a case of channelling your energies, same as you would do in life. In your old life, you'd have to make one hell of an effort to do that, too, and hope you could reach high enough, push your body to its limits. It's no different for us now. If you think you can't do something . . . well no, maybe you can't *always* in your current predicament. But there's an awful lot you *can* do. And it feels good, doesn't it?'

'It does,' said Eve. 'Can we wait for them to come out? I want to make sure they're OK before we go.'

Ten minutes later, the door to the chapel opened and the man and his son emerged, accompanied by a young priest.

'Gosh, he hardly looks old enough,' said Eve.

'Shh,' said Luca.

'Thank you, Father, you've been a great comfort.' The man shook the priest's hand.

'God bless you,' said the priest. 'And I do hope your wife makes a speedy recovery.'

'So do we, Father, so do we.' Their faces were still sad, but Eve thought they seemed somehow more tranquil.

'They look a bit better, don't they?' said Luca.

'That wasn't down to me, though,' said Eve. 'It was that lovely young priest. And their faith.'

'But you helped them get there. You showed them the way. That's what this is all about, Eve. Guidance.'

Eve looked at Luca. His eyes seemed bluer than ever against his white shirt, and she couldn't take her own eyes off of them. The multitude of questions she wanted to ask him suddenly evaporated.

'Thank you, Luca' she said. 'Thank you for making me do that.'

With a smile, Luca took Eve's hand and led her back to the ward. And for the first time in a while, his touch made her feel warm inside.

14

'So, where's your body?' asked Eve as they walked back to ICU.

Luca hesitated. 'Not far from yours, actually,' he said. 'In another little room on my own, a bit like you.'

'Can we go and see you?'

'Why would you want to do that?'

'Well, it's always you coming to see me. I've never seen *you,* have I? The *real* you, I mean.'

'Are we not real like this?' said Luca, turning away from Eve, his face in shadow.

'Is there something you don't want me to see?' she said.

'No, not at all. Just feeling a bit self-conscious, I suppose.'

'But you've seen me at my most vulnerable. Everything laid bare. It's only fair I get to see you the same way.'

'OK then, if you really have to.'

Luca led Eve through the swing doors towards his room. A nurse came out as they went in. The room was very still and seemed darker than Eve's. The blind was down, and Eve thought they must be on the north side of the hospital. It was gloomy, not a pleasant room to be in at all. Not that any hospital room was ever particularly pleasant.

Eve gasped as she set eyes on the man in the bed.

Luca's human form bore little resemblance to how he looked now. Whereas the spirit Luca was tall and graceful, his body was shrunken and small, barely visible for all the wires and technology attached to him. Whatever trauma had put him there, he was a person thoroughly diminished.

'God, Luca, you're in a worse state than me,' said Eve, and then her hand flew to her mouth. 'I'm so sorry.' It wasn't his fault he looked so awful. No wonder he hadn't wanted her to come.

'Well, thanks,' said Luca. 'You really know how to hit a man when he's down.'

'I'm sorry. It's just that, well . . . now, here, you're so . . . um . . . what's the word . . .?' She couldn't help her eyes from scanning the spirit version of Luca up and down.

'Handsome?' Luca joked, but the smile didn't reach his eyes.

'Um . . . yes. Of course,' said Eve. 'What I mean is . . .'

'It's OK, you don't need to dig yourself any deeper. I know I look a mess.'

'I'm sorry,' Eve said again. She felt a familiar prickling of blood rising up through her neck to her cheeks, although she knew it was impossible that she was blushing. 'What's actually wrong with you? What happened?'

'It was a bit out of the blue for me, too,' said Luca. 'But not in the same way as you. Not an accident. I was attacked on my way home from work. A former client, actually. Someone I had defended.'

'Client?' said Eve.

'I'm a lawyer,' said Luca. 'Or was. Criminal defence lawyer, to be precise. And a bloody good one, too.'

'Don't say *was*,' said Eve. 'So, this client, why did he, or she, attack you?'

'He. He was a client from a few years back. He'd done time for aggravated burglary—I'd failed to get him off, obviously—and he decided to come after me when he got out. They think it's our fault sometimes. That they've gone to prison, I mean. Despite all the counselling they get inside, sometimes they'd just rather blame the justice system for punishing them than take responsibility for doing it in the first place.'

'That's awful. What did he do to you?'

'Pushed me into the Thames. There I was, walking across Blackfriars Bridge on my way to the station one evening, and he came up behind me and literally lobbed me over the side. Apparently, he'd been following me for weeks. Watching where I went and working out the best way to do me in.'

Eve sat down. 'Oh my God, that's awful.'

'One of the concrete plinths broke my fall. You know, the bits that stick out between the arches.'

'Oh, Luca. Were you unconscious when you hit the water?'

'Oh yes. But luckily for me—if you can ever be lucky when something like that happens—there was a police RIB which had just gone past, and they heard the splash. Turned straight round and came back for me. *So* lucky. A few minutes more and I'd have drowned.'

'Gosh. It's horrific. So how do you know all this? Surely you can't remember much?'

'I've picked it all up since. The police came and spoke to my parents, and I got more from other visitors. One of them was a policeman who was in that boat. Fortunately, he was a talker. He sat by my side and I watched him get it all off his chest. He'd never seen anything like it, he said. Told me how lucky I was to be alive. Then he cried his eyes out and there I was, standing behind him, trying to comfort him. Crazy really.'

'So did they get the guy?'

'Thankfully, yes. They picked him up pretty much

straightaway. There were loads of witnesses. Busy bridge in the middle of rush-hour. Apparently, it was all over the press, and I did see one or two headlines in the shop downstairs. He didn't get bail and it goes to trial in October.'

'It's horrendous, Luca. Makes my accident look like a walk in the park. And at least mine was just that, an accident. I can't believe someone would want to do that to you. Something so evil, when all you've tried to do is help him.'

'That's the way of the world, I'm afraid. I can't help everyone. Sometimes you know they're going down and you're just there for due process. It can make you quite unpopular.'

'So, dare I ask,' said Eve, 'what the prognosis is? When are you going to get better?'

'They've been a bit more upbeat lately, I have to say. And they're pretty certain they can get my arm working again, now. That's cheered me up loads.'

'Oh God, it gets worse,' said Eve, hands flying to her mouth. She looked at Luca's arm now, which looked perfectly normal. A little opaque, but normal. 'What happened to your arm?'

'It got pretty smashed up on the concrete on the way down. I don't know, maybe I tried to raise it somehow to save myself and my arm took the brunt of it. In the early days they were talking about amputation. They've operated on it a few times now.'

'That's awful.'

'I'm not sure if I could stand here, complete—in as much as we are complete at the moment—with all my limbs, anyway, and know that the body I hope to get back into one day is missing something vital. What would be the point of going back, if not to what you had before?'

'Surely life itself is worth going back for, whatever level it's on,' said Eve. 'There's more to life than just arms and legs. There's love, and relationships, and . . .'

'Well, my track record with those things isn't particularly strong,' said Luca, cutting Eve off. He turned and walked to the window.

Eve wanted to know more, but now wasn't the time.

'I think I'm going to have some scarring on my face,' she said. 'Not that it matters, of course. And I don't know what kind of disability my accident might leave me with, if any. No one's really mentioned that. But I will cope with it, whatever it might be. I didn't think I would be able to, but now I just want to get back, whatever I have to deal with.'

Eve stared into Luca's eyes, and he stared right back. He opened his mouth to say something. But they were interrupted as the door swung open and a tall, dark-haired woman sauntered into the room.

'Who's this then?' Eve said.

'That's Lauren, my ex.'

'Oh. Do you want me to go?'

'God, no, stay. I don't even know why she keeps coming.'

'Don't you want to be alone with her? You knew she was coming, didn't you? That was why you didn't want me to come in here. I'm sorry for pushing it.'

'I did know she was coming,' said Luca. 'She comes at the same time every week. But that wasn't why. It's just that I look better like this than I do over there, and I didn't want you to see me looking so terrible. It's not me in that bed. This is the real me, here. And no, I don't want to be alone with her. You and I both know it doesn't really work like that, anyway.'

'Do you still love her?' asked Eve.

'That's a bit personal.'

'She's very pretty.'

'Looks aren't everything.'

'I know that but, well, she keeps on coming, doesn't she, so maybe she still loves you.'

'Somehow I doubt it. Probably just some misplaced sense of duty. Although I don't know why; she finished with me about a year ago. It wasn't like we saw much of each other after that.'

'So, have you tried to touch her? You told me we can't touch those we love. Then you'd know, wouldn't you? Whether it's your head or your heart that's in charge?'

'Don't, Eve.'

'I'm sorry. But don't you want to know?'

'No. I think some things need to be left alone, don't you? We don't need to know everything that fate has in store for us, or we'd never get out of bed in the morning. I'd rather take my chances in life.'

Eve sighed and turned away from him.

'What's up?' said Luca.

'Nothing. Just frustrated with it all. Don't get me wrong, it's lovely to have your company, but I think we've both got somewhere else we'd rather be, don't you? I mean, you could get back with your beautiful friend here, I've got Nathan, and . . . well, what kind of life is it really, this state of limbo we're in?'

'Not much of one, a lot of the time,' said Luca, his voice cracking. 'But I'm enjoying your company, too. You're OK.'

'So are you.'

Their eyes locked again, this time for just a little too long. Then, Eve laughed awkwardly.

'Anyway, I suppose I'd better get back. Things to do, places to go, people to help. You know how it is.' She turned and walked to the door.

'Eve, don't go,' muttered Luca, but it was too late.

It always was.

15

Eve left Luca's room and kept walking.

She didn't want to go back to her own room yet, in case she also had visitors. She couldn't cope with another well-wisher's tears, and as much as she loved to see her family and Nathan, she needed a little time to herself.

There was so much commotion coming from the entrance hall that she felt compelled to go and investigate. She would have preferred to have Luca by her side for security, but they had come this far when they'd helped the father and child and she felt no pain then.

She had to be brave and try it on her own now.

This part of the hospital was normally buzzing with noise and activity, but today felt different. There was music coming from somewhere, and applause, too. Eve squeezed through the crowds to find a busker, a young man with a guitar and a bright mop of unruly red hair. He looked perfectly at home there, perched on the end of a bench, strumming his guitar and singing. The onlookers were enjoying the impromptu concert and their good humour was infectious, lifting Eve's spirits.

A pair of security guards, puffed up with authority, sidled up to the busker. Then a nurse in blue scrubs approached. She touched one of the guards gently on the arm and smiled up at him.

'He's not doing any harm,' she said. 'Can't we leave him? Just for a few more minutes? Look at the faces of the little children.'

Oh, she's good, thought Eve.

The crowd had formed a large semi-circle around the

busker. A row of children with rapt faces sat on the floor, legs crossed, mesmerised by the talented young man.

'Is he Ed Sheeran, Mum?' asked a teenage boy. Eve noticed how thin and pale he was.

'No, love,' laughed his mother. 'He looks a bit like him, though. Shall we stay and watch till it's time?'

'It's like a private concert, isn't it?' said the boy.

The woman smiled. 'Your brother would love this, too.' She glanced at her watch. 'I hope he's getting on OK. That exam must be about halfway through by now.'

Eve's thoughts were drawn to her own pupils. If she hadn't lost all track of time since her arrival here, then public exams must be in full flow by now.

'He'll be fine. He's ace at everything,' said the boy, his eyes wide.

'You're right there, my love,' said the mother, pulling him close.

Eve wondered what awful thing had brought them here. She thought suddenly of Will and his family, hoping that life was improving for them.

She listened as the man sang several more songs.

'Right, thank you everyone,' he said. 'But I think it's time for me to go now.' He threw a hat onto the floor, where it was immediately deluged with coins, as the two security guards began to circle again.

'Mum, can I put some money in?' said the boy.

'Of course,' said the mother, reaching for her purse. 'Are you ready to go?'

'Sure. Let's get this over with.' The young boy stood up on frail legs and let his mother assist him through the doors and out of sight.

There is always someone worse off than you, Eve, she thought to herself.

Frustrated

'Oh, Eve, whatever am I going to do?' Nathan said on his last visit.

'Just stay with me,' Eve replied inside her head. 'Please keep coming in to see me. I love you and I miss you.'

She didn't mind if his visits were less frequent, as long as when he did come, he sat beside her, held her hand, and spoke to her. He had never been one for sickness and hospitals. She didn't want this to drag him down, or to affect the relationship they would continue when she got out of here. Things would soon return to normal for them, she knew they would.

Her parents, on the other hand, came too often. She mightn't be able to see the strain on their beloved faces, but she could hear it in their voices. That morning they had been more upbeat than usual, as if they had made a pact outside the door to sound more positive when they went in.

'We've taken Buster to live with us, Eve,' her mother said, patting Eve's hand. 'Just until you're well enough to come home again. Which will be really soon, we're sure of it.'

'Oh God, Mum, you're putting on your brave voice now, aren't you? Which must mean you're expecting me to be in here for ages.'

If they were making long-term plans for her cat, then things couldn't be good. Thoughts of Buster made Eve wish she could cry.

'I miss you, Buster,' she said inside her head. 'I miss your furry cuddles. I miss how it feels to bury my nose in your coat and rub your tummy. And that smell you have, like a freshly-washed teddy bear.'

Since her sight had been withdrawn, Eve found that her senses of smell and hearing were far more acute than normal.

Her mother's familiar scent was one of the most comforting and took Eve straight back to her childhood.

'Mum, you still wear that Gardenia perfume, don't you? I can't believe I haven't noticed it before,' Eve said. 'You always used to wear it when Hattie and I were little. Where on earth do you get that from these days?'

Eve had more confidence in her mother's ability to track down a former Avon lady with a garage full of the stuff than the likelihood of her ordering it online. Mary Chapman was genuinely terrified of the internet.

At the end of visiting time, Eve's door opened again, and she heard Nathan's familiar footsteps.

'Oh, darling, you made it,' Eve said. 'I knew you'd come. I've missed you so much. Here, sit down and tell me all about your day.'

But his greeting was all she heard before the death-darkness came again.

16

By late afternoon, Rob Barclay could wait no longer to call Sarah and find out how George's appointment had gone. The office was hot and humid, the day had dragged (as it always did during George's appointments), but still he would be unable to leave for another hour.

It was traumatic to think of his little lad lying in a hospital bed while the unpleasant process of dialysis took place. It was a horrible thing to have to endure several times a week and Rob would have given anything to trade places with George. He was finding it increasingly difficult to grasp the meaning of a world where children had to suffer like that.

With a sigh, Rob stood up to close his office door, leaned against it, and pulled his mobile from his pocket. He yanked his tie loose and wiped a hand around the back of his neck.

'Hi love, how did it go?'

Sarah sounded like she was still driving. 'Oh, same as usual.' She sighed. 'We're on our way home now. He's shattered.' Rob could hear her voice quavering. 'His nice nurse was back in today, though. She always manages to cheer him up a bit.'

Rob sighed. 'I wish I could have come over for a while. To be honest with you, I've been useless here. Have you heard from Will?'

'He messaged earlier. He's back home now. It went OK, apparently, although he didn't say much. You know Will.'

'Maybe we should do something nice with him this

weekend, now that exams are nearly over?' said Rob. 'You or I could take him out somewhere, a film and pizza maybe? Or if I can get Mum to come up and sit with George, then we could both go?'

Sarah sighed. 'One day we'll be planning things like that with George in tow, too, won't we? We'll be back to a proper family of four, doing normal family things. Won't we, Rob?'

His wife craved reassurance. 'Yes, we will, my love. One day this will all be behind us, you'll see.'

'Let's suggest it to Will tonight. Bet he'll jump at the chance.'

'I'll have a think about what to do and I'll call Mum on my way home,' said Rob.

When he locked the door to his office behind him ninety minutes later, Rob's team was still bent furiously over their laptops.

'Go home at some point, won't you?' he said as he passed. 'I'm off. Hope you don't mind me leaving you to it. I've been pretty hopeless today, I'm afraid. Thank goodness for you lot.'

'No worries,' they chorused. 'Night, guv. Hope the little lad's OK.'

'Thanks, guys. See you tomorrow.'

'We'll be here. In different clothes, just so you know we've been home,' said one of the team, waggling his eyebrows mischievously.

'Glad to hear it,' said Rob with a smile. It wasn't in their job descriptions to keep his spirits up, but that didn't stop them from trying.

As he headed across Westminster Bridgc, Rob could see a crowd gathering in the distance. He instinctively reached inside his jacket pocket for his phone and looked about quickly, scanning the area for imminent danger. When he heard clapping, he relaxed a little, realising that it must just be some itinerant musician or other. He completed his check of the vicinity, in case this was a distraction technique and the real threat lay elsewhere.

Always work.

Buskers were not permitted to stop on the bridges anymore. The pavements simply weren't wide enough to support a crowd and now that the concrete and metal barriers were in place to protect pedestrians from potential terrorist attacks, no obstructions were allowed. It made him nervous if he saw too many people congregating in one place. He would have to send this man on his way, in the interest of public safety.

'Sir, you really can't stop here. There's a no busking rule on the bridges now, I'm afraid,' Rob said, forcing his way to the front of the crowd and reaching into his pocket for his ID.

The young musician had a mop of red hair and dancing eyes. Smiling up at Rob, he continued to play, the tight-knit group around him cheering and egging him on. It dawned on Rob that sometimes Londoners needed a little bit of brightness in their lives, and looking at their faces, he didn't have the heart to assert his authority any further.

Not immediately, anyway.

'OK, just one more number, then,' Rob conceded, at which point the crowd burst into rapturous applause. They turned round to applaud Rob as well.

'Got any requests?' the busker asked him.

'Let them choose,' said Rob, smiling. He would stay and listen, just to make sure this talented young man really did move on afterwards.

'How about "I Fought the Law,"' shouted one cheeky bystander. The crowd laughed. All too aware how a pleasant situation can quickly turn threatening, Rob was thankful they were laughing with him, not at him.

'"I Shot the Sheriff,"' shouted another.

'No, something more recent,' said Rob, rolling his eyes. 'My youngest likes Ed Sheeran. Know anything by him?'

'Great choice,' said the busker.

The crowd fell silent as the young man started strumming the opening to "Castle on the Hill".

'Perfect,' said Rob, settling towards the back to listen. He really would need to move them on after this number, but for now he would stand and enjoy the music, and just be an ordinary Londoner for a while.

He would think of George.

As the song played on, he gazed down the river at a familiar scene, one he saw daily but scarcely ever really looked at. There was so much beauty in this place, but in the face of the ugliness of the world he was exposed to in his job, sometimes he forgot.

The song came to an end and Rob snapped out of his reverie.

'Thank you,' he said. 'You really are very good, you know.'

'Thanks, Officer,' said the singer. 'I'll go now, though. I know I was pushing my luck, but they seemed to like it.'

'They certainly did,' said Rob. For the first time all day, there was a genuine smile on his face, and as he carried on across the bridge, he felt suddenly more optimistic about what the future held for him and his family.

For George.

17

Five Weeks After the Accident

Five weeks. Was it really only five weeks? It felt like forever. Time was a weird concept in the hospital. Some days flew by, others dragged. As the weeks passed, Eve mentally ticked off missed family events.

In the past few days alone, there had been her father's and her little niece, Abbie's, birthdays. Her dad's birthday would have been as quiet an affair as it normally was, she imagined—a meal out with his family in a bistro somewhere. Or would it? Could she imagine them going without her? Probably not. Their hearts wouldn't be in it. She didn't like to think of them trying to put a brave face on things for her father's sake, sitting there, staring at their food, looking for something to celebrate when actually there was nothing.

Abbie would have had a wonderful party, though, Eve was sure. She wouldn't expect anything less of her sister. Hattie had taken Eve's accident hard, but Eve could imagine that hordes of screaming six-year-olds, all high on sugar and dancing to pop music would be a great distraction. Eve should have been there to help Hattie cut up sandwiches into tiny, crustless triangles, which would later go uneaten in favour of Party Rings and Iced Gems. She should have been standing by her sister, smiling indulgently on the side-lines, mopping up spillages, rousing the little guests to sing a discordant 'Happy Birthday' and taking proud auntie photos as a pink-cheeked Abbie blew out her candles.

Then there were the things she and Nathan had planned together.

Carefully chosen events that they had been looking forward to for ages. Eve had even managed to secure a pair of tickets to see *Hamilton* at the theatre, via a friend who worked in the industry. She had been so excited; Nathan too. The night for that had come and gone two weekends ago. Did Nathan still go to see it, Eve wondered? Alone, or with a friend? Or would he have sold the tickets, or given them away to some friends who could use them? She would like to think that the joy he had displayed when she came home with them wouldn't have survived her accident.

Eve and Nathan had booked a holiday, too. They planned to leave for a fortnight in Croatia as soon as the school year was over. That trip was less than a month away; would she be back in time? Somehow, she doubted it. Even if she did wake up, she probably wouldn't be well enough by then.

How wonderful it would be to feel the sun on her face right now. To lie by an azure pool and read to her heart's content, her hand occasionally brushing Nathan's as they smiled at one another in their happiness. Nodding to the pool attendant when their cocktails ran a little low. Dining on the terrace and watching the sun dip behind the mountains.

It was a million worlds away.

Would Nathan have cancelled it by now, assuming that she wouldn't be better in time? Or deferred it even? Perhaps they could go later in the year instead. October half-term, maybe? It would still be warm enough. Nathan would have thought it all through, she was sure.

And then there was their anniversary. Two years since their first date. Two years tomorrow, in fact.

Nathan would come and be with her for that. She knew he would want to sit by her side, reminiscing about their early days together, as they so often did, and telling her how much he loved her and was missing her. And there'd be flowers. Nathan always bought flowers for special occasions. Beautiful ones. Huge bouquets.

But he wouldn't be able to bring them into her room because they didn't allow flowers in ICU. *Dangerous for patients.* Eve failed to understand how anyone ever got sick and died as a result of flowers. Many of her visitors had tried to bring her some. She would really love to see some flowers, have something to brighten up her room.

Nathan had to come tomorrow. He'd remember their anniversary. He was good like that. Though to be fair, he was better when he had Eve there to jog his memory about dates. It amused her how sometimes he even needed a nudge from her to remember his own family's birthdays and anniversaries. Eve didn't mind, though. She enjoyed shopping for presents.

She slumped to the floor with a sigh. It was so frustrating. There was so much she needed to get back for, so much to look forward to. All she wanted to do was get better and get on with her life.

The following morning, Eve woke as the *swish-swash* of the double doors at the end of the corridor announced the beginning of visiting hours. It was followed by the *click-clack* of loved ones' footsteps as they dispersed around the ward.

Finally, her own door swung open as Nathan marched in.

'Happy anniversary, darling,' Eve said, hovering close to him as he approached the bed. 'You're here. You remembered.' She leaned forward and put her hand on his chest, planting a kiss he would never feel on his cheek.

'And how are you today?' Nathan asked, sitting on the side of the bed.

What had happened to his *darling girl*, Eve wondered. Today of all days, she was his darling girl, surely?

'Looking the same as ever, aren't you? Poor girl.' He was about to pat her hand but his own hovered mid-air, then he withdrew it and stood up. He beckoned to someone to come in.

'Are you sure it's OK?' said a woman. 'I won't disturb her or anything?'

'She can't hear you,' said Nathan. 'Don't worry.'

'Who are *you*?' Eve said between gritted teeth.

'Carolina, this is Eve,' said Nathan, presenting Eve's inert body to her as though she were an exhibit in his gallery.

Eve circled the woman, taking in the glossy, blow-dried hair, the smart work suit, the slim legs, the heels. Not only was she a vision of loveliness, but she wore high heels—on a Tuesday! Nathan considered high heels the height of elegance and moaned about the stubby-heeled shoes that Eve wore to work.

Who was this woman, and how did Nathan know her well enough to bring her into Eve's hospital room? Her private space. On their anniversary, of all days.

She reeled back, pressing her hands against the wall for support.

'Oh Nathan, she's very pale,' said the uninvited guest,

leaning over Eve's body. Her face was pinched with fear, as though what Eve had might be contagious.

Eve hated that the woman had an exotic name. Why couldn't she just be a normal Caroline? *Carolina.* Nathan pronounced it *Caroleena.* It had the summery whiff of the Mediterranean about it, as did her accent.

'Poor Eve, when are you going to show some signs of improvement?'

Nathan perched on the side of the bed again and touched Eve's face with the back of his hand. Eve thought he was checking if she was still alive. How convenient it would be for him if she weren't.

'It's heart-breaking, isn't it?' he said. He looked up at Carolina, his eyes puppy-dog wide. 'She looks the same every time I come in.' A slight quiver edged his voice. 'Still no change. This is so damned frustrating, Carolina. Now you can see what I'm up against here, can't you?'

'What do you mean, what *you're* up against?' said Eve. '*I'm* the one who's fucking stuck here, not *you*!'

'What was that?' said Carolina.

'What?' said Nathan.

'I thought I heard someone.'

'Probably just the nurses in the corridor,' he said. 'They're always in and out, fiddling about with her. Honestly, it doesn't stop. Sometimes I think they just do it to make it look like something's actually happening in here.'

'I'm sure they're far too busy for that,' said Carolina with a nervous laugh, peering through the window onto the corridor.

'They're trying to make me better,' Eve said slowly, as though explaining it to a person of limited intellect. 'It's what they do.'

'There. Listen. Did you hear that?'

'No, my love,' said Nathan. 'What was it?'

'Voices. Like someone talking behind the wall. All kind of muffled.'

And then it dawned on Eve. She slapped the palm of her hand on her translucent thigh.

'You can actually hear me, can't you, Carolina?' This woman, to whom Eve had taken an instant dislike, could hear her! She knew Carolina couldn't understand what she was saying, but she knew Eve was there.

She could feel Eve's presence in the room.

'Nathan, shouldn't we be going?' said Carolina, wrapping her arms around herself as though a chill had descended. She glanced nervously around the room.

'If only you could see me, too,' said Eve. 'We could really have some fun then, couldn't we?' To appear to Carolina as some kind of ghoulish shadow in the corner, mysterious and terrifying, would have been perfect. Eve knew it would have sent the woman running for the hills.

Carolina couldn't see her. But she could hear her, and that was a first. Eve puffed up with pride. For the first time in this new existence of hers, she felt she had the upper hand until, with a pang, she realised what Nathan had said to Carolina.

He had called her *my love*. How could he? Nathan wasn't one of those people who naturally called everyone *love*.

He stood up and wandered to the window, hands in his pockets. 'It's such a waste,' he said, gazing down at the street below. 'She should be out there, doing what she does best, not stuck in here like a vegetable. Are you really still in there, Eve? Or have you left us already?'

'Oh yes, Nathan, I'm here all right, and I can see you,' said Eve. 'I can see *both* of you. I can hear everything you're saying. And I don't like it one bit.' Eve placed her hand gingerly onto Carolina's shoulder and the woman flinched.

'Come on, Nathan, we're going to be late if we don't go soon,' said Carolina, taking hold of Nathan's hand. 'Have you got the tickets?' She glanced back at Eve's body and shivered.

Eve couldn't believe he was taking her out. On their anniversary, of all days. How could he stoop so low? And then it dawned on her that he hadn't even remembered. He had no idea how special today should have been for them both.

He really didn't care at all.

'Yes, don't worry,' said Nathan, patting the breast pocket of his jacket.

'Come on, then,' said Carolina again.

'Can't get out of here quick enough, can you, *love*?' said Eve.

With one last glance over his shoulder, Nathan followed Carolina to the door, resting his hand in the small of her back.

As the door closed behind them Eve lunged at her lifeless body.

'You useless thing! Why can't you get better, get up and show him that you're coming back? Fight that woman for him?' She lay sprawled across the bed, her ethereal fists pounding at her human head. But she knew it wouldn't make any difference. She couldn't make herself get better, and she couldn't make Nathan choose her.

The tears Eve so wanted to cry wouldn't come.

Her cheeks remained bone dry, as always.

18

Eve was still lying on her bed an hour later when her parents arrived. She sat up quickly and looked at her human form; mercifully, it seemed unaffected by the pounding it had received.

'Mum, Dad, you'll never believe what he's done,' she wailed, climbing off the bed.

'She looks a little brighter today,' said Mary, as she did every time they came to visit. 'Doesn't she, Douglas?'

'Yes, dear, if you say so,' he said. His stock reply. 'Have you heard from Nathan this week? He said he was coming so maybe we've missed him the last few times we've been in.'

'Oh, he's been in,' said Eve. 'And about bloody time, too. But, Dad, it wasn't just him. He had this woman with him. Wouldn't like to speculate or anything, but I reckon he's lining her up as the next girlfriend, now that this one is out of action.'

Nathan couldn't bear to be single. He'd had a girlfriend almost continuously since he was sixteen. He had told her soon after they met, though not all of them had been serious. Apparently, he'd only finished with Eve's predecessor the week before she came to the gallery with her students, but she wondered now how credible that explanation was. What if the poor woman had still been on the scene when Eve came along, only to be dumped when Nathan decided he fancied a change?

Given the day's events, she couldn't help her harsh reassessment of the situation.

'He's turned out to be a good man, hasn't he?' said Mary. 'Despite our earlier misgivings, I mean.'

'Well,' said Douglas, 'I suppose he has. He's stuck by her, so we have to give him credit for that. He can come across as a little brash sometimes, but I think his heart is in the right place.'

'No!' yelled Eve. 'He isn't good. He isn't sticking by me, and he's hardly been in much at all. And when he does come, he hates it. Can't get out of here quick enough. But today! He brought this woman. *Carolina!*' Eve rocked her head from side to side as she announced the name of The Other Woman. 'He's taking her out tonight. On our anniversary, of all days. How could he do that to me? Today is our second anniversary, Mum. It's two years since he told me he'd never met anyone like me. I *lit him up*.'

The door whooshed open.

'Mr and Mrs Chapman, good afternoon,' smiled Miss Thompson.

'What is it, Lucy?' said Eve to her surgeon, her voice flat. She hoped this was just a regular visit; she couldn't cope with any more bad news today.

Eve felt she knew Miss Thompson well enough now to be on first name terms with her, even if Lucy couldn't return the informal mode of address.

Douglas' brow furrowed. 'Is everything all right? I mean, is there something you need to tell us?'

'No, not at all, just popping in for a regular check-up on our lovely Eve here,' said Lucy. 'I am happy to tell you, though, that we're very pleased with her. She's doing well, and her vital signs are improving. All we need now is hope, and a little bit of luck that things will start to speed up.'

'And that's good, is it?' scoffed Mary. 'Even though you're basically saying that you can't do any more for her? Everything else she has to do for herself? And some of it's down to *luck*?'

'I'm sorry, Mrs Chapman. It is very frustrating, I know,' said Lucy. 'The wait can feel interminable, but already she is doing a lot more for herself than when she first came in. I'm sure you've noticed that there are not so many tubes attached to her now. She's breathing unaided and all we need to do is wait for her to wake up in her own time. If she's lucky then it could be soon, or it could still be weeks away yet, we just don't know. But it *will* happen, I'm sure of it. She's young, and otherwise fit and healthy. We just need to wait for her body to decide it wants to fight back.'

'That *is* good then, isn't it, Douglas?' said Mary, but the smile Douglas gave her failed to reach his eyes and he shoved his hands into his pockets.

'Oh, Dad, don't be like that,' said Eve. 'I *am* doing OK. I'm much better than I was. You heard what Lucy said as well as I did. I'm going to get better, I know I am.' Eve put her arms around him and gave him a hug. All wasted, she knew, but it raised her spirits even if she couldn't raise his.

Lucy was gone as quickly as she had arrived.

'So, Mum, what should I do about Nathan?' Eve asked, sitting down next to her mother.

'So, back to the subject of Nathan,' said Douglas.

'Well, he's clearly making an effort, but I do think he should be here more,' said Mary. 'Eve needs visitors all the time. Remember what Miss Thompson said about voices stimulating the brain. This has gone on long enough now. We all need to do more to try and bring her back. Shall we get him over for supper and sort out some sort of rota with him? Make sure one of us is here for her at every visiting session? What do you think?'

'Yes, if you think it's a good idea, love.'

Poor Mum, thought Eve. She was deluding herself if she thought Nathan would go and see them on his own, even before Carolina came on the scene.

Nathan had a polite but distant relationship with Eve's parents, and they had always welcomed him into their home, despite their misgivings about him. More recently, Eve tended to visit her parents when Nathan was working late, preferring to have them all to herself. It made life easier for everyone.

'I think it would be a good idea,' Mary went on. 'We can't come every day, it's just too far. And Hattie does what she can, but she has Abbie to think about. I know he's busy, but it's much easier for him to get here than it is for us.'

'Oh Mum, he won't come for supper,' sighed Eve. 'And I don't even think he'll be back here to see me anymore.'

'Hmm,' said Luca, as Eve recounted Nathan's visit later that day.

'Is this the point where you tell me you saw straight through him, right from the start?' grunted Eve.

'No. No, I'd never do that,' said Luca. 'I don't know him well enough. But if he can give up on you so easily, it says something about his strength of character, doesn't it?'

'But we were so happy together,' said Eve.

'Back in a normal world you were, where there were no obstacles,' said Luca.

'We had loads in common, same taste in a lot of stuff. We laughed together, all the time. We had so much fun.'

Eve thought back to the good times they had shared, the mischief they had wreaked. They'd only been going out for a few weeks when they went on a shopping trip together. Nathan had suggested the Wonder Room in Selfridges.

Eve watched in awe as assistants in Hugo Boss suits hovered, intimidating enough before she'd even glanced in the cabinets full of diamonds and fancy watches, all out of their price range.

Eve popped her handbag into the crook of her arm—even though it was only a cheap high-street offering—and pulled herself up to her full height before announcing:

'Isn't this the one you like, darling?' The watch had a price tag of fifteen thousand pounds.

Scenting the whiff of a sale, an immaculate assistant was immediately beside them. 'Would you like to try it on, sir?'

'We're just looking at the moment, thank you,' said Nathan.

'Yes, he'd like to try it on, please,' said Eve. She nudged Nathan to hush any protests.

As the assistant extracted the watch from the cabinet, he said: 'And for the lady?'

'Diamonds,' said Eve, with a toss of her hair. 'Always diamonds.' She didn't dare catch Nathan's eye.

'Well, we have a lovely diamond-studded ladies' Omega Seamaster. Would you like to take a look?'

The two of them paraded around the room with

thirty-five thousand pounds worth of watches on their wrists.

'Perhaps we should pop upstairs and have some lunch first, darling?' said Eve, feeling the need to extricate herself from the situation. 'While we think it over?'

Once they were out of earshot the pair of them collapsed into fits of laughter. 'Oh, you were good in there,' said Nathan. 'I don't know how you managed to play it so cool.'

As they left the restaurant later Nathan said, 'Let's avoid the Wonder Room on the way out, shall we?'

They whizzed through the perfume department, dodging the sales assistants armed with spray bottles until one of them pounced and ensnared Nathan. Eve succumbed and bought him some aftershave, and every time she smelled it on him afterwards, it took her straight back to that day and made her smile at the memory. Things *had* been good. *Very* good, for most of the time.

'But did you ever have to deal with any big challenges?' Luca asked. 'Any major problems that tested the strength of your relationship?'

'Um, no, not really, I suppose. We did have a patch when he was having a tough time at work. For a while he even thought of jacking it all in, going off and doing teacher training or something. I told him we could do it, that we'd manage if we moved in together, but in the end he never took it any further. Things were a bit tricky then. He was really tense, you know. We argued a bit, but before we knew it, things were back on track, and he didn't mention it again and everything kind of settled down.'

'That's fairly minor, though, in the grand scheme of things,' said Luca. 'People go through a lot worse. It wasn't a real test of your relationship. Other than demonstrating that he was reluctant to give up his independence.'

'Well, um, I suppose. I hadn't thought of it that way,' said Eve, furrowing her brows. Something seemed to click behind her eyes, and she sighed. 'Two years together and we were no closer to something permanent than we were at the start.'

'I'm so sorry, Eve,' said Luca.

'Don't feel sorry for me. I've been the fool in all this. Couldn't see past the end of my nose in our rosy little relationship, could I? What a fool I was. And what a fool he's made of me.'

'He hasn't made a fool of you. Not at all. If anything, it's shown what a coward he is. He doesn't deserve you.'

'Doesn't stop me loving him, though,' said Eve.

Luca stood up and crossed the room.

'So, you said this Carolina woman could hear you? That's pretty amazing. I suppose you had rather strong feelings about her, once you'd worked out what was going on?'

'Yeah, you could say that.'

'Well, you remember how I told you that your loved ones can't feel you? Maybe because you disliked her so intensely and so immediately, your energies could be felt by her. They were kind of concentrated on her.'

'That makes sense, I suppose.'

'This woman could feel you in the room because you hated her, whereas Nathan couldn't, because you still love him.'

'Yeah. Back to what I said earlier. I'm a fool, aren't I? I do, though. I do still love him, despite all this. Oh, what am I going to do?'

'Don't panic just yet, Eve. Is there a chance all this

might have an innocent explanation? She could just be a friend.'

'Oh, I don't know. I would like to give him the benefit of the doubt, but there was definite chemistry between them. And he was taking her out on our anniversary. He'd even forgotten it was our anniversary. The ultimate kick in the teeth.'

'I'm sorry, Eve.'

'Please don't pity me,' shot Eve, turning her face away from him.

Luca crossed the room and leaned on the windowsill, staring down at the street below. 'Then don't tell me your troubles,' he said quietly.

Eve turned back to him.

'No, I'm the one who should be sorry. You listen to me ranting on and then I bite your head off. You're the only friend I have right now. I should be nicer to you.' She put her hand on his arm and a tingle ran through her fingers. 'Friends?'

'Yes, friends, of course we are,' said Luca. 'Always.'

'Not for always, I hope,' laughed Eve. 'And I mean that in the nicest possible way. Do you think we'll remember each other when we get out of here?'

'Who knows,' said Luca.

I hope so, thought Eve. Luca couldn't read her thoughts, after all.

At least, as far as she knew.

Hopeful

'Yes, don't worry,' said Nathan.

'Come on, then,' said a female voice, and the door swung behind them. Eve cursed the fact that she hadn't managed to extricate herself from the death-darkness until the final few moments of Nathan's visit. Who was this woman? She hoped she was just one of the medical team, calling him outside to tell him something in private.

'Thank you for coming, Nathan,' Eve said inside her head. 'I'll try to be a bit more awake next time.' She wished she knew what day of the week it was, or how long she'd even been in here. Probably just a few days, maybe even a week or so.

'This has gone on long enough now,' she'd heard her mother say earlier. How long was long enough? It couldn't have been that long, because she'd know otherwise, wouldn't she?

If only her parents could be as positive about things as Nathan was. All he wanted was for her to get better, but some days they were all doom and gloom.

'What will we do if she doesn't come back to us?' they'd say.

Sometimes the death-darkness was better than listening to their negativity. It had to be hard for them, though, having her stuck here like this. In London, a long way from their home.

But they didn't need to worry, because Nathan was looking after her. Talking to her probably, too, although sometimes she missed that if she was still asleep. She felt safe in his love. He wanted her back with him and he'd make sure she got the best treatment and got better.

She knew he would.

19

'So, what did you used to do for fun, back in the day?' asked Luca.

He had taken Eve to the A&E department. It was the first time she had visited—other than for a fractured wrist as a child—and she couldn't believe how busy it was, compared to the rest of the hospital.

Luca leaned back in his seat, feet crossed, hands in his trouser pockets. As though he was sitting in the park on a Sunday afternoon.

'I liked to paint,' said Eve, turning towards him. 'I converted my spare room into a studio so whenever I had the chance, I was in there.'

'What kind of stuff?' said Luca.

'Acrylics mostly. Fairly abstract stuff. I loved it.' She sighed. 'I'd just managed to get a gallery on the King's Road to accept a couple of pieces, actually. I was so excited about that.'

'As you should be. That's pretty major,' said Luca.

'What about you?' said Eve. 'What was your *thing* when you weren't lawyering?'

'Well, I'd love to be able to say I was a concert pianist, or a virtuoso cellist in my leisure hours, but I wasn't. I do play the piano, though. Badly, most of the time, but hey, I enjoy it. My neighbours less so.'

Eve laughed and then fell silent, looking away. 'I know why you brought me here,' she said a few moments later. 'It's a distraction technique, isn't it?'

'Sure is. Is it working?' said Luca.

'Maybe.'

They watched as a man pushed a woman past them in a wheelchair, clutching a surgical pack to her bleeding stomach. A father, face white with panic, ran in with a limp child in his arms as a tearful teenager in cricket whites with his arm at an awkward ankle staggered through. The walking wounded and the worried well at every turn.

'Plenty to look at, anyway,' said Luca.

A dishevelled man rose from his seat near Eve and stumbled to the desk. 'Four hours now,' he said to the booking-in nurse in a gravelly voice. 'Four hours I've sat here. I'm as sick as this lot and they're all going through before me.'

'Sir, we will get to you as soon as we can,' said the nurse. 'Could you please sit down? We will call you when it's your turn.'

'I wonder how many times a day the poor woman has to say that,' said Luca. 'I didn't want you moping in your room all day, by the way.'

'I wasn't moping,' said Eve. 'But I can't stop thinking about it, Luca. I mean, who on earth would want to go out with someone whose partner is in a coma? What kind of person would do something like that? She must be really desperate.'

'Eve, stop trying to analyse the whole thing,' said Luca. 'Wait till the next time Nathan comes in and see what happens then.'

'Somehow I don't think there'll be a next time,' said Eve.

'Oh no, look at this,' said Luca, sitting up straight. The automatic doors flew open and a man on a trolley was pushed through, a drip attached to him. 'Ambulance case. Looks nasty.'

'This is the hit-and-run we phoned in,' shouted one of the paramedics. 'Male, forty-five, multiple contusions, possible internal bleeding.'

'Straight through,' said the admissions nurse. 'They're ready for you.'

'Shall we go and watch?' said Luca.

'What, the operation, you mean?' said Eve.

'Well, you watched your own, so why not this one?'

'No, not today. Let's go and check on him later, instead.' Eve sighed. 'Do you think she feels sorry for him?'

'What? Who?'

'Carolina, of course. I can just imagine him playing the sympathy card at work, everyone fawning over him. Women falling at his feet. Pathetic. It's all so underhand, isn't it? I bet he feels that because he can't officially dump me, it's fine just to move on. I wonder if he'll bother to explain it to me when I wake up? Do you think I'll remember it, or will he get to dump me all over again, to my face? Maybe he won't even have the nerve to do that. Maybe he'll just disappear off the planet.'

Luca placed his hand on hers. Once again there was that strange tingle.

'I wish there was something I could say or do that would make you feel better.'

'You do help, thank you. I know you're trying your best, and I'm sorry you have to listen to me ranting on about him the whole time. It's just that I can't concentrate on anything else at the moment. This is all so unlike Nathan. He's such a kind, caring person so I'm having real trouble reconciling his behaviour to the person I know. The person I love.'

'Well, then wait and see,' said Luca. 'If he comes in

next time and everything's fine, then you've no need to worry. And if he doesn't come in, then you'll know where you stand. Anyway, come on. Let's go for a walk.'

'Where are we off to now?'

'Oh, just doing our rounds. We're like the doctors, in a way, aren't we?'

'How do you know when people will need you, Luca? Have you got a kind of sixth sense for it, or something? I mean, every time I've been with you and we've helped someone, it's seemed pretty random.'

'Sometimes you know beforehand. Normally that's what happens with the bigger things. Other times you just feel a pull. Remember how you were with that man in the room next to you?' said Luca.

'Len. Yes. He was lovely. It's weird, isn't it?'

'Yes, but nice, too. It's a good feeling when you can help people.'

'It is. But why do we have to do it? What makes us this way?' said Eve. 'We can't help ourselves, can't make our own bodies get better any quicker, but we can do all these amazing things. They're just little things really, but they seem to make such a difference to other people. To their emotional state. To their souls, almost. Why, Luca?'

'Why, indeed,' said Luca. 'It's like a calling, isn't it? One day it will become clear to you. Clearer, at least.'

'Can't you tell me now?'

'We have work to do. Explanations are best given when we've some quiet time. We need to keep an eye on that poor guy, the hit-and-run. God only knows if we'll be able to do anything for him, but there are bound to be some distraught family members in need of comfort.'

Eve stood side-by-side with Luca as, together, they peered through the window into the operating theatre. The floor was awash with blood and the surgeons' faces told a tale of desperate last measures.

'Really, we've got very little to worry about compared to some, haven't we?' said Luca.

'He's not going to make it, is he?' whispered Eve, hand to her lips.

'I don't think so,' said Luca. 'Look.'

Above the man's body the air quivered. Eve couldn't really say that she had definitely seen a spirit leave his body—it wasn't a peaceful process, like Len's passing—but there was something, some kind of presence. This presence looked torn, somehow, as though it couldn't decide whether to stay or go.

'He's a fighter, that's for sure,' said Luca. 'His spirit is trying to get back inside.'

'But failing,' said Eve. 'That's so sad. He's not very old. His poor family.'

Eve and Luca had spent some time in the family room, trying to give what comfort they could before realising that these poor relatives—a wife and twin boys of around eight or nine—were too shocked, too distraught to be receptive to the gentle comfort they had to offer.

'It's going to be a lot for them to deal with,' said Luca. 'You're right, we're very lucky in comparison.'

'We'll get back, I know we will,' said Eve.

'Let's hope so. And when we do, we've both got great lives to go back to, whatever or whoever might be in them when we get there,' said Luca.

'Even if it is all over with Nathan, I had a good life before all this.'

'Yes, you did.'

'I'd cope. I'm fine with being on my own. I have so much other good stuff in my life.'

Luca looked her directly in the eye. 'It will take you a while to get over Nathan, Eve. Longer than these brave words of yours. But you're going to be fine, whatever happens.'

'Is there anyone in your life now?' Eve asked suddenly. 'I mean, Lauren's still hanging around but . . .'

'Nope. No one. But I'm hoping that . . .'

He stopped short as the shimmering over the man's body began again. This time it was more violent, and as the medical staff reached for the paddles to shock him, it seemed to hang back, to wait in a corner of the room, before once again taking up its position above him.

The medics shook their heads, looked up at the clock, and a nurse scribbled down the time of death. Eve expected the shape over the bed to have gone, but it was still there.

'Why hasn't it gone yet?' she said to Luca.

'It doesn't always go straight away. I suppose it's like it needs to check that it's OK to go, that there's nothing more that can be done for him. I've seen it like this a few times now.'

'Oh, God, it's so sad,' said Eve.

Where the air particles had shivered and shaken, suddenly there was a stillness over the body. A nurse began to detach tubes and wires from the man, and the rest of the team left the room, their heads bowed.

'What a huge responsibility,' said Eve. 'Someone's life hanging in the balance like that, and you're the one who has to save it. Or not.'

'They've done their best,' said Luca. 'But sometimes that's just not enough.'

Eve sighed. 'Should we split up?' she suggested. 'I'll do the family and you take care of the medics? I think they need our help too, don't you?'

'You really are getting the hang of this, aren't you?' said Luca, smiling at Eve. 'Go on then, off you go.'

An hour later, they reconvened outside the operating theatre.

'He's still in there,' said Eve, looking at the forlorn shape on the trolley, a sheet now covering his entire body. 'Why haven't they taken him away?'

'The donor team have just been in and harvested what they needed,' said Luca. 'They took his heart, lungs, liver, and kidneys. Four people will get a second chance at life thanks to him.'

They watched as the porters arrived to take the body away.

'It's just so final,' said Eve. 'So sudden. That poor guy probably went off to work this morning, not knowing that he'd never see his family again. I bet he would have said different things to them, had he known.'

'I know I would,' said Luca.

'Me too,' said Eve. 'Me too.'

20

Six Weeks After the Accident

'So, dog or cat?' asked Eve. They were sitting on a bench in the foyer of the hospital, watching the world go by. As they did so very often now.

'What do you mean?' said Luca.

'Are you a dog person or a cat person?'

'Both, I think.'

'You can't say that. You need to choose.'

'Why do I have to choose? I like both.'

'No, you have to choose. I want to know,' said Eve.

'Dog then. You?'

'Cat.'

'Well, I'm glad we've cleared that up.'

Eve giggled. 'I've got a cat. Buster. Does that mean that if you met me in real life, you wouldn't like me because I like cats better than dogs?'

'No, I never said that. You were the one that brought this up, remember? What are you trying to do, Eve, analyse me from my pet preferences?'

'No, I just want to know, that's all.'

'Well, if it makes you feel better, we had both when I was growing up, and I loved them equally. Fido the dog and Fluffy the cat.'

'That's so original.' She rolled her eyes.

'Well, I didn't choose them, did I? I was only a kid. If I was choosing, then it would've been something with a little more gravitas. Something from Greek mythology, I reckon. Aphrodite or Artemis, something like that.'

'So posh.'

'I'm not posh.'

'You are. You use words like *gravitas* in your speech.'

'Sorry.'

'Don't apologise. I like it.'

'Glad to be of service,' said Luca.

'Have you ever been outside?' said Eve. 'While you've been like this, I mean?'

'Yes, I have. Why do you ask?'

'It's that pull you spoke of. I'm really feeling it. I'll need to go a little bit further soon, I think.'

'Just be careful. Don't rush into anything.'

'I won't, but I want to try. Maybe not today, but soon.'

'That's really good,' he said. 'Progress.'

'Does the whole thing with the magic touch work outside, too?'

'Yes, but seriously, wait till you're ready.'

'I will.'

Luca looked away with a sigh.

'What's up?' Eve asked.

'Oh, just thinking. Regretting. You know.'

'Regretting what?' said Eve.

'You shouldn't be here, Eve.'

'What do you mean, I shouldn't be here?'

'I mean, I'm glad you are. For me. For company. But you're not supposed to be. This wasn't meant to happen.'

'I don't follow you.'

'You should be out there, back in your real life, doing what you do, not stuck in here, not knowing when you're going to get better.'

'Neither of us should be here,' said Eve, and placed a

hand on his arm. 'It's just some cruel twist of fate that's put us here, isn't it? There's no point sitting around, moping about it. We have to make the best of what's been dealt us. That's what you were always telling me in the early days, when I was trying to understand it all.'

Luca suddenly slapped his hands on his thighs and stood up. 'Anyway, this has been lovely, but going out is exactly what I need to do right now.'

Eve found the change in his demeanour quite jarring. 'Oh, you're off. OK.'

'You won't try anything silly while I'm not here, will you? Wait for me, Eve. When you're ready to go outside, I'll come with you. Promise?'

'Yeah, I suppose so,' said Eve. 'Where are you going, anyway?'

'There's someone I need to help. Maybe I'll get to do the job properly this time.'

'What do you mean?'

'I'll catch you later. Take care, Eve.' And with that, he was gone. Eve watched him rush down the hospital steps, and as he crossed the road, it was almost as if he just faded away.

The urge was still strong.

Eve just wanted to stand near the open doors and sniff the fresh air, or at least pretend to sniff it, to see if she could remember what those smells were like. She yearned to breathe in freshly mown lawns, flowers, the earthy smell after a downpour. But even if she closed her eyes and focused on her sense of smell, there was nothing there. Nothing at all.

Despite Luca's warning, she walked over to the automatic doors, half of her bracing herself to go further, the other half knowing she should pull back and wait for another day.

A heavily pregnant woman, her face contorted in pain, staggered past, leaning on the arm of her anxious partner who was carrying a huge holdall.

'Good luck to you both,' Eve said to them. 'I hope it goes well. I might pop in on you later and see what you had.'

A little girl clutching a large bouquet of flowers with a bright pink 'It's a Girl!' balloon walked past. 'Don't you look pretty,' said Eve, bending down to speak to her, as though the girl would hear her. 'Are you off to visit your new sister? How exciting!'

Eve stood up as the girl and her father moved on, and when there was a gap in the flow of people, she stepped gingerly towards the automatic doors.

Nothing happened.

Of course nothing happened. Of course they didn't open, because she wasn't real. She had no body, no weight, no *gravitas*.

So, what now? Wait until someone else came in and the doors slid open again, or just walk right through them? She could do that. She'd done it before, but only when Luca had dragged her through, and she hadn't had time to overthink it. It shouldn't hurt, but that explanation he'd given her about having resistance to solid matter—like sitting on a chair or leaning against a wall—frightened her. Knowing her luck, she would crash into these doors and make a complete fool of herself. Not that anyone would witness it, but even so.

Eve set her sights on the world outside. It was right there, through the glass, just out of reach.

She decided it might be better to close her eyes and

just walk. She stepped towards the doors and there was a whoosh as they swung apart, and a new group of people came in.

She didn't know if she had gone through them herself or passed through as someone else caused them to open.

But she was outside.

She'd done it.

21

It felt so good to be away from the hospital. Not just to prove to herself that she could do it, but to satisfy the urge that continued to tug at her. Luca had told her he needed to go and help someone, and Eve had a niggling feeling that she had been called out for a similar reason.

She just didn't know what that reason was yet.

She looked around, as though seeing everything for the first time. This was the London she knew so well and used to take for granted, and it was a wonderful feeling to be a part of it again.

Elegant buildings, modern glass structures rubbing shoulders with ancient stone turrets. A glorious blue sky latticed with vapour trails. Tips of trees in the Archbishop's Park swaying in the gentle breeze. The hustle and bustle of the busy street, horns blaring and a siren whining somewhere in the distance.

And people. So many people. Eve forced her body to mimic the movements of inhaling deeply and exhaling slowly, almost remembering how good it felt.

She walked slowly down the steps and glanced behind her, back at the hospital. She knew she mustn't stray too far, not on this first foray out. What would happen if she ran out of energy and couldn't get back inside, couldn't reach the safe haven of her room? How long could she leave her body for? As much as she wanted to go forward, she didn't want to take too many risks. Not at this stage. Not until she understood more.

She followed the flow of pedestrians along Lambeth Palace Road, watching in awe as normal everyday life unfolded around her. Every commute, every jog, every bus ride was a special gift to mankind, and just like those people around her now, she had taken such freedoms for granted. Now that she couldn't jump on a bus or hail a cab, it left an aching feeling of loss in her stomach.

When Eve saw a young couple holding hands, she felt the loss of her former life even more keenly. She watched as the young man leaned over to whisper something in the woman's ear, his eyes full of fire. His nose caught her cheek, tickling the woman, and she raised her hand to brush her face, laughing.

How she envied these people and their real, ordinary lives, their ability to touch and feel and love. She would sacrifice every future bus trip or taxi ride or daily commute just to have that sensation again.

She moved on, observing how no one made eye contact. How they furtively looked away or glanced to one side. The streets were a sea of people, but each individual was an island, intent on its own destination. Now, Eve could look deeply into these people's eyes and not suffer their sudden downwards glance, embarrassed that they might be at risk of engaging with someone.

Eve decided then and there that she would be very different if she got back into her body. She would be that person who looked up and smiled, that person who struck up conversation, just because.

She headed towards Lambeth Palace, its Tudor turrets towering above the low-rise office buildings. She was conscious that it was a long way from the hospital, but this was the way she felt she must go.

She hadn't felt any pain, so she tried to keep her cool. She didn't want to turn back yet, presuming she would know when it was time to return. The small hospital room that had been her sanctuary felt like a prison cell, now that she was out here in this vast and wondrous space.

When Eve spotted a party of school children, a serene feeling of certainty and knowledge settled upon her. She knew that this group was who she had been sent out to help. Something was going to happen, and she would be the one who would prevent it.

She heard the rumble of the motorbike, watched as it tore over the bridge and swung around the corner.

She knew what she had to do.

When Eve ran to the crossing, squeezed past the remaining children, and put herself between the teacher and the motorbike, she wondered if this was the end. Maybe this was what Luca meant about being the chosen ones—that they were sacrificial lambs, sent out into the world to prevent bad things from happening to other people. For the first time ever, her actions felt like a matter of life and death.

Eyes tightly shut, Eve heard the rider's muffled groan beneath his helmet as he realised that he was going to career into a party of children. There was a screech of rubber on asphalt and Eve felt the impact deep in her core.

For a moment, there was silence. She thought she had failed, but when she opened her eyes, it was as though she and the bike had become one. Her form was wrapped around the machine, cushioning it like a giant brake pad. She ached in a way she'd never experienced before, but compared to what metal could do to real flesh, the effect was miniscule.

Cocooned by Eve, the bike came to a perfect halt. Other than a short skid-mark on the road, there was little evidence of the speed at which it had been travelling and the sheer force with which it had been stopped. She had managed to summon enough power—direct her energies, as Luca called it—to stop a motorbike, something she could never have done in her human form.

How could she possibly have so much strength when there was so little to her? It was phenomenal.

Eve unwrapped herself from the bike and watched the rest of the children walk to the pavement on the opposite side of the road, followed by another teacher. She noted the expression of near-missed horror this woman shared with the other adults.

'How on earth . . .?' said the teacher.

'Shh,' said another. 'I have absolutely no idea, but let's keep that between us for now, shall we?'

Now there was just the motorcyclist to attend to. Freed from the invisible force which had enrobed him, Eve watched as he drove a few metres more before pulling over and wheeling his bike towards the Riverside Café on the embankment. She followed him and as he pulled off his helmet, shaking out a mane of long, dark hair, he became a she. Tucking her helmet under her arm, the biker walked unsteadily to the café and ordered a coffee.

'Double espresso please, Antonio,' she said to the barista.

'You all right, Nadia? You look like you've seen a ghost.'

'Yeah, I'm OK. Near miss at the crossing. Nothing a drop of caffeine won't sort out, though.'

When Nadia sat down on the wall by the SOE monument, Eve joined her. As the woman sipped at her coffee, hands trembling, the colour began to return to her cheeks. She took a deep breath, letting it out as a sigh.

'It's all right,' Eve said, placing a hand gently on her

shoulder. As she did, Nadia looked in her direction, seeing right through Eve. Then she adjusted the collar of her leathers and flexed her shoulders, as though something was prickling inside.

Eve stayed with Nadia until she finished her coffee and her breathing returned to normal. The woman tossed her empty cup into the bin, waved to Antonio, and headed back to her bike. She hesitated for a moment before wheeling it to the roadside and climbing on. Eve stood behind her as she fastened her helmet.

'Take care, Nadia,' Eve said as Nadia started up the bike. 'Be safe.'

Then she watched as Nadia sped off into the distance.

Remembering

The smell reminded Eve of something . . . perfume . . . aftershave . . . but she couldn't place it.

Sniffing any harder or breathing more deeply wasn't an option because, other than the shallow breaths she already took, her nose and chest wouldn't work anymore than they were.

At least the breathing machine was gone now. The metallic click-click *had offended Eve's eardrums, and that feeling of her lungs being artificially inflated and deflated was too . . . well, she had no words to describe it. It was like nothing she'd ever felt before. If she'd been able to move, she knew she would have tried to yank those tubes and wires off her body, sit up and tell them that she didn't need any of their help, that she could do it all on her own.*

But that smell. What was it?

And then it came to her. It was the aftershave that Nathan used to wear, the one she had bought for him. It wasn't anything expensive, just something they both liked the smell of when they'd been out shopping one day and he'd been mobbed by sales assistants. Recently he had switched to an expensive designer brand, but she'd never liked that quite as much.

Had he been here? Wearing his old smell? She hadn't heard him, but that didn't mean he hadn't come. A lot of men must wear that aftershave, though. It could be pure coincidence.

'Nathan, help me,' she called.

Something was pulling at her arm now, making her surrender her delicious memories in favour of the deepest of sleeps.

PART 3

MAKING A BREAK

22

Six Weeks After the Accident

Eve was bursting with pride as she walked back to the hospital, but as she neared the steps to the entrance it was as though someone had punched her in the stomach. She doubled over in pain, grabbing a lamppost for support.

'Oh my God. Someone help me,' she gasped, even though she knew nobody could hear her.

'I'm here,' said a voice behind her. She almost collapsed with relief.

'Luca, thank God. I don't think I can get back.'

'Shh, you'll be fine. Come on, lean on me.'

Luca put one arm firmly around Eve's waist and draped her arm over his shoulder. She was surprised at the sensation this gave her—not of touch, exactly, but a kind of glow, as though the heat from his form was warming hers. When she had touched Luca's hand in the past, it felt different than this, like her hand was sitting on his, floating above it. This feeling was far more intense and seemed to fuse their bodies into one stronger entity.

He gave her the strength to make it back up the steps.

The glare from the sunshine had turned the doors into a pair of full-length mirrors; Luca steered her away from them. 'Close your eyes,' he said. 'It'll make going through the doors a lot easier.'

'OK,' she said. 'But it didn't hurt on the way out.'

'It's just safer for now,' he said, 'while you're so weak.

Shut them now and I'll tell you when we're through to the other side.'

There was a whoosh as the doors opened to disgorge a young family and Luca led her carefully through.

'You can open up now. You OK?'

'It hurts,' she said, clutching her stomach. 'But it was like I got some of your strength, hanging onto you. Is that how it works?'

Luca noticed a small white feather lodged in Eve's hair, but as he reached to flick it away it disappeared.

'It seems to be what happens, but I don't really know why,' he said.

Eve turned to face him.

Luca's eyes really were a startling blue. She noted, too, how his hair curled upwards quite endearingly over the collar of his shirt. At that moment, she wanted nothing more than to put it between her fingers and feel how silky it was.

The thought made her gasp and she pulled away from him, embarrassed that he might have noticed her staring.

'Are you all right?' he asked.

'Um . . . yes . . . thanks,' she stuttered. 'I think I'm good on my own now. Thank you. I . . . um . . . I'd better get back and check on that body of mine.' She was speaking too fast. And walking faster than she had the strength for.

'Are you sure you're OK?' Luca asked again.

'Quite sure,' said Eve. She kept her eyes firmly in the direction of travel, not daring to make eye contact with Luca.

Eve hoped her voice didn't betray the confusing mass of emotions that had suddenly overcome her. She blamed it on the immense sense of relief she felt when Luca came to her rescue. Didn't people often develop feelings for those who had saved them? It was just a touch of hero-worship, nothing more than that.

It would pass.

A quick check of her body revealed that nothing had changed. She was no medical expert, but she had come to recognise what constituted 'normal' for herself, and the lines on the screens continued to pump out the same repetitive patterns of peaks and valleys.

She collapsed onto the floor in her usual spot, her back against the wall. Luca sat down beside her. Despite her earlier awkwardness, Eve didn't want him to leave her yet.

'Thank goodness,' she said, letting out a huge sigh. 'And thank you, Luca. I don't know what happened to me out there. It was all going so well. There was this group of schoolkids and a bike and he, I mean she, was going too fast and then . . .'

She couldn't continue. Luca smiled as her eyelids drooped. Her head lolled onto his shoulder, and he propped her back up. But when it flopped there a second time, he decided to leave it.

He was in no hurry to go anywhere. He could wait until she was rested.

'You did well today, Eve,' he said, stroking her cheek. 'Now you're starting to see what this is all about. Sleep well, love.'

He wasn't sure if she heard him or not, but it didn't matter.

When Eve awoke there was a strong male presence in her room. Luca had gone and Nathan was sitting on the side of her bed next to her body.

'Oh, it's you,' she said, blinking the sleep from her

eyes. 'Didn't think you'd have the nerve to show your face around here again.' She pulled herself upright and stood over him, willing him to feel her close by. 'So where is she then? Couldn't she face you parading your sick girlfriend in front of her anymore? Perhaps she does have a conscience, after all. Unlike you, it would seem.'

Nathan's face was pale and there were dark shadows under his eyes. Eve thought it probably had more to do with a run of dizzying social events than from worrying about her.

'What are you doing here, Nathan? Have you had a change of heart, or is the lure of a hospital ward just too much to resist?'

'I can't stay long, Eve. I'm so sorry,' said Nathan. 'I hate to do this to you, but I'm just no good with illness and infirmity. I mean, what if you come out of all this with special needs of some sort? It's not my thing, being a caregiver, and I know you wouldn't want me to hang around to see you like that, would you?'

'How do you know what I'd want, Nathan? I'm not convinced you've *ever* known what I wanted.'

'You'd understand it was for the best that we end things now. You were always so kind, Eve, so caring, and I'd hoped I would be able to cope with this, but . . . I just can't.'

'So, you think that coming here and talking to my comatose body absolves you from everything you're about to do—or have probably already done—with Carolina?'

'I've got my own life to think about, Eve. I have to move on. Carolina has been an absolute rock through this.'

'And *you* should have been *my* rock, Nathan. I just wish I'd seen through you. Mum always said you weren't sincere, but I didn't want to hear it. She said anyone worth their weight would commit to their partner more than you did, but you just weren't prepared to compromise, were you? Everything always had to go your way, or it didn't go at all!'

'I just can't do it, Eve. Let's face it, they can't tell us what's going to happen to you, if you'll get better or not, and what kind of recovery you might make. I'm afraid it's just not me, looking after someone in a wheelchair, with demands that I can't meet.'

He shuddered. Eve thought he was probably imagining having to attend to all her basest needs.

'I hope that one day, if you wake up . . .'

'*When* I wake up,' shouted Eve.

'. . . then you will find it in your heart to forgive me.'

'I will *never* forgive you! What you're doing is the lowest of the low. I never imagined for one minute that you could be this heartless.'

Eve watched as a solitary tear trickled down Nathan's cheek. She didn't feel sorry for him—why should she? He was abandoning her. He didn't love her enough to wait and see if she would come back to him.

'You don't deserve me, Nathan,' she said, her voice dropping to a broken whisper. 'I thought you loved me. I thought things were good between us, that we had a strong relationship.'

'I'm so sorry, Eve. I didn't deserve you. I just don't think our relationship was strong enough in the first place to survive something like this.'

'Just go, will you?' said Eve.

'I'll go now,' said Nathan. 'Goodbye, Eve.'

He opened the door and Carolina walked in.

'How dare you bring her here!' shouted Eve.

Nathan put his arm around Carolina and kissed her on the cheek.

'Did you tell her?' said Carolina. 'Explain how you feel?'

Nathan nodded meekly. 'I did. It was awful, Caro, but I feel so much better now that the weight is off my shoulders. I know she can't hear me, but it was therapeutic, all the same. I don't feel good about this, but I hope you understand my reasons for wanting to come.'

'Oh, for goodness' sake, you two make me want to vomit,' spat Eve.

'There's that noise again,' said Carolina.

'What noise? Are you hearing things again, my love?' said Nathan.

'Oh, she can hear me all right, because I HATE her,' shouted Eve. 'And I HATE you too, Nathan Kellerman. Just go. NOW!' She charged at him with all her might, knowing he probably wouldn't feel a thing.

But as she hit him hard with her shoulder, he stumbled.

'Oh, God, Nathan, are you OK?' said Carolina, grabbing his arm. 'You poor thing, you're weak with emotion. Come on, let's get you home.'

Eve was awestruck. Nathan had stumbled, and she had made it so.

Carolina glanced nervously over her shoulder as she pulled Nathan from the room. As the door swung shut behind them, Eve collapsed into a heap on the floor.

23

'It was awful,' Eve wailed into Luca's shoulder. After Nathan and Carolina had left, she went to seek him out and had been relieved to find him in his room. He was quick to take her in his arms and comfort her.

He said nothing. Simply stroked her hair.

Eve spoke through rasping sobs. 'He's a despicable person if he can do something like that, and I know I should be glad to be rid of him, but it hurts so much. I really loved him, Luca.'

'Shh,' said Luca, wrapping his arms around her even tighter. Eve could feel the glow coming from his body, strengthening her own.

'I wish I could cry properly,' moaned Eve. 'This dry crying thing is rubbish. I never realised before how therapeutic it was to have a good sob. But we can't even do that properly, and it just makes it even worse.'

'No, but you can remember the feeling. It'll still help you.' Luca took a deep breath. 'Now, I'm only going to say this the once, Eve, and then never again, and not because I'm trying to prove I know better or anything, or to lecture to you, but you *are* better off without him. You'll come to realise that when you go back into your body, I know you will.'

'But what if I don't remember this when I wake up? What if I don't remember what he did, and then I have to find out all over again that he's dumped me? That's like being dumped twice over, isn't it?'

'We can't know what we'll remember if we do get back out there, but for now not being with him is actually the right thing for you. He was no good for you, Eve, you're worth a hundred of him. You're a much bigger, much better person than he will ever be. And you're loved. You're loved so much by so many people, and you'll get over this. It might seem like the end of the world right now, but look at the wonderful life that you have, look at what you still have to go back to.'

Eve sat upright and pulled away from Luca so that she could look at him properly.

'How do you always do this, without sounding like Mr Know-It-All? Because you never do. You just sound like a wise person who I know I should really listen to. If someone had come out with all that stuff back in my real life, how Nathan was bad for me, I'd be better off without him and all that, then I wouldn't have wanted to hear a word of it. But when it comes from you, it's different, somehow. Why is that?'

'Because I'm looking out for you, Eve,' said Luca, his face serious. 'It's my job to look out for you. And my pleasure, obviously.'

He looked directly into her eyes. They were both so still, their faces so close. Something shifted in Eve's stomach, a memory of fluttering butterflies, tiny stirrings which she knew weren't really there at all. Was he about to kiss her? Surely not—it would be atrocious timing. But part of her still couldn't help hoping that he might, inappropriate as it seemed.

He was her teacher in all this, after all. Her mentor.

And suddenly, he looked so, so sad.

She pulled back from him slightly. 'Luca, what is it?'

'It was me,' said Luca. 'I tried to protect you. Tried to stop you having the accident. I failed, and now you're in here and I'll never forgive myself for that.'

'What do you mean?' Eve said. And then realisation dawned on her, and she leapt to her feet. 'You mean . . . you mean . . . I was one of the people you were trying to help? That's it, isn't it? And you failed. I was meant to be saved by you, but the accident happened anyway. Christ, this is what you've been getting at, isn't it? All those cryptic comments, all that "we're the chosen ones" stuff. It's all about that, isn't it?'

'Yes, it is,' said Luca. 'You weren't ready to hear about it before, but now I think you are. Now that you've seen the skills we have, and what we can do, I think you will understand. You've saved people too, Eve. You went out there and protected those children, and I know you felt compelled to do it, just like I do. You didn't know why you had to do it, or how, but you did it, all the same. We have a special power, that was what I meant by the chosen ones. We can do things that other people can't. While we're in this state, this nothingness, we can do an awful lot of good.'

Eve kept Luca's gaze, her pupils swivelling from side to side as she tried to make sense of what he was saying. Her mouth opened and closed a couple of times, as though she wanted to speak but couldn't find the right words.

'Are you OK?' said Luca. 'I know it's a lot to get your head round.'

She sat back down, and suddenly laughed out loud.

'It was you, wasn't it?' she said, spinning round to face him again. 'The voice I heard. *Eve, don't go*, it said. That was you. Your voice. In the bathroom, and then when I was going out of the house.'

The sensation had been no more than a gentle brush, a breath of air on the back of her neck, a feeling of something there but not there.

It was real, though. She *hadn't* imagined it.

And then in the evening, as she entered Charing Cross Tube station and headed towards the steps in those cursed new shoes, that sensation had come again. She lost her footing and reached out. She grasped frantically, but instead of meeting solid matter, something which might save her, her hands brushed at thin air, arms flailing like a non-swimmer out of her depth.

Time had slowed down—frozen in mid-air almost. The wide stairway down into the depths of the Underground was teeming with people going in both directions, but not one of them was able to break her fall.

She couldn't remember if she had cried out, but for her, it was like something from a silent movie.

'People say their life flashes before them in moments like that,' Eve said. 'Well, it doesn't. I had no time, Luca. No time to recap on if I'd lived my life well, any regrets I'd had, loves won or lost, joyous moments, moments of tragedy. None of that.'

She'd tried to grab at the handrail that separated the two sides of the staircase, but the momentum of her fall caused her body to tip forward. Headfirst she hit the handrail, and headfirst she plummeted further into the depths. Then it was her head that reached the final step first, whose sharp metal edge would determine her fate, slicing into it before the rest of her body caught up, neck twisted and limbs contorted.

The blackness of death beckoned to her, obliterating everything she thought she knew.

For anyone who witnessed Eve's fall, it was over in the blink of an eye. For them, the frozen horror of her face might return to them briefly the next time they walked the same way, wondering how on earth it could have happened, and if she'd made it out alive.

For Eve, it had been a lifetime in mere minutes of trying not to die, hoping for a miracle, praying to a God she had never truly believed in.

'There was nothing. Just nothing,' she said finally.

'Oh Eve, I'm so sorry. I let you fall. I let you fall and it's all my fault that you're here, like this.'

Eve jumped up. 'Let me just have a moment, will you, Luca?'

She paced around his room, running her fingers through her hair. Finally, she came to a standstill and looked at him. He was still sitting on the floor, head in his hands. When she spoke again, Eve sounded very sure of herself, composed.

'This whole thing is massive, Luca. Beyond belief, really. But it wasn't your fault. How could it have been? It was nothing more than an accident. Whether you were meant to save me or not, it was my fate for that day. Wrong place, wrong time, and all that. I made some snap decisions, did things I shouldn't have, and that's what happened.'

'But . . .'

She raised her hand. 'Let me finish. It wasn't like you pushed me. You can't blame yourself for it. You did your best. The fact that you didn't manage to stop it doesn't make it your fault.'

'But it *is* my fault, Eve. I didn't save you. I didn't manage to hold on to you. I let you fall. And I have to live with that. Just put yourself in my position. Imagine if those children had been hurt, if you'd failed to stop that motorbike the other day. If you were two seconds too late, or not strong enough. How would you have felt about that, if you'd seen it happen before your eyes and couldn't do anything about it?'

Eve looked at him searchingly.

'I need to know more, Luca. I need to understand why we must do all this. Are we part of some great masterplan here? How do we know who we have to save and when? Or why? Why are we chosen? How do we . . .?' Her voice trailed off as she stared into the distance.

'I don't know, Eve. I don't know how it all works. Why we were chosen, or if we were really chosen at all. But when we're called to help, it's the most compelling feeling I've ever had in my entire life. And I know you've felt it too.'

And truly, nothing *had* ever felt more compelling to Eve than this urge.

This urge to help.

24

Back in her room, Eve was still in shock.

Luca had been the one calling to her that day, telling her not to go. He was meant to have saved her from the accident. His was the strange voice she couldn't quite fathom if she'd heard or not. Now she knew she most certainly had.

She couldn't believe that she hadn't worked it out sooner. She hadn't recognised his voice when she first met him in the hospital, but now it seemed bizarre that she hadn't. Of course it was him, his voice was just the same.

Then something else hit her with a jolt, juddering in the place where her heart ought to be.

She ran back into Luca's room, bursting straight through the closed door to find him where she had left him, slumped on the floor.

'It was you,' she said. 'On the train. You were the man sitting opposite me on the Tube that morning.'

'Yes,' said Luca. 'I don't quite know how you managed to see me. It doesn't happen a lot. Occasionally someone we're watching can sense our presence, like you did that day, but most of the time they don't even realise they're being looked after. They don't really need to know. That's the whole point of it, really. They carry on with their lives and we look out for them.'

'I can't believe I didn't realise. Why didn't I recognise you when I first saw you in here?'

'I suppose you have other, more dominant, memories of that day. Just think about how many people, strangers, you might glance at in the course of a day. Unless something happens to jog your memory, then most of those faces are instantly forgotten, aren't they?'

'Yeah, I suppose.' A shiver ran down her spine. 'Still, even so.'

Luca sat quietly, waiting for her to speak again.

'So how long had you been watching me?' said Eve.

'A while. It started not long after I got here.'

'But why me? People hurt themselves all the time, so why was it me you had to help? There must be people far worthier of your attention.'

'It was my duty. You were the one I had to watch.' Luca stood up. 'Come with me.' They left his room and walked a few steps along the corridor. 'It's time for you to know.'

'Know what?' said Eve as they stopped in front of a door. 'Whoa! This is the Gents' bathroom. I can't go in there.'

'You're invisible. It'll be fine.'

'No, Luca, you don't get it. I'm not worried about being seen. It's just that no woman in her right mind *ever* wants to set foot inside a Gents' loo.'

'OK then. Point taken. In that case we'll go into the Ladies'.' Luca had a wild look about him. This wasn't some kind of prank. This was serious.

'But why?'

'Just bear with me. I'm going to show you something that might come as a bit of a surprise to start with. Close your eyes for a moment.'

Eve walked hesitantly as Luca led her into the toilets, her eyes closed. They shuffled to a halt in front of a long mirror.

'Say something, Luca,' said Eve.

'Open your eyes.' He put his hands firmly on her

shoulders, rooting her to the spot. 'You can look now.'

And so, she opened them.

'No,' she gasped. 'No, I don't understand!'

She reeled back, freeing herself from his grip, then clutched at her stomach, as though in pain.

'No, Luca. Why? Why didn't you tell me this before? Oh my God, I can't believe it. You should have told me first. It's too much! You should have told me this!'

And without waiting for a reply, Eve turned and fled from the room, passing straight through the wooden door.

'Eve, don't go,' he called, but it was too late.

He was always too late.

25

Eve couldn't believe it. Couldn't believe Luca had let so many weeks go by without telling her. How could he keep something so mind-blowingly important from her?

She staggered out of the toilets and kept going, out through the foyer and towards the exit, avoiding her reflection in the glass doors as she left the hospital. She couldn't face seeing it again, that monstrous thing.

Her vision was blurry. She couldn't walk straight, couldn't think straight. She was glad no one could see her, lurching along the street like a pathetic drunk.

She kept walking. She didn't know where she was heading, but she needed to get away from him, away from the truth.

It wasn't Luca's fault she was like this, but he could have told her sooner. He could at least have prepared her for what she was about to see, instead of dragging her to a mirror and forcing her to face up to it, there and then. She didn't know how she felt about him anymore. She'd thought he was her friend, but if he was then he should have been honest with her from the start.

Friends didn't keep enormous secrets like that.

She walked and walked with no particular purpose, but when she passed Lambeth North Station, she realised she had come quite a long way, the furthest she had been from the hospital. A walk that in her human form would have been just a few minutes suddenly felt a lot further. After her last experience of leaving the hospital, she was wary of going too far and not being able to get back. The pain before had been excruciating, and she couldn't always rely on Luca to rush to her aid when she needed him.

After this, could she rely on him for anything?

She considered the wretch she had become—a hopeless soul, disembodied, caught up in something that she would never understand, and with no idea if life would ever return to normal. If her body failed to gain strength and recover, would she be stuck like this forever? Permanently in a coma and permanently out of her body, with a huge responsibility for other people's survival on her shoulders? And what would happen if she died? If they decided to switch off those machines that were keeping her alive? Would everything end right then, even this meagre existence she knew now?

The blocks of newly built, luxury apartments soon gave way to shabbier, more downtrodden properties. Eve put her own problems behind her for the moment and slowed down, taking in the tall townhouses, which in Victorian times must have been grand dwellings. Now the columns of named push-button bells by front doors spoke of too many bodies sharing cramped conditions.

Like an anthill.

A group of small, dark-skinned children played in the street, too young to be out alone, Eve thought. Three youths on bicycles hung around on a street corner, practising wheelies and stunts, swinging their bikes out into the road and incurring the horns of passing cars.

In her old existence, Eve knew she would have felt threatened by that group. She watched now as they stopped their tricks and fixed their stares on a smartly dressed young woman carrying a laptop bag. They were full of false bravado and cocky in their assumption that she would be intimidated by them, and they were right.

The woman crossed the road, pretending to ignore them, but Eve recognised on her face the expression that would have been on her own, not so long ago. She would probably have crossed to the other side of the road, too.

Eve could hear the strains of a song coming from a basement flat and recognised it as one of Ed Sheeran's latest numbers. She followed the sound, opened a shabby gate that creaked on its rusty hinges, and walked down the steps. She felt like a burglar, and looking down at her feet, laughed at her ludicrous tiptoeing.

She stood in front of a grimy sash window, craning her neck to get a better look inside.

And then it became a defining moment for her. A burst of recognition, a *coup de foudre,* the second when she felt the true pull of fate. She realised that she was caught up in something far bigger than just her, far bigger than the tiny role she had been assigned in a hugely momentous thing.

Luca had chosen the right time to put her in front of that mirror, she knew now. It was all becoming clear. Because the man inside the shabby flat was *him.*

Of course it was him. The busker she'd seen before. The one with the mop of red hair who had entertained the crowd in the hospital foyer. It was he who now sat before her, on a battered sofa, in a gloomy basement flat, practising his repertoire in order to earn a few paltry coins for his troubles.

Eve was rooted to the spot, unable to take her eyes off him. Who, or what, had sent her here to him? Why, out of all the people in London, out of all the people living in this little pocket of the capital, had she ended up here, on his doorstep?

She stood transfixed as the young man played his

guitar. He really was quite outstandingly good. So talented that he ought to have made it big but hadn't, simply from lack of opportunity.

She peered in closer. The sofa he sat upon was grubby and threadbare, the hessian stuffing in its armrests spilling through to the outside. Behind him, she saw an unmade double bed, white sheets cascading to the floor and pillows still dented. A small kitchen area was largely concealed in the gloom at the rear; the window that Eve peered through was the only one in his tiny basement home.

Eve hoped he was warm enough in the winter; she could imagine the damp and cold seeping through these old walls, condensation on the rattling window only made worse by wet washing on a clothes horse and steam from the kitchen.

The young man paused for a moment and looked up as a young woman—not much more than a girl—approached him, clutching two bottles of beer. Eve watched as he took one, smiled up at the girl and took a swig. She was close enough to see the Adam's apple in his throat bob up and down as he swallowed. The girl leaned over to kiss him tenderly on the lips and they exchanged a few words.

He put out a hand and the girl took it, laughing as he pulled her down onto the sofa beside him. She tucked her slender legs up beneath her and pulled her long skirt over them, settling down as he picked up the guitar again. Despite the open sash window, Eve couldn't quite make out what they were saying. There was a sparkle in their eyes, a special light when they looked at one another.

He has love in his life, Eve thought. *I'm glad for him.*

She felt a pang of envy for the sensations these two could experience: hands held, lips brushing, the warm glow of skin on skin. When Luca held her hand or put his arm around her, she did feel something, only it wasn't the same, wasn't as satisfying as real human contact. But for now, it was all that was available to her, and it was comforting.

Eve was mesmerised by the music this man made, so easy and so fluent. So, it seemed, was his girlfriend, who sat and sipped her beer while he sang, his voice clear and melodious.

She was unable to take her eyes off the pair of them.

Eve lost track of the time. Many songs later, as a silent and invisible observer, a sharp pain in her side brought her back to reality. She knew she should head straight back to the hospital, or she may not have the energy to return unaided. She regretted her harsh words to Luca.

Eve didn't understand why she'd felt compelled to come here today. This young man seemed fine and clearly didn't need her help, certainly not in the same way that those schoolchildren had, or in the way that she had needed Luca. Despite his shabby surroundings, it was obvious that he was safe and happy, settled with his girlfriend in their little studio flat.

But she *had* to come. Had no choice in the matter. Some power had decreed that she should go, and so she had.

Clutching her side, Eve staggered back up the steps and out onto the street.

But still it bugged her.

Why him?

Wishful

This time, the scent was Cali's perfume. Eve felt the air particles settle around her as her best friend took a seat by her side.

'Hello, my fabulous friend,' said Cali. Eve felt a kiss on her cheek. 'How are you? We're all really missing you at school, you know. You need to hurry up and get better. I need my partner in crime back with me.'

Eve thought she heard a sniffle.

'Hello, Cali my love,' Eve said inside her head. 'I miss you, too. I want to know all the gossip. All the ins-and-outs of the staffroom. And, of course, how it's going with the lovely Milo. It gets a bit boring stuck in here.'

'And no one's missing you more than me,' said Cali. 'I've got some exciting news for you. Milo proposed! I've accepted, of course. You're the first one I've told. Other than my parents, obviously. He did the honourable thing and asked my dad. You should have seen him, poor love, he was petrified. I know we haven't been together for long, but at our age, and with my history . . . well . . . I just know it's right this time.'

Eve could hear the excitement in her friend's voice. She wished she could jump out of that bed and give her a hug.

'Anyway, the wedding is going to be in the spring. Got to get saving! No time to waste, is there? And you'll be better by then and . . . well . . . I wanted to ask if you would be my matron of honour?'

'Oh, Cali,' Eve said. 'Oh, my lovely, lovely friend. Of course, I will. I'd be delighted.'

'I'll ask you again when you wake up, of course,' said Cali. 'Just in case you can't hear me now. Although I really think you can, can't you?'

She put her hand on Eve's. So warm, so soft.

Eve tried to move her head, tried to make her eyes flicker beneath her lids—just a little would be enough—or force some small tears of happiness from their corners.

But nothing ever worked the way she wanted it to.

'I can hear you, Cali, and I'm so happy for you. So excited. I'll be back, don't you worry. I'll be by your side to look after you on your special day. He's a lucky man, Milo.'

'I'm so lucky, aren't I? And you never know, maybe it'll be your turn next?' said Cali.

'Nathan's never been one to rush,' said Eve. 'Although he's stuck by me in here, so you never know what'll happen when I get out and we get back to normal. Maybe me being like this will make him realise he can't live without me and that life's too short to wait.'

'I expect you being like this will make him realise he can't live without you,' said Cali. 'Life's too short. Just you wait and see.'

Eve's saddened heart suddenly flooded with hope.

26

'Hi, love,' said Sarah, hearing the click of the front door latch followed by her husband's distinctive footsteps in the hall. He was home earlier than usual.

'Little present for you,' Rob said. He lay a bouquet of huge, blousy peonies beside her, and kissed her on the cheek. She looked up from the onions she was chopping, tears rolling down her face.

'Oh, love,' he said, putting an arm over her shoulder.

'It's the onions,' she sniffed, trying not to put her messy hands on his suit jacket. 'They're beautiful, thank you. What have I done to deserve these?' She wiped her nose with the back of her wrist.

'Um, well,' he began. 'I know . . . I know I don't say often enough how much I love you, and how much I appreciate all that you do for us. But I do, I really do. Tough times, eh?'

Sarah gulped. She turned to Rob, rubbing her hands down the sides of her jeans and trying to smile through her tears.

'Yes, they have been. And I lied. It's not the onions.'

'I know,' said Rob.

'We'll be all right, won't we? Whatever happens?' After months of constantly bolstering everyone's spirits, strong words still flowed automatically from Sarah's lips, but she wished she had the conviction in her own heart to back them up.

Rob pulled her into his arms. 'Of course we will. Whatever we have to cope with, we'll do it together. All of us. All *four* of us.'

Rob and Sarah had made the heartfelt decision not to tell the boys just yet that George's kidney failure was now so severe that, if a donor organ didn't become available soon, there was little else that could be done for him. The dialysis would keep him going for a while longer, but it was never a permanent solution. The consultant had called them the previous evening to administer this latest blow in what seemed like a year of constant strikes against their little family.

They wanted to continue to give hope to George—and to Will—even though they knew this may be short-lived, so they decided to try to have as normal a summer together as possible, before reality sank its teeth into them. Their plan, however, was dependent on George staying well enough for them to pull it off.

The consultant did say that the immediate future was far from predictable—George's health could deteriorate quite quickly, or very slowly—and so they had opted for an optimistic outlook to such a vague prognosis.

Both Rob and Sarah wanted terribly to donate a kidney to George, but knew it was unlikely they would be a match, given the one major factor that neither parent had ever disclosed to the boys:

Will and George were adopted.

Sarah and Rob believed that their darling sons, who were actually true brothers, were still too young to comprehend the situation fully. A serious childhood illness of Rob's had left him infertile, but he and Sarah were adamant they would have a family, whatever it took and whatever means they had to go through. When several gruelling rounds of donor IVF failed, it seemed that adoption was the only way forward. Very soon after being accepted as adoptive parents, they were presented with their boys—one a toddler and the other a baby of just a few months. They felt blessed indeed.

When George fell ill, Sarah and Rob were the first to be tested as living kidney donors, but they knew their chances of success were minimal, as George had a rare blood type. Their worst fears were realised when neither they, nor any of their family (nor some very altruistic friends) proved compatible. They hadn't wanted Will to be tested as he was so young, but when he had insisted—and then wasn't a match either—it had only added to his despair of not being able to help his brother.

In desperation, they asked the adoption agency if it would be possible to trace the boys' real parents. Because George was under eighteen and didn't know he was adopted, all parties had to tread carefully. But further hopes were dashed when the agency informed them that the birth mother had died of a drug overdose a few years earlier, and no father's name was stated on the birth certificate.

Now it was a case of waiting. Waiting and hoping that something would happen in time; quite literally, that someone else would lose their life in order to save their son. Sarah felt ashamed for hoping, but if their darling boy was to be saved, then someone else's family had to be torn apart.

'We won't lose him, love, we won't,' said Rob. 'I've still got a good feeling about this, despite everything. And it's about time things started to go our way, isn't it? We're well overdue for a lucky break.'

He held his wife tightly in his arms, wishing they could turn back time to how life was before, when George was well and they were just a normal little family. Back when their lives were not defined by this awful disease.

'Hey, you two, get a room, won't you?' said Will, materialising out of nowhere, broad, bony shoulders slicing through the tension.

Rob and Sarah smiled indulgently as he headed for the fridge, grabbed a huge bottle of Diet Coke, and began to glug at it. With his other hand he reached for a family-sized packet of crisps from the cupboard next to the fridge. GCSEs were now over and between sleeping all morning, hanging out in town with his friends, and shooting virtual enemies upstairs on his computer, they had seen little of him.

'Everything OK, Mum? Dad?' He gave them both a meaningful look.

'Everything is fine, love,' lied Sarah. 'Your Dad and I were just talking about how glad we'll be when this is all over, when George is better.'

'He will get better, Mum. I know it. Call it brotherly intuition or something. He's got to get better, anyway. I need a proper opponent on the Nintendo Switch. It's so boring having to let him win all the time, just because he's ill.'

Rob laughed. 'You're so good with him. I can't imagine a lot of boys your age would have the patience.'

'He's my bro, Dad, don't stress. We've been together forever.' There was a lengthy pause and Will stopped in his tracks, the Coke bottle tucked under his arm. 'Even before you two came along.'

Sarah's heart dropped. Rob looked at his wife, eyes wide.

'What do you mean, darling?' asked Sarah tentatively.

'I know, Mum,' said Will. 'That we're adopted. I've always known.'

'Oh, love, why didn't you say so?'

'It's no biggie, that's why. I mean, you guys are my parents, right? You're the ones I love. The ones *we* love, so what's the point?' A handful of crisps disappeared into his mouth, and he chowed down noisily.

'But how did you *know*?' said Rob, hating the thought that Will might have overheard an adult conversation at some point, and then bottled this up for years. Goodness only knew what kind of damage that might have done.

'Because I remember her,' he said. 'Our birth mother. Not a lot, but I kind of remember someone. Before. A bit like a dream, I suppose. And then when you two weren't donor matches for George, well, that kind of spelled it out for me, I suppose. Like I said, no biggie.'

'Oh, Will, I don't know what to say,' said Sarah, moving towards her son.

'Nothing *to* say.' Will gave his mother a quick hug. 'Taking these upstairs, that OK?' He waved the bottle and crisp packet in the air. 'Oh, and don't worry, I haven't said anything to George. It was different for him. He was only a baby.'

And with that, Will turned on his heels.

'Oh my God,' sighed Sarah. She pulled out a chair and sat down hard. 'I always knew our kids were amazing, but sometimes they do or say something that makes you wonder how they can be so utterly perfect.'

Rob stood looking at the door his son had gone through, still speechless.

'Yeah,' he managed breathlessly, a few seconds later. 'Yeah, they are. Perfect.'

27

Eve stumbled back from the busker's house, clutching her stomach in pain, but as she neared the hospital and climbed the steps, her discomfort began to ease and a little of her energy returned.

She still couldn't quite believe that what Luca had shown her in the mirror was real. Although she struggled to understand why he had waited so long to show her something this important, it all made sense now. It went a long way to explaining this urge, this *need* she had to help people.

The low, early evening sun had turned the glass doors to the hospital into full-length mirrors and Eve knew that seeing her reflection again was inevitable. She decided to confront it head-on and stood up straight to get a proper look at herself. Then she turned to one side and peered over her shoulder and as far down her back as she could, as if she were trying on a new outfit in the changing rooms of a shop.

Maddeningly, her reflection disappeared every time the doors slid open to admit or disgorge someone new. She couldn't dispel the small sliver of hope that, during one of these intervals, what she saw might prove to have been a trick of the light and the next time round, she would look different.

Normal.

Human.

Eve's thoughts turned to Abbie, her little niece, when she was in her Christmas play last year. Wearing one of Hattie's old white nightdresses cut down to fit her, the cheap plastic wings her mother had ordered from Amazon, and a little halo of tinsel on her head, Abbie had looked angelic. At least, until the feathers started dropping off her wings before they even left the house. Abbie's face was puce with tears by the time they reached the school, and she stood with her arms folded, scowling throughout the performance, sporting a pair of almost bald wings.

There might not be a halo above Eve's head, but her own wings were certainly no cheap plastic offering. These were quite breathtakingly beautiful, reaching from about two feet above her head down to the backs of her knees. Large and small feathers interlocked in a complex pattern, fanning out to a fine, almost translucent bottom tip. If she stood face-on with her arms by her sides, they protruded well beyond the width of her body, even folded, as they were now. She couldn't begin to imagine how wide they would extend once unfurled. Eve reached out with one hand over her shoulder, hoping to stroke their soft, downy surface, but what she touched was thin air.

Of course she couldn't feel them. How could she? Otherwise, she would have known about them sooner. She was flabbergasted to think she had spent so much time curled up on the floor in her hospital room without knowing that these huge things were attached to her back. But if she could feel them, then they'd have been in the way. They would have dragged her down, stopped her moving about with such ease, caused her to question what was happening to her much sooner than she had.

What a dreadful shock it would have been, waking up one day to find not only your human form lying on a bed while you stood guard on the other side of the room, but also that you had mutated into an angel. She felt a sudden, overwhelming sense of gratitude to Luca for the protection he had given her, for breaking things to her gently and giving her the time to learn and understand, little by little.

'They are rather beautiful, aren't they?' said the man himself, coming up behind her and startling her. 'In fact, I think yours are even more beautiful than mine.' He stood by her side, and they stared into the mirrored doors together, like a well-dressed couple at a special occasion. 'I know it was a shock, but this is what we are. I just didn't want you to find out too soon. Not until I knew you were ready to deal with it. It was so hard avoiding mirrors, though. The more independent you became, the tougher it got, so I just had to make the decision to tell you, I'm afraid. When I thought you could handle it.'

'That's OK,' said Eve. 'I'm glad you made me wait. And that you were there with me. I don't know what I'd have done if I'd been on my own.'

'I was on my own when I first saw my reflection,' said Luca. 'It was really hard. I didn't think there'd be anything at all in the mirror, as no one around me could see me, so you can imagine the shock. And I had no one I could turn to, no one to answer all the questions that were racing around in my head.'

'You poor thing. It must have been awful. Thank you for taking care of me.'

'I try my best.'

'And then you have me shouting at you for your troubles. I'm so sorry.'

'It's OK. It was a lot to take in.'

'But I stormed off. That was out of line.'

'No harm done. I thought you might react badly to start with, but I would say you're coming round to the idea already, aren't you? And they suit you.'

'They do, don't they?' said Eve with a proud smile. 'I just hope I deserve them. Hope I can live up to them.'

'Of course you will,' said Luca.

'So why can't I see yours?' said Eve. 'Why do they only show up in mirrors?'

'Another one of the great mysteries of this new life of ours,' said Luca, smiling. 'How did you get on seeing Jimmy, anyway?'

'How do you . . . How did you know?' asked Eve. 'Were you following me? And how do you know he's called Jimmy? I didn't even know that.'

'I may not be quite myself at the moment, but what I do have is a very particular set of skills,' said Luca in his best Liam Neeson impression. 'And I know how to use them.'

'Ah, you like *Taken*, too,' said Eve. 'But can you use your skills as well as ol' Liam? That's the real question.'

'Probably not, but at least I'm as handsome,' said Luca.

Eve threw her head back with laughter.

'Don't laugh,' said Luca. 'It's true.' He flashed Eve a smile that made her stomach spin. 'Damn, now I'll have to stop using my pool of film quotes and start speaking like a normal person.'

'No, don't be normal,' said Eve, still laughing. 'Don't ever be normal. I like your particular set of skills. Perhaps you could teach me to use mine a bit better sometime?'

'Don't worry, it will all come with time. Don't try to run before you can walk . . . or fly.'

Eve's eyes shot open.

'Fly? You mean we can fly, too? Christ, Luca. This is crazy.'

'Yes, we can fly. They're wings, remember.'

Eve frowned.

'I haven't done it in front of you, for obvious reasons,' said Luca. 'It would have been a bit too much too soon, I think.'

'Er, yeah, probably.' Eve put her hands to the sides of her head. 'Oh God, this whole thing just gets more and more bizarre. Is there anything else you're planning to spring on me? Like we can shapeshift or travel through time or anything?'

'Er, no. That's enough though, isn't it?' he said with a grin. 'Don't be greedy.'

Eve laughed. 'You really are a tonic for the soul, Luca. Which is good, seeing as that's what we are. Souls. Floating souls. *Flying* souls.'

Eve held Luca's gaze for a moment too long, and felt she needed to break the silence.

'Come on then, let's put them to the test. Teach me how to fly!' she said.

'Er, no,' said Luca. 'They can only be used in appropriate situations.'

'And what exactly qualifies as an appropriate situation?'

'You'll find out soon enough. Come on, let's get you indoors, you look pale as a ghost.'

'You're so funny,' said Eve.

'You're welcome,' said Luca. He grabbed her hand and the pair of them slipped through the open doors.

28

Luca was so good at changing the subject. Deflecting her questions—or just downright avoiding them. No wonder he was such a good lawyer.

She'd never experienced a courtroom first-hand but had seen enough legal dramas to know how these clever people could twist words to their own advantage. Perhaps he still had things he didn't want her to know yet, although after everything he had thrown at her recently, she couldn't imagine what else there could be.

Luca escorted Eve back to her room. 'I need to know more,' she said. 'More about the wings thing, and the flying.'

'All in good time,' he said. 'That was enough for today. You're too tired to take it all in now.'

'Well, if you won't tell me about that, then please will you start at the beginning?'

'The beginning of what?' said Luca.

'The day of the accident. I want you to tell me what happened that day.' Eve's accident wasn't Luca's fault, and she'd told him that already, but she knew that it was still hard for him to talk about it. But perhaps talking about it was exactly what he needed in order to put it behind him for good. 'If you can bear to,' she added sheepishly.

'Well, I tried to warn you that morning,' said Luca, sitting down and folding his hands in his lap.

'I know you did. Remember, I told you I heard you in the bathroom, almost caught a glimpse of you, actually. You were a kind of presence, a movement of some sort out of the corner of my eye. It spooked me, but I thought I was imagining it. I would never have contemplated then that there was a whole . . . whatever this is . . . a whole dimension of something, way beyond my wildest dreams, and that you could be part of it. That *I* could become part of it, too.'

As Luca was about to speak again, an uncomfortable thought hit Eve.

'Hey, you weren't watching me in the shower, were you?'

She had meant it as a serious question, but Luca collapsed into fits of laughter.

'Sorry,' he said, his voice high-pitched. 'I just find it hilarious, after all you've been through, this is what you think of first.'

'But you were in my bathroom! I was there, wearing just a towel—if that—and you were standing behind me. How do I know you weren't in the shower with me even?'

'You don't, but you have to take my word for it, Eve, that I have never seen you naked. Although . . .'

Eve felt the old urge to blush as she caught Luca looking her up and down. Her non-existent insides turned to jelly, and she looked away quickly.

'So, you were saying?'

'Let's walk, shall we?' said Luca, pulling Eve to her feet.

As they walked along the pavement, Luca slipped his hand into Eve's. It felt the natural thing to do, so she left it there. She liked the sensation of their fused hands, and when she glanced down, although they were still translucent, they looked somehow brighter. More defined.

Eve glanced sideways at Luca. He cleared his throat before speaking again.

'So, that morning, I tried to warn you,' he said, looking up at the sky, which once again was a perfect clear blue.

'I know you did,' said Eve. 'We've already been over that bit. The shower scene, remember? Please don't get the giggles again.'

'No, not then. Later. When you came out of school. You were in a hurry, and you looked like you had somewhere you needed to be.'

'Yes, we were meant to be going to this ball at Nathan's work. At the gallery. I was going to go and collect the shoes I'd ordered, then go back to my place to feed Buster and get changed, and then get a cab back into town to meet Nathan. I tried to leave work on time but there was this boy in my art class who needed me.'

Eve told him briefly of Will and his family problems.

'I saw him with you once or twice,' said Luca.

'He's a good kid. So did you follow me around quite a bit?'

'I hung around the school gates a few times, waiting for you to come out, but I didn't go in. I thought that would be a bit like stalking. Not that you'd know I was there, obviously. But anyway. A bit like you with Jimmy, I suppose. You feel you don't want to overstep the mark. I went home with you a few times, too, but it took me ages to get the strength to go that far from the hospital. The end of the Northern Line is a fair old way out, Eve.'

She laughed.

'It was easier to watch you when you went back to Nathan's, but I hated it when you were with him. I knew from the start he wasn't right for you.'

'Were you jealous?'

'No, it's . . . I mean . . . no. I just thought he wasn't

good enough. I thought you were lovely, Eve. I still think you're lovely.' They stopped walking and Luca turned to face her. 'I'm sorry, it's just that it's quite emotional, telling you all this.'

'I know. But I'm glad you are,' said Eve. 'It's funny because I had no inkling of you till that final day. Did you know that something bad was going to happen then, or was it just to make sure I got home OK?'

'I was just doing my job. It was what I had to do. I knew I'd be needed at some point. It's like an instinct for us, isn't it? You don't know when Jimmy will need you. He might never need you in quite the same desperate way that you needed me, but you'll just know. Sometime very soon you'll feel the urge to go out looking for him again, and you'll find him, because somehow we always find the ones we're watching over.'

'It seems like this is all so clearly mapped out for us, doesn't it?' she said suddenly. 'I mean, if I hadn't had the accident, I wouldn't be here with you now, and I wouldn't be keeping an eye out for Jimmy. If you'd got better quicker, then you wouldn't be the one standing here with me. We'd never have experienced all this together.'

'Yeah, and you might have had a better guardian. One who managed to see the job through properly, and you'd still be living out there in the real world, in blissful ignorance. And we wouldn't be standing here, trying to make sense of it all.'

'Luca, when are you going to stop beating yourself up about this? I'm fine. I'm here, and that's OK. And you have to admit, there are so many other ways it could have gone, most of them a lot worse than this. Everything happens for a reason.'

'It sure does.' Luca took his hand from Eve's. 'I'm

really sorry, Eve, but I have to go now. I'm needed. You know how it is.'

And with that, he was gone. It wasn't until Eve saw his form fade completely as he reached the other side of the street that she remembered he still hadn't told her about the accident.

29

The following day, Eve decided to go to another of the morning neurosurgical meetings. She lived in constant hope of learning more about her case than she picked up from the chatter in her room.

Luca was already there. 'Oh, hello,' she said, sitting down beside him. 'Anything interesting today?'

'Yeah, but it would help if I understood their jargon a little more,' said Luca. 'Medics have even more code names for things than lawyers do.'

Eve smiled.

'Hoping for an update?' said Luca. 'If they're going to talk about us two it'll be at the end.'

'That's fine. It's not like I've got anywhere else I need to be.'

'Want to go and look at some cute babies after?' asked Luca.

'So, we go from head injuries to babies?' said Eve.

'It's got to be more uplifting than this.'

After half an hour, Ms Ormandie called a halt to the meeting.

'Thank you, all,' she said. 'Those accompanying me on my round, outside in five minutes. The rest of you, back to work.'

'We're just not exciting enough at the moment,' said Luca, downcast. 'We're not getting any better or worse, so we're left to tick over.'

'But they don't know that we have a purpose,' said Eve. 'While we're lying there in our beds, looking helpless.'

'Precisely. If only they could see our gorgeous spirit

faces hanging about, they'd know there was a reason for our comas.'

'But then we'd probably scare the living daylights out of them.'

'Yeah, would be funny, though,' said Luca. 'Anyway, let's go and see some babies. I need cheering up.'

The maternity ward was busy and loud.

'Do you want to watch a birth?' asked Luca.

'God, no, I think that's a bit too intrusive,' said Eve. 'And too bloody. Let's just go and look at the babies, like you said.'

'In here, then,' said Luca, pulling Eve through an open door. Inside was a large ward with a dozen curtained bays, most of them containing a new mother with a clear Perspex crib at her side.

'Oh my goodness,' said Eve, clasping her hands to her face. 'So much cuteness in one small place.'

'Come and see this one over here,' said Luca. 'Tiny little baby girl. Aww.'

Eve melted when she saw the expression on Luca's face. Something jolted deep inside her. 'They're all so tiny,' she said, leaning over the crib. As she did, the baby opened her eyes and looked directly into Eve's.

'She can see me,' said Eve.

'I don't think so,' said Luca. 'New babies can barely see beyond the end of their noses.'

'No, but she can. Look.' Eve peered at her again. The baby made eye contact, then her face scrunched into an angry grimace before she let out a new-born howl of anguish.

'I've frightened her,' said Eve, as the mother reached over to pick up her baby. 'I'm so sorry, baby. Didn't mean to scare you.'

'You hungry again, little one?' said the mother. 'Come on then.' Eve stood rapt at the end of the bed whilst the mother latched the baby on to feed.

'Looks like you've done that before,' said Eve.

'Fourth time round, you know what you're doing, don't you, Faiza?' said a passing nurse.

'Four children,' said Eve. 'Gosh. Good luck with that.'

To the side of the ward there were a couple of private rooms. Eve peeped through the porthole window into the first one. A mother lay on the bed, with a baby in the crook of her arm and a man, presumably the father, sat in the chair at her side, also cradling a baby. Two cribs stood side by side at the foot of the bed, one of them draped with a pile of clean white onesies.

'Oh my goodness,' said Eve. 'Twins, Luca, look. Those parents are going to need all the help they can get. Imagine the washing.'

'Yeah, and the poop. Tonnes of it.' He smirked.

Eve moved along to the next door. 'This woman is all on her own. Where's her baby?'

'Let's go in,' said Luca.

The woman lay on her side. Eve thought she was asleep, but her eyes were wide and staring into the distance. Her cheeks were pallid and her lank, unwashed hair straggled across the pillow.

'Where's her baby?' Eve said again. 'Why's there no crib?'

'It might be in Special Care,' said Luca. He leaned over the woman to look at the hospital bracelet around her wrist. 'Amy Shenton, it says. Let's go and look for baby Shenton, shall we?'

A feeling of dread hit the pit of Eve's stomach. What

if the baby wasn't there, or there was something seriously wrong with it?

'She needs our help, Luca, wherever her baby is. Let's stay with her for a minute first.' They sat on either side of the woman, and each laid a translucent hand on her arm. 'Do you think she can feel us? Sometimes you can tell, can't you, but she's not showing any reaction. Oh, Luca, I'm worried for her.'

'Come on then,' he said. 'Let's go and find her baby, put your mind at rest. The poor woman might just be shattered after a long labour and someone's taken her baby for a while, so she can get some sleep.'

Eve wasn't so sure. As Luca took her hand and led her towards the Special Care Baby Unit, she had a dragging sensation where her heart should have been. A long window gave onto the corridor, through which they could see four or five rows of tiny cots, most of them containing an even tinier human being.

'Oh, look at them,' said Eve. 'How can they be that tiny? That one over there looks smaller than a baby rabbit.'

'The wonders of modern medicine,' said Luca. 'Just think how many babies—and mothers—used to die in childbirth until not that long ago, really.'

They moved slowly between the incubators, looking at name tags and watching as nursing staff tended to their minute charges, reaching through long access tubes to administer drugs or comfort.

'I don't know how these nurses do it,' said Luca. 'I mean, I'm sure that in this day and age, most are success stories, but there must be a few who . . .'

They stopped in their tracks. An incubator by the window was surrounded by three medical staff and a man whom Eve assumed must be a father. His face was ashen, tears streaming down his cheeks.

'No, please, no,' said Eve, her hands flying to her mouth. They hadn't found Amy's baby yet, but Eve have a horrible feeling that it was this one.

Luca put his arm around her shoulder, and they watched as two nurses detached the last of the tubes and wires from the tiny baby with the tips of gentle fingers. Her little face was like porcelain, Eve thought. Utterly beautiful.

'We're so very sorry for your loss, Mr Shenton,' said the doctor. Mr Shenton's eyes were rimmed in red from crying. 'Would you and your wife like some more time with her?'

'No,' said Mr Shenton. 'No. I'll stay with her. Amy said her goodbyes earlier. I don't think she's strong enough to go through it again.'

'A porter will be along in a moment to take her down to the mortuary. No rush.'

'I'd like to take her,' said Mr Shenton. 'Will you let me take her? I don't want them putting her on some huge trolley like she's just another dead body. I know it's silly, but I want her to be with someone who loves her for as long as she can.'

The two nurses looked at each other. One nodded almost imperceptibly. 'I'm sure that will be fine,' she said. 'I'll come with you. Here, you take her now. Cuddle her close.'

The nurse handed the swaddled baby to her father.

'I can't believe she's not alive,' Eve said. 'Look at her, Luca, she's so beautiful. She still has little pink cheeks.' Though tearless, her own eyes prickled. As she looked up at Luca, she was convinced she could see his glistening too.

The father's eyes were fixed on the baby's doll-like

face as he leaned forward to kiss her on the forehead.

'Goodbye, my baby girl. My darling little Olivia. I'm so sorry we couldn't make you stay with us, none of us could. Mummy and Daddy love you so very, very much . . .' His voice cracked and the nurse reached forward, one hand to steady him and one on the baby.

'No, it's OK. I'm OK,' he said, taking a deep breath. 'I'll be fine. Let me do this one last thing for her.'

'Oh, Luca,' said Eve, leaning her head against his shoulder. 'What can we do?'

'I think there are some circumstances where people are beyond our help,' said Luca, his voice catching. 'But we can try.'

As the father stood cradling his baby, Eve and Luca encircled him entirely, their bodies wrapped tightly around his, so that their arms fused on either side. Eve could feel Luca's glow, but looking at the man, there was no sign that he sensed their presence at all.

'He can't feel us, can he?'

'We'll never know,' said Luca. 'But there's nothing more we can do for him now. Let's come back and check on him and Amy later.'

They released the father and watched the tragic little procession leave the room, walking slowly as though carrying the most precious parcel.

'Take it gently,' the nurse told Mr Shenton. 'I've got you.'

Feeling

Someone was brushing her hair. Eve liked it when they brushed her hair.

She wasn't keen on the bed baths, which were wholly undignified, but hair-brushing and face-washing were wonderful. Eve had always been particular about her hair, brushing it until it shone, every morning and every evening. She couldn't bear the thought that it might be left tangled or unwashed.

'There, now you look beautiful again, my lovely,' said Nurse Jasmine in her lilting Irish accent, tucking the long side of Eve's hair gently behind her ear. Eve could hear the smile in her voice.

If Jasmine was smiling, then maybe Eve was looking a bit better. She had become an expert at judging the subtle nuances in people's voices: hidden anguish was poorly disguised behind hesitance and stutters; smiling eyes could be heard through more rounded vowels; trepidation was revealed through a change of tack halfway through a sentence.

Fear was the hardest to disguise. Eve had often heard the pure, unadulterated sound of terror in the voices of her loved ones.

She knew the doctors had shaved part of her head for the operation. Now there was a definite prickle, as though the follicles were trying to push out new hair, just as her legs would feel if she hadn't shaved them for a couple of days. Her legs! How awful they must look by now. Although she knew she had far bigger problems at the moment, she couldn't help the small shudder of revulsion that ran through her inert body.

'You enjoyed that, didn't you?' said the nurse.

'You felt me move!' said Eve. 'You felt me shudder, didn't you? But please keep brushing my hair, I really love it.'

'I'll be back to get you looking lovely again tomorrow morning,' said the nurse. 'My shift's done for today.'

'I love your accent,' said Eve. 'You have such a comforting voice.'

'Bye, love,' said the nurse, and the door swish-swashed behind her.

30

'We need to go and check on Amy,' said Eve as she burst into Luca's room the following morning.

'Don't you ever knock?' said Luca.

'Very funny.'

'She might already have gone home, you know. They don't tend to keep women in for long on the labour ward, although she did look quite poorly. But you're right, we should go and see.'

'I couldn't stop thinking about that poor little baby last night,' said Eve. 'It's just so sad. How on earth does a parent cope with something like that?'

Back on the same section of the maternity ward, only two mothers from the previous day still remained. In the other bays, curtains were pulled back to reveal a new set of admissions and their tiny offspring.

Eve peered anxiously through the porthole window into Amy's room and was relieved to see that she was still there, now sitting fully clothed on her bed, an overnight bag at her feet. Her shoulders were hunched and her hands sat limp in her lap.

Next to her bag was an empty baby carrier.

'Here comes the husband,' said Luca. They followed him in and stood at the foot of Amy's bed. Clutching her stomach, she got up and raised a tearstained face to her husband's for a kiss.

'How are you, love?' His voice was tender. 'Did you manage to get some sleep?'

'A little bit. They had to give me something. They said I'm OK to go home when I want. I need to get out of here now, Steve. I just still can't believe she's not coming home with us.'

'I know. The boys are looking forward to having Mummy home, though. I've told them you'll be a bit delicate and they're to be helpful.'

'There's a lot he's not telling her, isn't there?' said Eve. 'Look at his eyes.'

Amy managed a weak smile. 'Thank goodness for them. But how are we ever going to get over this, Steve?'

'We will, sweetheart. It'll be tough but we'll get there somehow.'

Eve looked up at Luca. 'They will be OK, won't they?'

Luca nodded. 'They're a tight unit by the looks of it. We can't really do a lot to help them now. They just need time to heal.'

As the couple embraced, Eve and Luca wrapped them both in their arms, encircling them entirely. She hoped they felt the warm glow as much as she did.

'Come on then, love, let's get you home,' said Steve, stooping to pick up Amy's bag. Eve couldn't bear to look at the empty baby carrier he took in his other hand.

'Where to now?' asked Eve.

'After that,' said Luca, 'I think we need a distraction. Fancy another walk?'

'Good plan. And we have unfinished business, don't we? You said you have more to tell me about the accident. Only this time, please try not to get whisked away on urgent business.'

'I'll do my best.'

Eve couldn't remember a summer where every day had dawned so bright and seemed to last so long. Perhaps it was just that she had time on her hands to *notice* the weather these days. She longed to feel the tingle of the sun on her bare skin.

Together, they sat down on a bench in Archbishop's Park.

'So,' Luca said, 'where did we get to?'

'The evening of the accident,' said Eve.

'Well, I watched you leaving work,' said Luca. 'You came out in a bit of a fluster, and then a few paces behind you, the young lad, Will. I followed you down into the Underground, and then you seemed to change your mind, and you came back up and jumped in a cab. You'd forgotten about your shoes.'

'Yeah, I had to go and get them then, or manage without them. I mean, there were others I could have worn to the ball, and it wasn't the end of the world, but these new ones went really well with my dress and . . .' She looked up to see Luca's tolerant smile. 'Sorry, you don't need to know all that.'

'So, a pair of shoes changed your journey home,' said Luca. 'I waited for you to come out of the shoe shop. I was watching you like a hawk, worried that you might get jostled by the crowds and pushed over or something—it was a particularly busy Friday evening, wasn't it—but you were as cool as a cucumber, even in your fancy shoes.'

He stopped speaking for a moment and rubbed his jaw before continuing.

'We walked along The Strand for a bit. You had your shopping bag in one hand and your work bag on your shoulder, and I could tell the new shoes were pinching you, so you decided you needed a taxi. You spotted one and put your hand up but then the traffic wasn't moving so you waved him away and headed towards the Tube. I called out to you not to and to wait, but of course there was no way you were going to hear me, was there? I was so worried you might topple, land in the path of a car or something. I was really close behind you, all the way.

'As you went down the first few steps into the Underground I had my arm around your waist, but then there was a sudden surge of people coming up.'

He rubbed his jaw again and Eve took his hand in hers. 'Go on, it's OK.'

'But it wasn't the people that made me lose my grip, Eve. It wasn't their fault; it was entirely mine. I got distracted, you see. Because I saw another one.'

'Another one what?'

'Someone like us. A guardian. An elderly lady. Coming up the stairs as we started to go down. I didn't realise at first, but when I got closer, I could see that she was like us. Real-looking from a distance, but up close there was a bit of colour missing. Just like us.'

'What was she doing?'

'I don't know, really. Well, I presume she was watching out for someone who was going up those steps, but she was looking directly at me, too. She'd spotted me. I was so surprised to see her and too busy looking at her instead of concentrating on you. I lost my grip on you and . . . and . . . it was a momentary lapse of concentration, Eve. That was all it took, and I lost you.'

'It's not your fault, Luca. It wasn't before and it still isn't now.'

'But it is. I'd been so careful with you all day, and then when you really needed me, I wasn't there for you. You slipped out of my grasp and in all the crowd I couldn't hold onto you. I couldn't stop you from falling. I was looking elsewhere, and not at you. I was distracted. I'm so sorry, Eve.'

'Luca,' said Eve, her face serious. 'At no time have I blamed you for my being here, have I? You didn't push me or let me fall on purpose. You couldn't have known that the very second you saw that woman would be the second I needed you.'

'But it was my *job*, Eve, and I failed to do it. I'm sure you'd feel just as bad if the tables were turned, wouldn't you?'

'Yes, I probably would, but I forgive you, Luca. I've told you that before and I mean it. And I didn't die. I'll get better, I hope, and you will too, and we'll both get out of this place and life will return to normal.'

'That means a lot to me, Eve. But what if I fail again?'

'You won't,' said Eve. 'Come on, don't start doubting yourself just because of this.'

'But what if someone else I try to help ends up being hurt, or worse?' said Luca.

'You've saved others, and helped so many people,' said Eve. 'You've got it right more times than not. That was just a bad day. Everyone has off-days, don't they?'

'Yeah, I suppose, but they're not always a matter of life or death. I get the feeling *they* don't like it though. It's like they've demoted me, and I get all the rubbish jobs now, the little ones. The kind of thing I was showing you when you were first finding your feet. Helping people see stuff, pointing them in the right direction.'

'Who's *they*, Luca?' asked Eve. 'Who's responsible for all this?'

'Despite everything, Eve, I still have absolutely no idea. And somehow I get the feeling we'll never find out.'

Eve sighed. 'So *they* . . . is it *God*? Some kind of higher power . . . jeez, I would never have thought I'd be having this kind of discussion. Whoever *they* are, anyway, they expect us just to accept our lot, and that's it? They get to put us here and leave us for as long as they choose, and we never get to know *why?*'

'Something like that, yes,' said Luca.

Eve sighed. 'It's so frustrating. I mean, clearly we're here for a purpose, just that we never get to find out exactly what that purpose is.'

'Yep. It's like having an absentee boss who expects you to work it all out on your own.'

Despite everything, Eve laughed. 'Well, if we can't get any further on that subject, can you at least tell me more about the flying thing?' she said.

'Please don't tell me you've tried,' said Luca.

Despite her exhaustion the previous evening, Eve hadn't been able to resist experimenting. She managed to drag one of her visitor's chairs to the middle of the floor, which had been a long process, exacerbated by a helpful nurse who had moaned about the errant chair and moved it back to the bedside. Once Eve had finally positioned it where she wanted it, she'd had several attempts at jumping off, half-expecting to launch miraculously into the air and glide down, smoothly and gracefully. She knew the chair probably wasn't high enough, but she'd assumed it would all be very easy.

Then she tried to jump off her bed instead, which was slightly higher than the chair. She figured the added height might help. Each time she jumped, she expected something magical to kick in, that her wings would unfold and she would be overwhelmed with the sheer wonder of it, but still nothing had happened. Every attempt had instead landed her flat on her face, fortunately bruising no more than her dignity.

'You did, didn't you?' Luca pressed.

'Oh, all right. Yes, guilty. Can't you see the bruises?' They both laughed.

'You failed, then. Obviously.'

'Why obviously?'

'Because it's not exactly the wondrous gift you think it is.'

'I did fail. But shouldn't it be some kind of instinct, like it is with birds?'

When those beautiful wings she could only glimpse in a mirror turned out to be quite useless, Eve had begun to doubt if they even existed. How was she supposed to move them, control them in any way, when she could neither see nor feel them?

'I'm afraid it's not quite as easy as that, so please don't go launching yourself off the roof or anything silly.'

'I won't. It was just a chair. And a bed. Not the cupboard, though; I thought that was probably a bit too high. Still hurt, though. Well, my pride, at least. Although somehow, I did manage to hit my head on a light. Not quite sure how that happened. It made a real racket, too. I thought someone might come.'

She put her hand over her mouth to stifle a giggle.

'Just as well no one could see me, really. I must have looked like such an idiot. So, why can't I do it? Shouldn't it come naturally?'

'If only it were that straightforward, Eve. In fact, we can't actually learn. When we *want* to fly, then we can't, but if we *need* to fly, then it will happen.'

'Wait . . . say that again?' said Eve.

'If we need to fly because it helps us to help someone, then it will happen.'

'So why couldn't you fly to save me, as I fell down those steps?'

'I did,' said Luca. 'It was only a tiny way though. More like a big jump really, over people's heads, but it still wasn't enough. I couldn't catch you, Eve.'

'It does seem a bit of a waste of these amazing things, doesn't it? These gorgeous wings we can't see most of the time.'

'We're still pretty amazing without them, though, aren't we? All the things that we *can* do have to go some way towards making up for the things we *can't* do.'

'I suppose so.' Eve was silent for a few moments. 'But I still really want to have a go. Can't we invent some kind of emergency, right now, so that we can fly there?'

'Oh, Eve,' Luca said, laughing. 'Like I said, things never work out quite the way you want them to.'

Fear

Someone was in her room.

Someone eerily silent, who hadn't spoken or made any other sound at all. Just a dragging noise. Plastic scraping on linoleum. Slowly it roused Eve from the death-darkness into her own limited awareness.

It was coming closer, moving towards her bed. Why hadn't they said anything? There weren't even the breathy sounds of effort as they dragged the object across the room.

'Who are you? What do you want?' Eve yelled inside her head. Her body tensed, nerves clenched, heart pounding. 'Please don't hurt me!' She couldn't think of anyone who might want to hurt her, but she was a prone target, unable to defend herself.

What if someone had broken into the hospital, some madman—or madwoman? Someone she had crossed in the past and who was now out to wreak their revenge? Still, she couldn't think of anyone. She couldn't call for help, couldn't press the buzzer on her bedside.

Then the door opened, and Eve recognised the footsteps of her favourite nurse. 'Jasmine, save me! Help, please help!'

'OK, so what's been going on in here, then?' said Jasmine with a sigh. 'What's this chair doing over here?'

Eve heard her puff as she lifted it and moved it to the other side of the room.

'It's freshen-up time for you, lovely lady.'

Eve listened to the familiar sounds of Jasmine pulling a plastic apron from the dispenser on the wall and the snap of one latex glove.

'Oh, poo, I need one more of these. I'll be back in a mo, then we'll get you sorted.'

As the door swung closed behind Jasmine, the noise came again.

Where had this person been hiding? They were going to kill her, weren't they? Suffocate her with a pillow while she lay there, utterly helpless. But why did they need a chair? None of it made sense.

'Jasmine!' Eve called. The stapled wound on her head throbbed as the blood pumped too fast around her body. The dragging noise went on and on, a slow screech, like a fingernail down a blackboard, but still Jasmine didn't come. Eve wished she could put her hands over her ears.

There was a clatter of glass and metal, as though someone had knocked their head on a lightbulb. The intruder was on the chair, high above her. Eve pictured long fluorescent strip-lights running the length of the room. Maybe there was a logical explanation, and someone had come to fix one of the lights, but then Jasmine would have said something to the person, wouldn't she?

'I'm back, lovely,' said Jasmine, and the atmosphere lifted. 'What the . . .? How did that chair get over there again? Honestly.' Tutting to herself she righted it once more. 'Did you sneak in a late visitor, Eve? Naughty you, eh?'

Why couldn't Jasmine see the threat? Why didn't she chase the intruder from the room? Press the panic button? Call security?

Eve tried to relax as Jasmine wiped her face gently with a wet cloth, then picked up the hairbrush. As the prongs teased her hair across the pillow, her heart rate began to settle. Clearly the chair-dragger was no longer there, but would he be back? Was he hiding until Jasmine had gone?

Eve had felt safe in the confines of her room, a constant trail of medical staff traipsing through, but if no one had seen the imposter, how were they to protect her?

How would they keep her safe?

31

Seven Weeks After the Accident

When Eve awoke, she felt Jimmy needed her.

The hospital foyer was bustling, and Eve's attention was drawn to an elderly couple. Although impatient to go to Jimmy, Eve watched as the man led his wife slowly towards the lifts. The old woman's shoulders were hunched, and she leaned heavily on her stick.

Eve looked around to see if someone could help them. A hospital porter was pushing an empty wheelchair in the opposite direction; Eve had to make him notice the couple.

The porter was about to head through the doors into the corridor beyond. With her eyes tightly shut, Eve passed quickly through the doors and with all the strength she could muster, held them closed from the opposite side. Her shoulders tingled from the effort.

The porter was baffled that the doors wouldn't open and jabbed constantly at the door release button. Eve pushed even harder.

The porter muttered to himself, then looked around for help. As he did so, he spotted the elderly couple.

'Oh, young man, I don't suppose . . .' said the old man, catching the porter's eye.

'Of course,' said the porter. 'I was meant to take this through there but the door's jammed. Lucky for you, eh?'

The elderly lady sighed with relief as the porter gently

eased her into the wheelchair. He ushered the couple into the lift.

Eve smiled to herself and headed for the hospital exit.

Another job well done.

As the front doors slid open for someone else, Eve slipped through and out into the sunshine. She stood at the top of the steps, looking down at the street before her. Although the sense of urgency had somewhat subsided, she still wanted to check on Jimmy.

Today was just *a day* for him, she felt now, not *the day*.

Eve always thought London was at its best in the mornings, that it really shone before the crowds and traffic built up, before pollution masked the wonderful scents. She went through the motions of taking a deep breath, imagining how today might smell—the freshness of newly showered skin and her favourite perfume; a waft of dew drying on grass; the aroma of coffee and bacon from the café by the station. If she tried hard enough, she could almost make it real.

Passing a modern office block, she caught sight of her reflection in the glass doors. She didn't shy away from it anymore; now that she knew about her wings, she took every opportunity to look at them. And every time she did, she marvelled at their sheer magnificence and latent power. Today they glowed golden in the low, early sun, the upper tips a light champagne colour, down to a creamy white at the bottom. If only she could move them, could make them work as easily as turning her head or raising an arm, how much fun she and Luca might have.

And how ridiculous it was that she might never actually get to use them.

She sighed and continued on her path. She was conscious of a certain lightness in her step this morning, a contentment in the knowledge that what she had to do today was worthwhile.

Jimmy needed her.

She had a purpose.

But Jimmy wasn't home. Eve had to find him. She stood for a while on the pavement in front of his flat wondering how she might do that, before instinct compelled her to put one foot in front of the other and finally, she found herself on the South Bank, close to the London Eye.

She wasn't sure how she knew, but this was the right place.

The promenade was chock full of the usual street entertainers, buskers and artists, and a long snake of tourists queued for a ride on the London Eye.

Eve heard Jimmy's music long before she saw him. She followed the strains of a ballad past the merry-go-round, where a long line of spirited children waited with their parents, to the edge of the gardens.

From a distance she could see that a sizeable crowd had already gathered around him. Eve didn't recognise the song Jimmy was singing and presumed it to be one of his own. She paused to observe how totally absorbed he was, his eyes glazed as he stared into the distance.

Jimmy's girlfriend was by his side, wearing a long, diaphanous dress that wafted in the breeze to reveal delicately tanned and flip-flopped feet. Her hair was much longer than Eve had realised, almost down to her waist, sleek and smooth. She watched adoringly as Jimmy performed, and as he finished the number, he looked to her for approval.

Young and in love, they were completely immersed in the moment, absorbing the audience's adulation. At

Jimmy's feet lay an upturned hat brimming with shiny pound coins, and when Eve peered closer, several notes, too.

Enough to pay this week's rent, she hoped.

She closed her eyes as Jimmy's music transported her to another time and place, when she'd thought she, too, was as happily secure in a relationship as strong as theirs. But looking at the bond between Jimmy and this girl, she knew that what she'd had with Nathan was neither as ardent, nor as durable, as this.

Had she ever seen such a look of adoration on Nathan's face, and for that matter, had he seen it on hers?

Next time around—if she was fortunate enough to be given a next time—Eve wanted more. If any relationship she entered into wasn't as strong as Jimmy and his girlfriend's, then she would rather be alone. There would be no settling for second best. She had tried hard not to let the despicable way in which Nathan had ended things cloud how she felt about the two years they had been together, because there had been good times, many of them, but as Luca had pointed out, they'd never had to weather a storm together.

This was the first real test of their love, and he'd failed.

Jimmy looked at his watch and gestured to the girl. It was time for them to move on.

'Ready my love?' asked the girlfriend, as she helped him to pack up his guitar and scooped the money into the case. She put the empty hat on her head as the crowd yelled for an encore.

'Sorry, we have to go,' said Jimmy, smiling and shrugging his shoulders.

'Can't you just do one more song?' asked a young boy, tugging at Jimmy's sleeve.

'I'll be back tomorrow,' said Jimmy. 'Same time. Come and see me then, and I'll make yours the first request.'

'Do you promise?'

'I promise,' said Jimmy, ruffling the boy's hair as his father came to lead him away.

Eve wondered why the compulsion to find Jimmy today had been so strong, but the urge to protect this young man—and by default his girlfriend, too—was fiercer than ever. The bond between them was strengthening like an invisible thread.

'Come on, Jules,' said Jimmy, hoisting his guitar case onto one shoulder and draping his free arm over her shoulder. As the couple headed towards Jubilee Gardens, Eve was struck with sudden panic.

'No, don't go that way! Please, Jimmy!' she shouted.

'What was that, love?' said Jimmy to Jules.

'Didn't say anything,' she said.

'I thought I heard someone. Tell you what, as we've done so well today, why don't I treat you to lunch on the way home? We've got plenty of time, the interview's not until three.'

'Are you sure? I don't want you to be late.'

'Yeah, I'm sure. Corner Café OK? Nothing fancy, but you won't need to eat for a week.'

Jules laughed. 'You really know how to treat a girl.'

'It's the way I roll,' said Jimmy, pulling her closer.

Eve relaxed a little once they had changed direction. She couldn't watch every step they took or keep them away from every road. This was London, for goodness' sake, and they were sensible adults.

And then Eve realised something. Jimmy had heard

her. Had heard her calling to him, she was sure of it, just like she had heard Luca that fateful morning. Did that mean his hour of harm was imminent? Should she stick by him today in case she really was about to be called upon to rush to his aid?

'What do I do here?' she pleaded, directing her eyes to the skies. 'I'm just trying to do my job. I want to get this right.'

She hoped that the powers-that-be, whoever they were, were listening.

32

'Where have you been?' said Luca, startling Eve.

She had followed Jimmy to the café, leaving him and Jules once she felt that danger wasn't imminent. Arriving back at the hospital, she was exhausted and had fallen asleep immediately.

'Jesus, don't do that!' she said, rubbing her sleepy eyes. 'I nearly jumped out of my skin. Or I would have, if I had skin to jump out of . . .'

'You have beautiful skin, captured in a perfect complexion of translucence,' said Luca. His eyes met hers and he didn't look away. When he reached out and squeezed her waist gently, Eve didn't pull back. 'Remember, I have seen your real skin. The alive version of it, back in the real world.'

Eve was thrown by Luca's compliments. When he squeezed her waist, she was surprised at the butterflies that danced in her non-existent stomach.

'Jimmy needed me,' she said, bringing the conversation back on track. 'And so, like a good guardian, I went to him. But there didn't seem to be a lot going on.'

'Just a chance to watch him, I guess?'

'Yeah, I suppose. How old do you think he is?' said Eve.

'I'd guess around twenty-one, twenty-two maybe? Why do you ask?'

'I can't bear the thought that something awful might be about to happen to him, and that's why I've been sent to watch over him. He's just starting out in life and trying to make a go of his music. He mentioned something about an interview this afternoon, too.'

'There's no age limit with this, is there? Although, thankfully, I haven't been called upon to look after any children. Not yet anyway. I think that would be doubly hard.'

'How old are you, Luca?'

'Thirty-nine. Or at least I was, when I had the misfortune to land myself in this place. I've had a birthday since. It was pretty tragic, actually, you should have seen it. My parents came in, plus Lauren, my ex, and a couple of close friends. They all sat around my bed looking pale and sad. They even brought in balloons, those awful helium things in the shape of a big 4-0, for God's sake. I don't know why they did it. They all know I hate birthdays. Maybe they thought that throwing a party by my bedside—even if only a very tiny one—might terrify me back to life. I hate parties. I suppose I should be thankful I escaped having to throw a big one for my fortieth.'

'I'm not mad on parties either,' she said with a smile. Something else they had in common.

'I miss my life,' he said, suddenly downcast.

'Oh, Luca,' said Eve.

'It comes over you in waves, doesn't it? Like a kind of bereavement. Mourning the life you've lost. Sometimes you can't quite believe you're here and not there. Other times, you're too busy to think about it. And the rest of the time, you're just trying to make the best of things as they are now.'

'I know what you mean,' said Eve. 'I miss the kids. My pupils, I mean. I know my job isn't a matter of life and death like yours can be, but we both have people who rely on us, and we've left them behind. I feel like I've abandoned them, somehow. I want to be there with them.'

'Yeah. It's a bit like here, really. We don't have any say in who we can help—they just kind of present themselves. Sometimes it's easy to help them and other times it can be a bit more of a challenge.'

'You're right,' said Eve.

'I'm glad you're here, though,' said Luca. 'It would be pretty lonely otherwise.'

Luca edged closer to Eve as they spoke, and although his proximity didn't generate the same warmth that human closeness did, there was still a sensation of sorts. Their heads were almost touching and neither took any notice of the nurse who came in to carry out Eve's check-up.

When Luca ran his finger tenderly under her chin and tilted her face upwards, Eve could never have said that she was expecting it, but it wasn't a complete surprise either. Nor was she shocked when something resembling a shiver ran down her spine. As Luca looked deep into her eyes, she felt he could see into her very soul.

Knowing him, he probably could.

'You're a wonderful person, Eve. You'll get back out there, love, back to the real world and those who love you. I have a very strong feeling you will.'

Pinned to the spot by Luca's fixed blue gaze, Eve couldn't move. He leaned forward and brushed the lightest of kisses onto her lips. She closed her eyes, not moving an inch in case he stopped. She couldn't bear to miss a single second of this.

It wasn't until Luca pulled away with a sigh a few moments later that Eve dared to open her eyes again.

His expression was full of something she couldn't quite comprehend.

After Luca left—only because he was needed elsewhere—Eve didn't move, her mind trying to process what had happened.

She never realised Luca had feelings for her. Not *those* kinds of feelings. He had been the best companion she could ever have hoped for, and that wasn't just because he was her *only* companion. He seemed to genuinely understand her. So how had they come to this?

Her emotions raced, head whirring, spirits lifting as far into the air as she suspected those wings could carry her. It was a wonderful, euphoric feeling. Had he planned this all along? Had he come to her room with the intention of *seducing* her? How had she missed the signals? Had he even given out any signals?

Eve was normally good at picking up on signs, but it seemed her radar for matters of the heart had let her down this time. Maybe Nathan's recent rejection had desensitised her. She certainly wasn't looking for love or romance right now.

Or am I?

It was a wonderful kiss. She found it hard to put into words how it felt, compared to a normal kiss in the real world. Deep. That was the only word she could think of to describe it. Deeper than the normal touches they shared, as though the kiss travelled down to her very core and, at least momentarily, filled the void inside her.

And he hadn't only kissed her, she realised. He had called her *love*. She couldn't wipe the grin from her face.

What surprised Eve most of all was the realisation that she felt something for Luca in return. She had spent too many long hours quietly contemplating—and then processing—what had happened with Nathan to know that this wasn't a rebound reaction.

Back in her old life, she believed she had a strong relationship with Nathan. But now, she knew that it had all been a mirage and that a breakup had always been inevitable. That realisation helped her to put things into perspective.

But even so. She had been more than grateful to have Luca's friendship, and his love as a friend, but as for kissing and the notion of romantic love, well . . . it had never occurred to her that their relationship could develop into more, even though she had to admit to finding him very attractive.

But was he in *love* with her? Surely, he couldn't be.

He hadn't wanted to stop kissing her and had told her that.

'Damn it,' he'd said. 'I'm needed. I'm sorry, love. He needs me, so I have to go. I have a new person to watch. Name's Owen. You understand, don't you? Please don't go anywhere. We'll continue this later, OK?' He'd dragged himself up and looked down at her, knowing he needed to go before his resolve melted.

'Sure,' said Eve, her eyes glazed. She understood the calling.

Eve's emotions soared skywards again, but as soon as they peaked, she could feel herself slowly drifting back down to earth, just a little way to start with, and then everything sped up.

She was an angel with broken wings, plummeting to earth and an inevitable crash landing. And all because she'd started to overthink what had happened.

Kissing Luca was wonderful, possibly even the start of something amazing. Had it felt like this the first time she'd kissed Nathan? Was it terrible that she couldn't even remember? Surely every couple's first kiss felt like an iconic moment.

But what was the point of it all? It wasn't like there could be a future for her and Luca. Neither of them knew if they would get better and get out of the hospital. There were several scenarios she could envisage:

The first was that they were both stuck here forever—or for a long, long time—and they would grow frustrated with the fact that they were limited to the constraints of their present form. How could they cultivate a proper relationship if they weren't even proper people?

Second, what if one of them were to recover and go home, leaving the other one behind? The one lucky enough to escape might not remember that they had left a loved one behind in this other existence of theirs.

And third, if they both recovered, then this whole experience might be forgotten by both of them entirely. So, what would have been the point of it all? All this wasted emotion, shared between two people who wouldn't remember what they'd had together.

As much as she hated to admit it, Eve concluded that continuing with this was utterly futile, and that she had to do the right thing for both of them. And that meant telling Luca that it had to stop now. They had no future, so there was no point in getting too attached to one other, because the relationship couldn't go anywhere.

Friends. They had to stay friends, and nothing more.

The thought of saying those things to Luca made her chest hurt. She hoped it wouldn't come as too much of a shock to him, that perhaps he had reached the same conclusion himself. It wasn't like they had made a commitment to each other or anything. It was only one kiss, after all.

But what if he really was in love with her? Would he understand then?

He'd be fine with it, wouldn't he?

Of course he would. It was the sensible thing to do . . .

Wasn't it?

33

Eve hurried along the road, away from the hospital and towards the Corner Café, full of renewed energy. The place had become a favourite haunt of Jimmy and Jules, especially if Jimmy had a good day playing on the streets.

A summer breeze whipped up from nowhere. It made cyclists wobble as they took corners too sharp. It flapped at armfuls of shopping bags, banging them into their owners' legs. Eve heard a woman curse as her hair flew skywards, and Eve longed for those warm gusts to brush her face, too.

Perhaps they would blow away all thoughts of Luca, and that kiss, from her mind.

Several police officers were chatting buoyantly, tucking their caps under their arms as they entered the café. Eve nipped through the door behind them. She watched their chests swell instinctively to inhale the aroma of all-day breakfasts, bacon frying and coffee brewing, and imagined how good that must feel. Stomachs rumbling as they queued to place their orders.

Jimmy and Jules were at a table by the window, their heads together, totally absorbed in one another. The sun beamed in the narrow window behind them, spotlighting them as though there were the only couple in the café.

Between them sat a large plate of bacon and eggs; Jimmy was tucking in, and Jules picked at it sporadically with a fork, which she waved in the air between mouthfuls.

Eve squeezed into a seat close by so she could listen to them. If the huge smile on his face was anything to go by, Jimmy was in high spirits; his eyes darted from side to side with excitement.

'So, you start next week then, that's fab!' said Jules, stabbing at a piece of bacon.

'Yeah, I've got the early slot to start with. I suppose you could say I'm more of a warm-up act than the main attraction,' he grinned. 'Hang on, let's not kid ourselves here, I *am* the warm-up act, but hey, it's a start, isn't it?'

'Come on, you'll be amazing. All the early punters will be in, fresh out of work and heading off for a drink. And then they'll hear you and they won't be able to leave. I bet you the management will be begging you to take their nine o'clock spot before too long!'

'Let's not get ahead of ourselves, babe. It's a start, it's regular income, and no one will come and move me on because they don't want me singing there. Or at least, I hope they won't.'

Jules laughed. 'Of course they won't. When's it going to dawn on you just how good you are, Jim?'

Jimmy put down his knife and fork and leaned across the table. He took Jules' face between his hands and planted the tenderest of kisses on her lips.

'I love you, future Mrs Thorne. One day. One day, when I'm rich. When I really deserve you. And then I'll do it properly, get down on one knee, buy you a gorgeous ring, all that stuff. Just you wait.'

'You don't need to wait till you're rich, babe. I don't need a ring and an expensive party to know how much you love me.'

Eve could see it in Jules' eyes. It was blindingly obvious that this woman would marry Jimmy tomorrow and settle down with him forever, even with what little they had.

'Go on, Jimmy, ask her,' said Eve out loud, all to herself. 'Get on with it. Make your lovely girlfriend happier than she's ever been. Don't waste a moment, will you, because you never know what tomorrow will bring.'

I should know.

And then a tiny thought, like an annoying itch, started chipping away at the corner of Eve's mind. They had nothing but their love, these two, and they were happy with that. Could she and Luca be the same? Could there be some hope for them, despite everything? They had nothing either, except the strength of their friendship and a growing feeling that it could be more.

Should Eve take her own advice and just *get on with it*?

They're real people, said the rational side of her brain as she gazed at Jimmy and Jules. *It's different for them.*

She was still resolved to go back and tell Luca they couldn't do this. It was the sensible thing to do, to knock this crazy, fanciful notion on the head before it even began.

She just needed to pull herself together and *get on with it.*

A man sat down at Eve's table, taking the seat next to hers. She was relieved he hadn't squashed in on top of her. She had visions of being pinned to her seat until the man finished his breakfast, or trying to slide ghost-like out from under him. The downside to being invisible was that no one respected your personal space.

Still slightly uncomfortable with how close the man was, she squeezed round to the other side of the table, where she had to twist a little to watch Jimmy and Jules.

'Number sixty-three, full English?' yelled the waitress, and the man raised his hand. 'There you go, deary,' she said, putting a huge plateful in front of him. 'Your tea's coming in a minute. You enjoy that, lovey.' He thanked her and tucked in.

There was a niggling feeling at the back of Eve's mind that there was something very familiar about this man, but she couldn't place him.

The man was good-looking in a rugged way, and there was something very physical about his presence. She could imagine him doing a job that required strength, maybe in the forces or something like that. He looked mid- to late-forties, greying but in the distinguished way men seemed to carry off so well. He tucked into his food but seemed somehow distracted, as though the meal was not his main focus. He kept glancing across at Jimmy with a furrowed brow as though he, too, was struggling to recall a face or a name.

The man put down his knife and fork and mopped up the egg on his plate with a piece of bread. As he took a large glug of tea, his curiosity finally got the better of him and he leaned over towards Jimmy's table, clearing his throat.

'Excuse me,' he began.

Jimmy looked up guiltily, as though he had been caught doing something he shouldn't—the default reaction for someone who spent their life busking, forever waiting for the tap on the shoulder and the order to move on.

'Don't I know you?' asked the man. 'I hope you don't mind me saying so, but I think I've seen you somewhere, though for the life of me I don't know where. Do you work round here?'

Jimmy chuckled, quickly swallowing down a mouthful of toast.

'Well, I kind of work all over,' Jimmy said enigmatically. He flicked a glance at Jules. 'I'd like to think it's because you've seen me singing somewhere, but . . .'

The man glanced at the guitar case propped beside Jimmy's seat.

'Of course!' He banged his hand on the table. 'You were on Westminster Bridge the other day.'

Jimmy laughed, delighted to have been recognised. Eve wished he could see how proud that made her.

'You're really good,' said the man. 'Far too good to be singing on street corners. Or even bridges.'

'Thank you, that's very kind,' said Jimmy quietly, suddenly humbled. 'It can be tough. I just need that big break, you know? I don't know if you're interested, but I've just got a regular gig at a club in Covent Garden. It's nothing fancy, but I'll have the stage to myself for a whole hour. No one will move me on, not like they do at the moment.' He fumbled in his pocket and pulled out a business card for the club which he scribbled on before handing it to the man.

'Oh thanks. I'll definitely look you up,' said the man, studying the card. 'Yes, I'd love to come and see you perform properly. My wife and boys would, too, I'm sure. My lads are really into their music. And I'm sorry you get moved on all the time,' he added rather sheepishly, Eve thought, glancing away from Jimmy and looking out of the window. 'I'm so sorry about that.'

'Not your fault, mate,' said Jimmy. 'Goes with the territory.'

'I suppose,' said the man. 'Anyway, work beckons. Great to meet you, and all the best with the new venture. I hope it works out for you.'

Jimmy stood up and shook the man's hand.

'Thanks,' he said. 'You're very kind.'

The man waved his goodbyes to the woman behind the counter. 'Thanks, Pat.'

'See ya, love, same time next week, eh?'

He nodded at her and headed for the door.

Eve also stood to leave. With a final glance back over her shoulder at the young lovers, and a deep sense that she wouldn't be needed today, she squeezed out behind a couple of builders with strong Eastern European accents, whose yellow hard hats swung from their arms as they pushed open the doors.

Broken-Hearted

Eve hadn't heard the dragging noise anymore. She had lain awake for hours, waiting for it to come back, waiting for the hand of death to strike, but whoever or whatever it was, it hadn't come again.

Nor had Nathan.

Was he really so busy at work that he couldn't squeeze in a short visit? Or had Eve fallen asleep, so exhausted after the terror of the day before that she hadn't heard him?

An awful thought suddenly occurred to her. She tried to brush it off, unable to believe that he could do such a thing but . . . he wouldn't have . . . no . . . he really wouldn't have . . . would he? Had he gone on their holiday? The one to Croatia that they had planned so carefully together. Eve had no idea how much time had elapsed, but it was the only reasonable explanation she could think of for his long-term absence.

No, he'd never do something so inconsiderate. If things had been the other way round, there was no way she would have gone without him. She'd have cancelled, rearranged, whatever it took to eventually share the holiday they had so looked forward to.

Eve heard her parents burst into the room.

'Hello love, you're looking a little better today, aren't you now?' said her mother. Her voice betrayed the raised cheekbones of a forced smile.

'You always say that, Mum,' said Eve. 'And I bet I don't look any different at all to the last time you came in.'

Eve heard the creak of plastic as her mother sat down beside her.

'No thanks to that dreadful boyfriend of hers,' said her father. 'Sorry. Ex-boyfriend.'

'What do you mean, Dad?' said Eve. 'He's still my boyfriend, he's just not been in for a while, that's all, but he will, when he has the time. Of course he will. Try not to judge him, please.'

'Fancy doing the dirty on her while she's in a coma, of all things. What kind of despicable person must he be to do something like that?' said Mary.

'We always knew there was a dark side to him, didn't we?' said Douglas. 'Looks like we were right all along.'

'She's better off without him,' said Mary. 'She'll soon find someone nice once she's out of here and all better, you'll see. Someone who really deserves her.'

Her father laid his hand over Eve's and squeezed gently. It was warm and comforting and Eve wished she could squeeze it back, to give him some reassurance. She felt a prickling at the corners of her eyes and a sudden dampness.

'Oh, Mary, look!' said Douglas. 'She's crying!'

Eve had no control over the tears that began to leak from her eyes. Her hands ached to reach up and brush them away.

'Nurse, come quickly! Come and see!' shouted Mary, opening the door. 'Oh Douglas, this is wonderful. It means she can hear us. Maybe she's been able to hear us all this time.'

'Yes, but that means . . .' began Douglas.

'That means she must have heard us talking about Nathan just now,' said Mary, clapping a hand to her mouth. 'Oh Eve, my darling, I'm so very, very sorry you had to hear this way.' Mary rushed to Eve's side and stroked her hair away from her face, kissing her on the forehead.

As Jasmine came into the room two more fat tears escaped from the corners of Eve's eye and rolled in tandem down her cheeks.

'How wonderful!' said Jasmine, smiling at Eve's parents. 'This is a huge step forward.'

Eve wished she could turn and hide her face from them all, and that the death-darkness would come and return her to oblivion once more.

'I've always been able to hear you,' she said. 'And sometimes it's torture. Please, just put me back to sleep.'

34

Eve hoped Luca was back in his room. Her mind was made up and she was resolved to tell him that they had to stop whatever this thing was that was developing between them.

'Oh, God,' she said, looking to the heavens. It surprised her how readily she now called upon God's help. 'Why this? I don't need love on top of everything else.'

As she ran through her prepared speech yet again, she thought she could feel real tears springing to the corners of her eyes, but she knew it was just another remembered sensation, and cursed its lack of substance.

Luca *was* back in his room, but his appearance shocked Eve. He was sitting on the floor, his back against the wall, a vague shadow of his already shadowy self. Shoulders hunched, face ashen.

'Luca, are you all right?' she asked, rushing to his side.

'I think I just overdid it, chased across town too quickly. And after all that, Owen was fine when I got there. I hung around for a while in case it turned into something, but it didn't, so it was a bit of a wasted trip. But hey, when we're called, we have to go, don't we?'

Eve sighed with relief. 'Oh, thank goodness you're all right. You gave me a scare.'

'How are you?' asked Luca, sitting up a little straighter. 'Have you seen Jimmy?'

'Yeah, he's fine.' She paused, knowing what she really should be saying to Luca, but unable to say it—not yet, anyway. It was far too harsh when he looked so shattered. 'He was at the Corner Café.'

She paused, staring into the distance before speaking again.

'I wish I could eat bacon again. Or even just smell it.'

'Yeah, that would be good, wouldn't it?' said Luca. 'Owen was eating when I got to him, too. Why do they torment us so? Do you know, I stood there, watching him, and I realised I really miss the whole physical thing of being able to eat. Not just the smell or the taste, but the total satisfaction it gives you. The chewing. The swallowing. Feeling full.'

'Oh, it's all about the smell and the taste for me,' said Eve, knowing she was procrastinating.

Taking a deep breath for courage, she started again.

'Luca.' Her voice sounded small and insignificant. 'We have to talk about what happened.' But her resolve to do what was right kept slipping further away with every second she spent in his company. He looked so lovely, so vulnerable—so *loveable*, for goodness' sake. How could she possibly tell him?

'Yes, we do,' said Luca. He spun round to face Eve and knelt up on his haunches. 'I loved kissing you, Eve. I couldn't bear that I had to break it off. All I wanted to do was stay there, kissing you all day.'

'I loved kissing you, too,' said Eve. 'But . . . that wasn't what I was going to say. Bloody hell, Luca, I had this all planned out. I was going to tell you we need to stop this before it starts but . . .'

'But what?' He tipped his head to one side.

'But . . . actually . . . I really like you. A lot.' She sighed again. 'I was going to ignore all that stuff, my feelings and your feelings and the kiss and just tell you that we can't . . . '

Luca put a finger to her lips. He got to his feet, still a little shaky, and pulled her up to him.

Whatever tiny vestige of resolve Eve clung to now deserted her completely. Somehow her legs remembered the feeling of turning to jelly as she melted into Luca's arms. It felt so right being there.

It *felt,* and actually being able to *feel* was more important than anything in this strange existence. The ability to feel something in a world of limited sensations.

Sod the future, or lack of it, she thought as they kissed.

The here and now was what mattered.

'Had you planned that?' asked Eve afterwards, her eyes twinkling. 'You knew what I was going to say, didn't you, and you wanted to stop me.'

'Well, maybe,' said Luca, a smile tugging at the corners of his mouth. He started walking round the room. 'I've wanted to kiss you for a long time. Right since the beginning, really. Which I know would have been wholly inappropriate. I've never felt like this about anyone else I've watched. About anyone else, *ever*, come to that. It was all different with you. I knew you were special, Eve. I suppose I was waiting for the right moment to declare myself. I'm just relieved you didn't run . . . or fly . . . a mile in the opposite direction.'

'It was a bit of a surprise, but when you kissed me, I kind of realised I'd been wanting you to. Does that make any sense?'

'Yes,' he said, reaching for her hand. 'Moments of joy are few and far between in here. We have to take happiness where we can, don't we? That's my excuse, anyway.'

His eyes had a new depth to them, and his voice slurred with emotion—love, lust, whatever it was. He was glowing all over, and so was she.

'I've loved you since I first set eyes on you,' said Luca, coming to a halt in front of Eve. 'I've never felt anything this strong before. You might find that hard to believe, as I've had to keep it to myself for so long, but that's exactly how I feel about you. I know that you were the reason I was put on this earth. And not just because they chose me to look after you.'

'Gosh, Luca. *Love.* That's pretty huge,' said Eve. Now she was the one pacing the room.

'The trouble is, you just shouldn't be in here,' said Luca. 'If I'd done my job properly, then you would be out in the real world, where you belong, and not stuck in here with me. It still kills me to think about it. But it also kills me to think of you still with him. With someone who didn't deserve you.'

Eve stopped pacing.

'I know what you're thinking,' said Luca. 'But you have to believe me, Eve, that I didn't let your accident happen, just so I could have you here with me.'

'Luca, that thought hadn't even crossed my mind. And in any case, if you hadn't tried to save me, I might have died. I know you're genuinely sorry that I'm here. I know you'd still rather I was out there, but I'm not, so let's just make the most of what we have, here and now, shall we?'

'I love you, Eve, and that's all I have to say in my defence.'

'Ever the lawyer,' said Eve.

'I know I've sprung all this on you,' said Luca. 'I know it's a lot to take in and maybe too soon for you to love me in return. You need time to think about it, but I . . .'

'I'm done with thinking,' said Eve, pulling him to her and kissing him. She knew exactly what she wanted.

35

Eight Weeks After the Accident

Eve and Luca had barely left each other's sides in two days, but now he pulled away from her with a jolt.

'I'm so sorry, Eve. I've a feeling I'm *really* needed this time. I think it was a false alarm the other day—either that or someone up there doesn't like us kissing—but now I have to go. Would you like to come with me?'

'Of course I'd like to,' said Eve. 'Come on then, let's get a move on.'

They fled hand in hand through the hospital exit and out onto the street.

'So where is he?' asked Eve.

'West End,' said Luca. 'Come on, we need to fly if we're going to make it in time.'

'I'm going as fast as I can,' Eve protested, running along beside him. 'Your legs are longer than mine.'

'I didn't mean it in the metaphorical sense,' said Luca.

Eve ground to a halt.

'You mean *fly*, as in . . . *fly?*'

'Yup. Do you think you can do it?' He pulled her level with him.

'How would I know, I've never done it before,' said Eve, her voice quaking. 'Maybe you should go on without me. I don't want to hold you up or anything.' But then she looked down at the ground, only to find it was no longer where she expected it to be, firmly beneath her feet, but several metres lower than it had been a few seconds ago.

She felt as though she were suspended in cotton wool and as light as the air around her.

'Oh my God, Luca! We're doing it . . . we're flying . . . no, I can't do this . . . I'm scared!'

'You're *already* doing it,' said Luca with a chuckle. 'Don't look down, just keep your head up and eyes forward.'

'This is amazing!' said Eve as she relaxed into it. 'Utterly amazing.' She turned her head slightly to look at her wings. There was a rush of air and she veered sideways. 'Woah, that wasn't so nice.'

'Look in the direction of travel,' said Luca. 'And believe me, those wings of yours look magnificent.'

Now that they were in use, both sets of wings were perfectly visible. They were even more spectacular in real life than they had been in the mirror. Eve was surprised at how vast Luca's were; her own were less easy to see without going off balance. Milky white, ivory and silver, their colour varied as they passed through sun and shadow.

Truly heavenly.

She lost her initial fear very quickly. Being up here, high above London, was a serene and beautiful feeling, like nothing else she had ever experienced. It felt strange, but so right, to soar above the heads of all those unsuspecting people below.

Luca pulled her higher still. 'This is amazing,' she cried over the roar of the wind, her voice coming in gasps.

'Isn't it?' Luca shouted back.

She dared to glance down as they crossed the Thames. Far below, a boat passed under Westminster Bridge. She wondered how the passengers might react if they were to catch a glimpse of these two aerial curiosities as they coasted on pockets of warm air above the city, wings glinting golden in the sunlight.

As they soared higher the city began to look like a map, the curve of the river revealing itself as it snaked eastwards. 'I can't believe I'm doing this. It's incredible. You never told me it would be this good.'

'It's pretty special, isn't it?' he replied. 'Now, shh. Listen.'

'For what?' she asked. They came to a stop and seemed to hover amid the clouds, bobbing softly with each flap of their wings. 'It seems pretty quiet to me.'

'My point exactly. Who would have thought that just a little way above noisy London, it could be so quiet? So peaceful,' said Luca.

'Where did all the noise go?' she wondered. Other than the occasional car horn or siren, there was very little to be heard.

'It's magical, isn't it?' said Luca. 'Concentrate now, though, we're nearly there. Landing can be a bit tricky when you haven't done it before, and we've gone quite high. Hold on tight and I'll guide you in.' He faked speaking into a headset, as though he were a pilot. 'Diaz and Chapman, cleared for landing. All OK?'

Eve didn't know whether to laugh, or gulp with fear. 'Yup, I'm OK. Just a little *terrified*. Please don't let go of me!'

'I won't.' He looked across and gave her a huge smile. 'Now, we'll come in pretty fast. Make sure you put your feet together and try to bring them forward when we're about ten metres from the ground. And bend your knees as we land. If you've ever done a parachute jump, you'll know exactly what to do.'

'But I haven't,' said Eve. 'I don't really like heights.'

'Now you tell me,' laughed Luca. 'But don't worry, you'll be fine. It's not like you'll break anything if you land badly. I've done it awkwardly before and it kind of winds you, even though you've not an ounce of air in your body. Here we go.'

Eve screamed in both terror and elation as they dived. Land was approaching far too quickly. They swooped over the Eros statue in Piccadilly Circus and cleared the heads of the shoppers milling along Regent Street, before landing on the pavement with barely a bump.

'Nice one,' said Luca. 'Anyone would think you'd done this before.'

'Yes, it was rather good, if I say so myself,' said Eve, puffing up with pride as she dusted herself down. 'That was out of this world, Luca.'

'You OK to go on? We're on foot from here. Come on.'

'Where are we going?'

'In here,' said Luca. They turned up a side street and Luca pulled her through the door of a restaurant.

'Do you know what's happened?' said Eve. 'What kind of danger he's in?'

'No idea. There's no email that goes out. It's a case of get-there-and-see.'

'Where is he?' said Eve.

'In the kitchen, probably. He's a chef.'

'Oh, no. More food to look at and not be able to eat. Torture.'

Luca grabbed her hand and the pair of them passed through more doors—*not again,* thought Eve—and into the kitchens.

'That's Owen, over there,' said Luca, pointing to a tall man with hair tied back into a short ponytail. He stood at a workstation, preparing something Eve couldn't quite see, and occasionally shouting instructions to other members of staff.

For a few moments, nothing untoward happened and Eve began to wonder if it was another false alarm. But Luca was a coiled spring, ready to pounce.

It happened so quickly, Eve barely had a chance to register the sudden shift in atmosphere. Luca reacted like a lightning bolt, leaping into the fray. There was a flash of steel and Eve watched in horror as a woman lunged for Owen. He hadn't seen it coming—she must have crept in via the back door and run across the kitchen unnoticed.

Luca seemed to know what was going to happen a split second before it did . . .

As the woman raised the blade to bring it down into Owen's shoulder, Luca grabbed a pan from the stainless-steel counter. He groaned with the effort of having to pick up something so solid, before throwing it at the woman with all the strength he could muster. Owen remained oblivious until he heard the crash of the woman, the knife, and the pan falling to the floor. He spun round sharply, his own knife clattering on the stone floor.

The woman appeared to be unconscious, and the rest of the kitchen sprang into action. A crowd formed around Owen, who was pale with shock. A female colleague calmly took charge of the situation, directing the chaos.

'Dial 999, Filip!' she yelled. 'Pascal, you grab her. She's waking up. We don't want her doing a bunk.'

Pascal sat on the woman, pulling her arms together behind her back and holding them at the wrists. She began to squirm, but there was no way she would be able to escape from under him.

Eve heard Filip asking for police and an ambulance. Owen seemed unharmed, but Eve couldn't be sure what condition the woman was in.

'Who is she?' asked Eve.

'Former employee with a grudge,' said Luca. 'And his girlfriend for a while, too. He dumped her, then sacked her a couple of weeks back. Bit of a mess, really.'

The woman was awake now, groaning on the floor beneath Pascal. A burly man in chef's whites instructed Pascal to get off and he yanked her to her feet, bracing her in an arm lock. She writhed and wriggled before submitting with a scowl.

'Look at them now,' said Eve. 'They'll be wondering for ages who threw the pan and saved his life. It'll give them something to talk about, anyway.'

Luca simply grinned.

'It was amazing, Luca. *You* were amazing. Just imagine if we hadn't quite got here in time. A split second really was all it took to make a difference, wasn't it?'

'I got it right this time, at least.'

'So do you think you're off the hook with Owen now?' she said. 'Or will you always be his guardian? How does it work?'

As the room swarmed with police and paramedics, Eve and Luca moved to one side to watch.

'Only time will tell,' said Luca. 'I'll just have to wait and see if I get summoned anymore, I suppose. Who knows? Anyway, my job is certainly done for today, so shall we go?'

'You were brilliant. Yeah, let's go.' Eve closed her eyes as they passed straight through the double swing doors, hand in hand.

'We don't have to fly back, do we?' she asked as they emerged onto the street. The first time had been amazing, but the idea of being that high up again made her squeamish.

'Why, didn't you like it?' said Luca, a smile playing at the corners of his lips. 'I thought you loved it earlier?'

'Oh, I did, but I'd rather have both feet on the ground on the way back, thank you very much.'

'I'm just teasing,' he said. 'There's no emergency now, so we won't be able to fly anyway. Look behind you. Our wings left us as soon as we landed.'

Eve looked over her shoulder. She was a bit disappointed not to see those beautiful wings anymore.

'All back to normal,' said Luca. 'We could enjoy a nice gentle stroll back through London. Should we pop into a few shops, maybe stop for afternoon tea somewhere fancy?'

'Wouldn't that be nice?' She grabbed Luca's arm and pulled him to a stop in front of Ladurée in the Burlington Arcade, where they both stared longingly into the shop window.

'What I wouldn't give for one of those little chocolate tarts,' said Luca, pointing.

'Oh no, pistachio macaron for me any day. This is a bit like when you're on an extreme diet, isn't it, and you can't stop obsessing about food.'

'Diet of literally nothing, not even air,' Luca said with a shrug. 'I miss chewing. I miss swallowing. I miss having something to do with my tongue. But that seems to have changed over the past few days . . .'

He squeezed Eve around the waist and leaned in to kiss her, and once again she felt that strange sensation. It was almost an electric shock, only there was nothing about it that made her want to pull away.

They strolled through the streets with their arms around each other, fused in their togetherness. She looked up at Luca's handsome face, hoping that when the time came for her to help Jimmy, she would rise to the challenge as admirably as he had today.

'Shall we cut through St James' Park?' asked Eve. 'We could pretend the ducks can see us and pretend to feed them.'

'Good plan,' said Luca, then suddenly, '*Oh!*'

He bent double and Eve lost her grip on him.

'Luca, what is it?!'

His form began to fade in and out, like a projection where the film reel sticks.

'Luca, say something!' said Eve. 'Tell me what's happening!'

'I don't know. Eve, help me.'

'I don't know what to do,' cried Eve. 'What should I do? Tell me!'

'Get me back,' he said. 'You need to get me back to the hospital. Fly us, Eve.'

'I can't. I don't know how.'

'Yes, you do. Look.'

Eve glanced over her shoulder to see her wings ready and waiting. Luca's were there, too, but so much paler than before.

'You have to, Eve. It's the only way.'

36

Eve didn't know how she found the strength to transport Luca back to the hospital.

She wrapped her arms around him as they flew over London and held onto him for dear life. The tingling sensation she normally felt when they touched was still there, but very faint now. She had to get him back.

Never before had she doubted her own abilities quite so much. Usually when something went wrong, he was by her side to help her. Now, he was powerless to help even himself and as he weakened further, Eve knew it was all down to her.

Luca's room was a hive of activity. His bed had been collapsed flat and hordes of medics clustered around him, working frantically.

She and the faded version of Luca now stood at the foot of his bed, wings gone.

'What are they doing to you? What's happening?' she asked.

He was fading, but he was still there with her. She clung tightly to his hand; there was some substance, some strength left in his grip. She just had to keep holding on and holding on, but when she next turned to him, he had faded to an even weaker and hazier shadow of his former self.

Luca was the ghost of a ghost.

Suddenly Eve understood what was unfolding. He was dying and they were trying to save him. That was why they were all working so desperately, why they all had such blind panic in their eyes. They were failing, he was dying, and Eve felt as though her life was over, too.

As she held fast to Luca's hand, with just an essence of him remaining, his human body was slipping away, and there was absolutely nothing she could do about it.

'Eve,' Luca whispered finally, with fear in his voice.

'Oh God, Luca. Please, you can't die. You just can't. You can't leave me.' But Eve knew they were both utterly helpless in the face of all this. A sob of despair escaped her throat.

For a moment, Luca faded in again.

'I don't think I have a lot of choice in the matter,' he said, his voice low and quiet. 'Eve, I don't want you to witness this. You have to go now. Please don't let this be your last memory of me.'

'No!' screamed Eve. 'No! You can't give in like this. Luca, please don't just accept it. Where has your fight gone? Why aren't you trying harder to stay here? Stay with *me*?'

'I'm so sorry, Eve.'

He took both her hands in his and she was convinced she could see tears glistening in the corners of his eyes, even though she knew it was impossible.

'Luca!' she yelled now, as he started to fade once more. 'Luca! Stay! Please stay with me!'

Then she shouted at the medical team, even though she knew her cries fell on deaf ears.

'Come on! Do something, will you? You're supposed to be the experts and you should be helping him and you're not! You're letting him slip away, and you can't, you just can't. Please don't let him die!'

Without warning, his outline became more solid, and she was filled with hope again.

'That's it, Luca! Come back to me!'

But what he said next ripped her heart in two.

'Eve, my love. I think it's time to say goodbye. You really do have to go. Please don't stay here and watch this. It's too painful.'

'No,' said Eve. 'You're going to stay here with me. And I'm staying here with you. Don't give in!' The place where her heart used to be felt hollowed out and raw, a cold shaft driven into her very soul.

The resigned smile Luca gave Eve spoke of a fate already accepted. As he led her to the door and pushed her through, she clung to him, refusing to let go.

'Please don't cry,' said Luca, but his voice was so quiet now that she could barely hear him. 'I love you, Eve, more than I've ever loved anyone.'

Eve's chest was racked with sobs, so dry that they really hurt. Now on the opposite side of the door, agonising pain kicked in. Pain like she knew she would have felt in her mortal body. Her heart was breaking, and it tore her apart from the inside out. She screamed at the doctors again, but what good would it do?

Why wouldn't he let her stay? She needed to be with him in his final moments, but he had cast her aside.

She turned to look through the porthole window, expecting to see his faded form still standing by the bed, but it was gone. He had left her. Luca had slipped away from her, and she hadn't even been there to see him go. To watch as his beloved spirit form merged with the mist over his body and dispersed, just as she'd seen before.

'No!' she wailed, banging invisible fists on the door. 'Luca! Come back. Please come back.' She staggered to the seating area and collapsed, all her energy spent.

It was hopeless. Everything was hopeless. She was hopeless. She hadn't been able to help him, hadn't been strong enough to keep him there with her.

Eve couldn't bear to look up and watch the medics leaving his room. She couldn't bear to see their despondent faces, the look of failure for a life lost before its time. Luca's special nurse, Janice, had left a few minutes before; Eve presumed they had sent her to call his family and break the dreadful news that he was dead. That after a long battle, they had lost him.

She had lost him.

It was all too much.

She couldn't stay any longer. Couldn't be here when his family arrived to say their final farewells. Couldn't bear to watch them wallowing in their grief. She had her own despair to deal with and she needed to be alone now. She wouldn't go back into his room, wouldn't look at that empty and inert shell, with its expressionless face and dead eyes. She wouldn't allow that to be her final memory of Luca. She couldn't believe that he would never smile at her or make her laugh again.

It was all too much.

She ran from the waiting area, careening past the nurses' station where Nurse Janice had her back to Eve, speaking on the phone. Eve couldn't care less that she disturbed the air enough to lift a pile of papers from the desk as she passed. Down they fell, like confetti fluttering to the floor.

She put her hands tightly over her ears so that she wouldn't hear Janice's soft words of condolence as she spoke to Luca's parents. Eve could picture the bereft faces on the other end of the line. How would they cope without their beloved son? What would they do now that he was gone?

'Luca, my love,' she whispered to no one. 'I never even told you that I love you.'

37

As the Barclay family sat down for dinner, George commanded their Amazon Echo: 'Alexa, shuffle songs by Ed Sheeran.'

'Shuffling songs by Ed Sheeran,' Alexa responded, and the beat of "Bad Habits" kicked up.

'Oh, that reminds me, Georgie,' said Rob. 'I forgot to tell you about this guy I met. A musician. I bumped into him in the Corner Café last week and I knew I recognised him from somewhere. Turns out I'd seen him busking in town. He's really good. He told me he's got a job at this club in Covent Garden. And he gave me a card, look!'

Thankfully Rob had tucked the card safely into his wallet, and it was still there.

'He plays a lot of the stuff you like, George. This song, for one.'

Sarah put down her knife and fork and took the card from her husband. 'Cellar Door,' she read. 'Interesting. Where did you say you saw him?'

'He was busking on Westminster Bridge the other week. I was going to move him on, but he was so good, I didn't have the heart. Well, I let him play a few songs first, anyway.'

Sarah frowned. 'I don't suppose he has a big mop of red hair, does he?'

'Yes, he does. Very distinctive looking chap. Have you seen him too, then?'

'Well, it would be a massive coincidence, but there was this guy . . .' She turned to George. 'Georgie, do you remember him, that busker we saw in the hospital?'

'Yeah, he was amazing. I bet it's him. And now he's going to be famous, and you've met him and so have we and . . . he was ace!'

Sarah hadn't seen her son this animated in a while. Even though he had only picked at his food, hardly eating more than a couple of mouthfuls, it cheered her up immensely.

'So, he's got a regular spot at a club now, that's great news,' said Sarah. 'Wouldn't it be fab if it was the same guy we saw, Georgie? There are a lot of buskers in London, after all. Look, he's written his number on the back.'

'It's him, I just know it,' said George. 'If it's the guy who looks like Ed Sheeran and plays loads of his songs, then it *has* to be him, doesn't it?' He flung his knife and fork down with a clatter. 'Can we go and see him, Dad?'

'Oh George, that would be great, but it's in a bar, sweetheart. I'm not sure you and Will would be allowed to go inside.'

Sarah could see the cogs turning in her husband's head. A knowing look passed between them.

'Leave it to me, Georgie,' said Rob, tucking the card into the back pocket of his jeans. 'I'll see what I can do. I can't make any promises, though.'

'Dad, you're the best!' shrieked George. 'We have to go and see him. I'm his biggest fan, after all.'

Rob and Sarah laughed, their youngest son's good humour utterly infectious. No words could communicate what George's raised spirits did for their renewed sense of hope.

38

Luca's nurse, Janice, had been asked to break the news to his parents.

She had spent many long months looking after Luca and had grown close to him, even though the conversation was very one-sided. She didn't know him—couldn't know him—but she had a feeling somehow that he was a good person and that the world needed him back. His doctor told her it was only right that she should be the one to make the call.

'Mrs Diaz?' she said. 'Hello there, good afternoon. This is Nurse Janice Taylor from St Thomas'. No, no need to worry. Far from it. In fact, we have some very good news for you. I'm so pleased to be able to tell you that Luca is showing signs of coming out of his coma. Yes, yes, it's wonderful, isn't it? Yes, he's awake, off and on. Still very drowsy, obviously, but all the signs are pointing in the right direction.'

There were delighted whoops down the line, and Janice felt tears spring to her eyes. It was wonderful to be able to convey some good news for once. She took a deep breath and pulled herself together.

'Yes, yes, he is. Certainly. Wonderful. Yes, come in later. It would do him a world of good to see you. Yes, lovely. We'll see you later this evening, then? OK. That's great. Goodbye Mrs Diaz. Thank you. And to you. Goodbye.'

As she turned to put the phone back on the desk, Janice felt a rush of air, as though someone had left a window open.

A pile of papers lifted off the counter and scattered like confetti, but she didn't mind the extra work, not today. With a smile on her face and joy in her heart, she scooped them up and patted them down into an orderly pile.

Then, she set off to find out where the draught had come from.

Mourning

When Eve awoke, her heart felt like it was made of lead. Pressing down inside her chest cavity so that she couldn't breathe. Her room was still and silent. No one was there to hear the irregular blips from the machines as they registered the changes in her vitals.

She felt so very alone.

Nathan had left her, she knew that now, and the tears had continued for some time, to her parents' joy and to her own dismay. Crying whilst completely immobile was desperately hard; her body ached to bend double, to thrash and grind and give vent to her feelings. She wanted to leap from that bed and hurl herself across the room. Grip her fingers in her hair. Wail in desperation.

But she had to be content with lying there rigid as slow, burning tears streamed down her face, to be blotted away by her mother.

'It's a miracle, isn't it?' Mary had said. 'She can hear us, so it must mean she's on her way back.'

If only they knew how she had lain there, day after day, week after week, hearing everything they said—at least when the death-darkness didn't have its grip on her.

'This is nothing new, Mum, Dad,' she wanted to say to them. 'I'm a prisoner in here. I always have been. I can hear you, feel you, but that's it. That's all I'm allowed for the moment.'

But this feeling, this empty feeling today, was something new entirely. It had nothing to do with Nathan. This was a different ache, deep in her heart, stronger than the loss of separation, as though someone dear to her had died suddenly.

It felt as though the very core of her soul had lifted out and deserted her, leaving her empty and grief-stricken.

She was grieving for something or someone, but she didn't know who or why.

She'd had enough now. Enough of lying here, waiting for something to happen. She needed to get out of this place. She had to get better. The death-darkness wasn't coming as often, so surely she was well enough to wake up now.

'Get me out of here,' she wailed inside her own head. 'I have to get out of this place. Please!'

The tears came again, alongside another huge wave of loss. This time she could feel the pressure of a sob lodging in her chest, then rising up and bursting out through her mouth with an audible gulp.

But no one was there to hear the first noise she made. No one was in her room to exclaim with delight at another stage in her recovery. Another bodily function that she was now able to perform again.

Enough now.

She had to get out.

PART 4

MAKING PEACE

39

Ten Weeks After the Accident

Eve missed Luca. So very much. Minutes, hours, and days were longer and lonelier without him.

In the immediate aftermath of his departure, she spent far too much time confined to her room. Other than the usual family members and a dwindling group of friends who paraded through at visiting hours, she hardly saw anyone. And when she did see them, it did nothing to lift her spirits. These visitors, too, were waiting for something to happen, and it never did. Their doleful faces dragged her down.

She still ventured out to check on Jimmy when she had to—her conscience wouldn't permit otherwise—but she would return quickly. Shoulders hunched, head down, back to her hermit-like existence.

It occurred to her that Luca would have been appalled at her recent behaviour. She could hear his voice in her head, telling her to pull herself together and go and do something useful.

'Eve, this is not what you're here for,' he would have said, his hands planted firmly on her shoulders. 'Jimmy needs you. And he's not the only one. You need to get out there and help people, in any way you can. It'll take your mind off everything. Off of me.'

It was as though he was in the room with her, but it was torment to know he wasn't, and never would be again.

Hard as it was, she complied. She started going round the hospital, helping people in any small way she could, just like Luca had taught her to. The trouble was that everything she did now in this half-life of hers always led her back to thoughts of him.

He'd taught her this, introduced her to that, showed her this, taken her there. He was the one who'd tried to keep her away from mirrored doors, for fear that she would catch sight of her reflection and it would terrify her.

He was so good, so admirable, such a wonderful person, and she missed him desperately. She could never hope to be as good as he was, but she owed it to him to at least try. Nothing would stop her from missing him—she would miss him forever—but she had to carry his love in her heart and get on with her life, such as it was.

But she was lonely, and having no one to talk to—no one that could hear her—was driving her mad. So, she went out looking for a friend, hoping there just might be someone else like her in this huge hospital, if she cared to look hard enough—but she hadn't bargained on it being so difficult to distinguish the real people from the ones like her.

Up close, she and Luca looked quite different to *proper* people, the ones whose spirits still lived inside their bodies. At first glance and from a distance, they all looked much the same. All had human form and mannerisms and moved in the same way. It hadn't really crossed her mind until now how to spot the difference.

And then, one day, she found someone.

Eve watched her for a little while, just to make sure. Sometimes the woman looked fully formed, but other times there was a glow to her, as though her essence hadn't yet decided where it wanted to dwell. Ultimately it was the woman's air of hesitance, the look she had of being out of her normal environment, that convinced Eve she should pluck up the courage to speak to her.

'Hello,' Eve said.

The woman glanced over her shoulder to see who Eve was talking to, then looked back again, her brow furrowing.

'You mean . . . you mean . . . you can actually *see* me?' the woman said, her face lighting up. She was petite with neat braids of black hair, and eyes that danced as the light caught them.

'Yes, I can,' Eve replied. 'I'm Eve. Pleased to meet you.'

'Hi, Eve, I'm Ellie. So, I'm not imagining all this, or in some kind of weird dream thing or . . . I don't know. I've no idea what's going on here, to be honest with you.'

'Are you new?' asked Eve.

'New? I mean, I suppose so. I haven't a clue, really. I just seem to be here, not knowing how I got here, or anything. But that's my body, lying on the bed in there.'

'It's a lot to take in, isn't it?' Eve said. 'Just don't try to go too far away from it to start with, will you? I made that mistake, and it really hurt. Stay close by for a while.'

'Oh,' said Ellie, 'I didn't know that.'

Eve put her arm gently around the other woman. 'Why don't we go back into your room, and I'll tell you a bit more about all this?'

Eve needed to tread with compassion, just like Luca had with her, and she knew that the ultimate tribute to him would be for her to take Ellie under her wing (quite literally, in fact). She needed to introduce Ellie to this existence and educate her about who they were and why they were here. Just like Luca had done for her.

Once again, it all came back to him. To Luca. Everything always did. She couldn't do anything, think about anything, without it being a part of the memory of him.

'It's very confusing to begin with,' said Eve, sitting on the floor in Ellie's room and pulling Ellie down next to her. 'But we have some very special skills that we can use to help people.'

'Oh, really?' said Ellie. 'What sort of skills? I feel pretty useless at the moment. Can't do half the stuff I used to.'

Eve told Ellie as much as she felt was appropriate for now about her own situation and the small acts of kindness she had been able to perform, even early on.

'Oh goodness, I never thought I would be able to do anything other than just hang around here, waiting,' said Ellie. 'So do you think those people could really feel you?'

'In a way they could. Sometimes the help we give them is a physical thing, like when I moved the sign for the guy who wanted to find the chapel. Other times, it's more like they sort of sense our presence: a touch on the shoulder, a shiver down the spine, that kind of thing. We can help them make the right choices.'

'That's incredible,' said Ellie.

'It's a bit daunting to begin with,' said Eve. 'I'll help you, though. You won't have to do it on your own. I had someone very special looking after me, at least until recently.'

'So, there was another one like us. What was her—or his—name?'

'Luca,' said Eve. Her stomach churned at the mention of him.

'Where is he now? Are there more? A whole community, or something?'

'No, I don't think there are many of us. In fact, you're only the third one I've met.'

'Where's Luca now?' asked Ellie.

'He's gone. He died. And I miss him so much,' said Eve. She felt the familiar prickle at the corners of her eyes and knew it wouldn't take much for her to crumble again.

'Oh, I'm sorry,' said Ellie, putting her hand on Eve's arm. 'I didn't mean to upset you. Did you . . . um . . . did you love him?'

'I did,' said Eve.

'Oh, Eve.'

Ellie put her arm around Eve's shoulder, and there was that strange tingling sensation, like she used to feel with Luca. She could still remember how it felt.

How *he* felt.

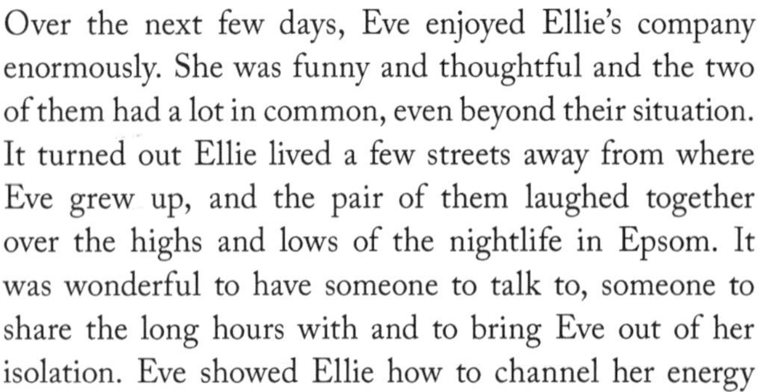

Over the next few days, Eve enjoyed Ellie's company enormously. She was funny and thoughtful and the two of them had a lot in common, even beyond their situation. It turned out Ellie lived a few streets away from where Eve grew up, and the pair of them laughed together over the highs and lows of the nightlife in Epsom. It was wonderful to have someone to talk to, someone to share the long hours with and to bring Eve out of her isolation. Eve showed Ellie how to channel her energy and it astounded her every time, just like it had amazed Eve in those early days.

She hoped she would never forget the sense of pride she had felt, the first time she helped Ellie to take care of someone. A small boy in the foyer had lost his parents and was wandering around, his face streaked with tears.

'I can't believe no one has stopped to help him,' said Ellie.

'Humans—real humans, I mean—are quite absorbed in their own lives, most of the time. It's not that they're purposefully ignoring him, they just haven't noticed.'

'What can we do, though?' said Ellie. 'We can't leave him like that.'

'Look over there,' said Eve, pointing to a distraught young woman, whose head swivelled madly from side to side, eyes wide on her pale face.

'Samuel!' she yelled. 'Samuel! Where are you? Please don't hide from Mummy. Come on Sam, please!'

'I'm not sure what I can do, though,' said Ellie. 'I can't steer the boy to her, can I?'

'You can,' said Eve. 'Think how it worked with me and that sign. You need to move something physical so that it catches her eye.'

A cleaning trolley had been left unattended and Eve could see the cleaner chatting to someone a few feet away. The tall brooms and mops prevented the mother and boy from seeing one other.

'I need to move that trolley?' said Ellie.

'Exactly,' said Eve. 'Luca used to tell me to channel all my energies and I didn't know what he meant to start with, but when you've done it once, you know exactly what to do the next time. Only harder.'

Ellie stood up straight and focused her attention

on the trolley, then charged at it. As she passed straight through it, Eve remembered the frustration she had felt when she was first learning. 'Don't worry,' she said, seeing Ellie's frown of disappointment. 'Now you know how to focus, you just need to do that about ten times harder.'

'Can you do it, Eve?'

The boy was howling now and Eve was surprised that the mother hadn't heard him, or that no one had come over to offer their help.

'No, you try again, Ellie. You'll get it this time, I'm sure.'

Ellie summoned all her strength once more, then battered into the trolley with everything she had. This time she hit the side of it hard and it edged a couple of feet. Ellie whooped with joy.

'I did it! I did it!' she shrieked and high-fived Eve.

'And look,' said Eve. The mother finally spotted her son, and the pair were reunited. 'Go and comfort them now. Put your arm around them.'

'Why? They won't be able to feel me, will they?'

'Just do it. You'll see.'

As the mother stroked her son's hair and held him close as though she would never let him out of her sight again, Ellie very tentatively placed an arm around her shoulder. The woman's eyes widened, her back stiffened slightly, and she glanced sideways as though expecting someone to be there. Then she smiled and looked down at the boy once more.

'She sensed you,' said Eve as Ellie returned to her side. 'You gave her a little bit of comfort.'

'She didn't really know what it was, though, did she?' said Ellie.

'They don't,' said Eve. 'It's just that feeling of

something passing over you—remember that back in the real world? A shiver of recognition or a brief sense of déjà vu, something like that? It's gone in an instant, but it pulls you up short for those few seconds and makes you stop and think.'

'So do you really think that every time we used to get those feelings in the real world, someone like us was looking out for us, too?'

'I suppose we'll never know, will we?' said Eve. 'But it would be nice to think that was the case. At least some of the time.'

'But why, Eve? Why are we here? What's the point of all this?'

In the end, Eve and Ellie's friendship was short-lived, and many of Ellie's questions remained unanswered.

A few days after meeting Ellie for the first time, Eve arrived at Ellie's room to find her huddled in one corner, confused and fading in and out. It brought back painful memories of losing Luca.

'Oh no, not you, too,' Eve moaned, trying to grab hold of her. But then it became obvious that Ellie wasn't dying, she was recovering. Her human form on the bed was starting to move, its eyes were flickering and there was a sudden buzz of excitement in the room.

And so, Eve let her go.

'You're going back,' she said to Ellie's fading outline, trying to conceal the sadness in her own voice. This wasn't about Eve; Ellie's recovery was the best outcome for everyone. 'You're getting better.'

'I'm sorry, Eve,' she said. 'You've been such a wonderful friend to me. I'm so sorry to leave you alone again.'

'Don't be silly. You're going back to your family, you lucky thing. Say hello to the real world for me!' Eve tried to add colour to her monotone voice. 'Goodbye, Ellie. I'll miss you.'

But Ellie had already gone.

Eve was determined not to mourn the loss of Ellie in the same way she had mourned Luca. It was very different anyway; she had known Luca for much longer and loved him as more than a friend. Eve couldn't resent Ellie's return to life.

Looking back at that dark time when Luca went away forever, Eve realised just how lucky they were to have shared so much time together. Nothing was forever, and either of them could have been whisked away at any minute, like Ellie. She and Luca had shared so much and declared their feelings for one another, and they had done so before it was too late.

But Eve couldn't help becoming despondent again. She once more found herself alone, with too much time on her hands for contemplation. Who knew what was in store for her now? Would she recover one day like Ellie, or pass on to another place like Luca? Or would she be held here in limbo until the doctors decided that no more could be done for her? And where would she go to then, when they turned off those machines that kept her alive?

Eve liked to hope that Luca's spirit lived on, somehow or other. That the essence of him, all that was good about him, endured on some spectral plane. She always used to believe that death was the end, plain and simple. But what she was certain of now was that there were a great many mysteries in this universe which were to be experienced only by a select few.

She was lucky enough to be one of those few.

She hoped her new philosophy on life would follow her back to the real world, should she ever be given the opportunity to return.

40

Jules watched Jimmy from the wings, her cheeks rosy with pride.

When the applause became deafening and the audience rose to their feet, she felt the emotion bubbling up inside, threatening to spill over. She hoped she didn't show herself up and cry, but Jimmy made her so very proud, standing up there on the stage with nothing between him and the audience but his guitar.

She'd been right about his future at the club. Within a couple of weeks, he was promoted to the prime nine o'clock slot two nights a week, and audiences were now paying to see him as the main attraction, not the warm-up act. It was all going so well, and he couldn't quite believe his luck. As far as Jules was concerned, it had nothing to do with luck and everything to do with talent.

'You were wonderful, babe,' she said as he left the stage with a final wave, his smile wide and his eyes gleaming with excitement. She put her palms on his chest and leaned up to kiss him.

'Do you think it was OK?' he said. 'I wondered if it was too much of my own stuff. Maybe I should have done a few more covers instead?'

'Nope, not at all. I was watching them, and they were rapt. You got a standing ovation, for goodness' sake. What more do you want?' said Jules. 'You'll have some record label boss sniffing round you soon, just you wait and see.'

Wrapped around one another, they headed for Jimmy's dressing room. It was no more glamorous than a shared space with the other headlining acts, but it was a start. He sat down in front of the mirror with a sigh.

'Phew, I'm shattered,' he said. 'Do you still want to go out or can we just grab a takeaway and head home?'

'You sure know how to party, old man!' said Jules, kissing the top of his head. 'Whatever you want, I'm not fussed.'

'In that case, I'm up for a curry and a night on the sofa with my gorgeous girlfriend. Better than anything else I know,' said Jimmy, grabbing Jules and pulling her onto his lap. 'Seriously, though, I can't believe how well this is all going.'

There was a knock at the door, followed by Jon, the club manager, sticking his head inside.

'Can I come in?' he asked.

'Of course,' said Jimmy. Jules jumped up off his lap.

'You were great tonight, Jimmy. They loved you,' said Jon. 'Any chance you could add a couple more sessions a week to your schedule?'

'I'd be honoured. Thanks, mate. Just let me know when, and I'll be there.'

'Great. I'll email you,' said Jon. 'At this rate, you'll be able to give up the busking.'

'Never,' said Jimmy, smiling. 'I love it. It gets my music out there, and everyone needs music in their lives, don't they? For free, as well as in places like this. Although obviously a little bit of cash in the hat comes in useful as well.'

Jimmy doubted Jon knew that the cash in the hat had been his only source of income until he got the job at the club.

'That's very generous of you,' said Jon. 'But I bet they're queuing up to throw tenners at you now, aren't they? You're starting to get a bit of a reputation around here, you know.'

Jimmy glanced down sheepishly, uncomfortable with all the praise.

'He's too modest,' said Jules, seeing her boyfriend's discomfort. 'I'm always telling him he's brilliant, but it'll take more than that for him to believe me. He just thinks I'm biased.'

She ran her fingers through Jimmy's unruly hair and planted a kiss on his cheek.

'You've got a very special talent, Mr Thorne,' said Jon. 'And a very special young lady, too. Hang on to her.'

'Oh, I will, mate, I will,' said Jimmy. 'She's one in a million, this one. Worth more to me than all the music in the world. And that's saying something.'

As she watched Jimmy pull Jules back onto his lap, Eve felt a churning in the place where her real stomach would have been. Pride, she supposed, mixed with the tiniest tinge of envy for the love they shared.

She had been to see Jimmy's last couple of gigs, standing close to Jules as they watched him from the wings. Today she had followed them back to the dressing room. She felt a little like a stalker, but she wasn't ready to go back to the hospital alone just yet. It was lovely to see the two of them together, even though it made her miss Luca even more.

Jimmy was in such a good place right now that Eve wondered if her time with him might be drawing to a close. Perhaps the crisis point in his life was never destined to be anything tangible at all. Maybe it had more to do with making sure he was settled in his personal and professional life. Spiritual guidance rather than physical. Although how she had contributed to his current success, she had no idea.

All she had done was watch from afar.

But Eve did appreciate how easily things could have taken a different turn for Jimmy. If he hadn't secured that job, then he might have struggled to continue paying the rent for his little flat. She had no idea what Jules did for a living, but the pair of them seemed to be living hand-to-mouth before the club gig came along.

So much could have gone wrong for them. They might have been rendered homeless. Jimmy could have been arrested for busking where he shouldn't. They could so easily have fallen in with the wrong crowd. Eve would have done her best to steer them in the right direction through any crisis that arose. But now? Did he really need her anymore, now that things were going so well? All she could do was presume that it would become evident to her at some point. She had to wait for guidance, just as much as Jimmy did.

And so, despite the emptiness in her heart, it was with a smile on her face and a certain pride of a job well done, that Eve headed back to the hospital.

41

Rob thought he'd see if he could sort something out with the young musician before he said anything to the boys.

The fact that this man, Jimmy, had written his name and number on the back of the business card was an absolute godsend, and that alone gave Rob his idea in the first place. If he could pull this off, if Jimmy was up for it, he could just imagine the excitement on his sons' faces. For once, fate was playing its hand in the best possible way, just when they could really do with something positive in their lives.

When Jimmy answered the call, Rob was relieved to hear that he remembered him from the café.

'I was wondering if you'd be up for doing a little private concert for my boys?' Rob said. It felt very presumptuous, calling him up like this, but there was no harm in asking, was there? At worst, Jimmy could just say no.

'I'd be honoured,' said Jimmy. Rob thought he sounded genuinely humbled by the request. He explained about George's condition, and why he so wanted to do something special for him, and for Will.

'I'm sorry to hear that,' said Jimmy. 'My little sister was in poor health when we were kids, so I know what it's like. It was really tough on all of us. It would be my pleasure to do this for George.'

'We'll pay you, obviously,' Rob said.

'Wouldn't dream of it,' said Jimmy. 'I'd love to do it for you, and I really don't want anything from you. If it helps George, then it's my pleasure. And you know, I reckon I might be able to persuade them to let me use the club. One afternoon, maybe, before they open up. So it'll be fine for the kids like that, won't it? Leave it to me and I'll speak to the management, see what I can do.'

Jimmy called back the following day. Rob took the call at his desk.

'Rob, we're on!' Jimmy said, sounding delighted. 'Next Thursday, four o'clock. We can have the place till five-thirty, then they need to kick us out so they can start setting up for the evening.'

'Oh wow, that's brilliant. Thank you so much. You've no idea what this means to us all. George has been through such a lot, and he loves you. He says you're going to be famous one day, you know?'

'Ha, I wish. Wouldn't that be nice, though? But hey, you never know.'

'One lucky break is all it takes. Hang in there. You're good, it'll happen for you, I'm sure it will. I really appreciate this, Jimmy, I can't thank you enough. We'll see you next Thursday, then. I'm going to call Sarah now and she can break the news to the boys. George will be absolutely stoked. And Will, too. Thank you. Thank you so much.'

Rob walked quickly out of his glass office and headed straight for the toilets. Emotion was building in his chest, and he couldn't bear for his team to see him crumple. It was all welling up inside him—relief, pain, gratitude, grief for what his little boy had gone through in the past year. All of it combined into one big melting pot and Rob felt he was about to explode.

Holding his head high, he made it into a cubicle, locked the door and leaned against it. The tears came silently but profusely. He'd had plenty of practice at crying quietly behind closed doors, shutting himself away to give vent to his emotions. He always tried not to cry in front of Sarah, tried to be strong for her, but sometimes it was just so hard.

Rob dried his eyes and splashed his face with cold water. Taking a deep breath, he walked back to his office, hoping no one would speak to him on the way. It wouldn't take much more than a kindly comment to start him off again.

He called Sarah, his voice still shaking.

'Love, that's fantastic!' she said. 'Oh, you clever thing, well done. I'll go and tell George now. Or do you want to wait and tell him yourself later? He's been a bit quiet today, so this'll really cheer him up.'

'Tell him now, that's fine. Isn't it nice of Jimmy? Restores your faith in mankind, doesn't it? Anyway, text me, let me know what Georgie says. And I'll see you all tonight. Love you.'

Encouraged

It was happening again. Someone was in her room. There were no footsteps, no opening and closing of the door, but somehow, they had made it inside. She had been awake the whole time, so she knew it hadn't crept in unnoticed. It was just there, by her side. Not quite a person, just a presence.

Was it the same intruder as before? Had they come back to finish the job? To murder her in her bed as she lay there, unable to defend herself? Perhaps this time they planned to hold a pillow over her face and suffocate her. She shuddered on the inside, but the reverberations didn't make it to the outer layers of her body.

There had been no sound, no disturbance of the air particles in the room. Humans were never completely silent, but this person was.

When it stopped by the bed Eve felt the lightest of touches on her hand, a whisper of cool gossamer against her skin, and there was the sense of someone leaning over her, studying her closely, looking for signs of life. In an instant, the fear left her, only to be replaced by the knowledge that this was a benign presence that meant her no harm. Her heartrate returned to normal and as the being moved around to the other side of the bed, she could sense it pausing, looking around, considering. Then a sigh. A real, audible sigh. Its first proper, human noise.

And then it spoke. 'I need to get out of here.' A female voice, soft and gentle, even through the fog.

'So do I,' said Eve, only her voice wasn't audible. 'Can you help me? Can we do this together?'

It touched her face this time, gingerly running a cool finger along the raised line of the scar on her cheek and trailing into her hair. She knew she had nothing to fear. Whatever it was, it wanted to help her. She felt like it belonged to her, or with her, this presence, although she knew that was a ridiculous idea. There was no way that something or someone outside the confines of her own body could have anything to do with her at all.

But it was there and that was how she felt. She and this presence were united in what they wanted. It wanted to get out and so did she.

It desperately wanted exactly what she did.

42

The sun inched slowly upwards as Sarah awoke, full of anticipation and nervous energy. She wanted the concert that afternoon to go perfectly, for both her children's sakes.

Rob called late that morning from the office to see how George was faring; his youngest son had still been in bed when he'd left for work.

'He's beyond excited, bless him,' said Sarah. 'Leaping about on the furniture, would you believe. I told him he should have a little sleep now, but you know what he's like, he thinks he can keep going. I just hope he's got the energy to get through it.'

'Of course he will. He'll be fine. Anyway, I'll be on time, don't worry. I'll see you outside the club.'

Sarah poked her head around the living room door. She was glad to see that George had dozed off at last. Rubix, their Labrador, was curled on the sofa by his side, whiskery jowls vibrating and legs twitching as he chased rabbits in his sleep. She laid the furry throw carefully over them both, bent to kiss the top of George's head, and turned off the TV before leaving the room. He still had plenty of time to rest before their big adventure later.

Everything would be fine.

'Mum, I'm home,' said Will, bounding through the front door. With a free period last thing on a Thursday afternoon, he was home in plenty of time to get ready for their outing. Sarah could see that his eyes were gleaming; he was just as excited as his brother.

'Hi, love,' she said, putting her finger to her lips. 'He's asleep at the moment, but I suppose I should probably go and wake him up.' She looked at her watch. 'Oh God, is that the time already? We need to be off in half an hour.'

'Sure thing, Mum. I'm going up to change.' Barely a minute later Will was back downstairs. 'Mum, have you seen my new jeans?'

'Try your bedroom floor. I've told you before, love, if you don't put stuff in the laundry basket, then it won't get washed. You'll just have to wear them as they are.'

'Yeah, yeah, yeah,' said Will. And then turning back towards Sarah: 'Thanks, Mum. Love you.'

'Love you too, darling,' she said, her heart swelling with pride. Will wasn't vocal with his endearments these days, so when he did say something heartfelt, it meant a lot. She knew all too well that there were worse things in life than a teenager with an untidy room. If only all of life's troubles could be dealt with by picking up your dirty pants from the floor.

'Come on, Will!' Sarah called up the stairs, looking anxiously at her watch.

Glancing down at George, she thought he looked pale, but his level of wellness varied so greatly from day to day. At least he was alert and more mobile than he normally was, although he had noticeably flagged and was now sitting on the bottom stair, head resting on the wall.

'You OK, love?' asked Sarah, unable to shake her habit of analysing his every move.

'I'm fine, Mum,' he said and sat upright again, no doubt worried that a show of weakness might mean his mother cancelling the trip. 'This is going to be brilliant. Have you got my phone? Is it charged up?'

The sudden excitement seemed to tire him out and he lolled against the wall once more.

'Yes, I have, love. And yes, it is.' And to her other son: 'Come *on*, Will.'

'Relax, Mum, I'm here,' said Will, appearing at the top of the stairs.

'The taxi's just pulled up,' said Sarah. 'Can you grab the bag? I'll see George to the car.'

'I don't need help. I can walk on my own,' said George. But Sarah stayed with a protective hand close to his elbow as George tottered to the waiting taxi like a shrunken old man.

George's animation on the journey brought home to Sarah just how housebound he had become in recent months. His regular trips to the hospital for dialysis, or to the doctor's surgery for check-ups in between, could hardly be classified as outings. It wasn't much of a life for a thirteen-year-old boy. She pulled down the jump seat and sat facing her sons, smiling as they chatted about what was to come.

'Yeah, we need to get him to play loads of Ed Sheeran,' said George. 'Do you think he'll play what we ask? Do requests and that?'

'Don't see why not,' said Will. 'It is our concert, after all. Dad says he writes his own songs, too. I can't wait to hear some of those. I'm the only one who's never seen this guy, remember. It's so cool, having a private concert just for us. It's sick.' Will launched into an air guitar performance, and his mother and brother roared with laughter.

George's eyes were still fixed on Will, but Sarah noticed the colour slowly draining from his face.

'Georgie, love, what's up? Are you OK?' She jumped out of her seat and knelt in front of him. George's head suddenly lolled and he flopped against her, unable to support his own weight.

'Can you sit down, darlin'?' yelled the taxi driver, taking a sharp turn and destabilising Sarah.

'My son's ill,' shouted Sarah. 'We need to get him to the hospital. Now.'

'So, Covent Garden's off, then, is it?' said the cabby with a sigh.

'St Thomas', please, quick as you can. He's very ill. He has kidney disease.'

'Oh, right. Sorry, Miss. No problem.'

Will shuffled over to the jump seat, and Sarah sat down next to George, laying his head in her lap. He was still conscious but only just, and he was murmuring incoherently. She placed a hand on his forehead, which was cold and clammy.

Nothing like this had ever happened before. George's illness had been terrifying enough for them at all stages, but it had been a steady progression. There had never been such a sudden turn for the worse. Although petrified, she knew she needed to keep it together for the sake of her boys. Luckily the hospital wasn't much of a detour from the route they had to take into the West End, and already they were only a matter of minutes away, provided traffic conditions remained kind to them. She knew there was no point in calling an ambulance and wasting even more time.

'Can you ring Dad?' she said to Will. 'Tell him to meet us at the hospital?'

'Is Georgie going to be all right, Mum?' asked Will, his voice fraught with fear.

'I don't know, love. I really don't know. Just call Dad, will you?' Will was almost as pale as his brother, his brow furrowed with worry.

Sarah couldn't understand this sudden turn of events; George had shown some genuine signs of improvement this past week or so. He'd seemed better in himself, happier and more perky somehow, and he'd looked a healthier colour, less jaundiced. The dialysis sessions this week had gone smoothly, and despite the doctors' concern over the summer, all the signs had been positive.

So why had this happened now? She could only hope it was a temporary hiccup that could be rectified with drugs, and she tried to chase away her fears with positive thoughts. Everything would be fine. It had to be.

'What about Jimmy?' said Will. 'Should we call him, too?'

Sarah had almost forgotten the reason they were in the taxi in the first place.

'Oh God. Will, I'm so sorry. We'll call Jimmy when we get to the hospital. I can't think about anything till I know George is going to be all right.'

'OK,' said Will, his shoulders drooping. Sarah knew he was trying to hide his disappointment for the sake of his brother. Poor Will, he had so few things to look forward to these days, and now this.

'How long did Dad say he'd be?' said Sarah.

Will looked puzzled. 'Well, he said he was already on his way to the hospital, and he'd see us there. Why would he be going there now?'

'I don't know, love. I can't think about that at the moment. We're here.' And then to the driver: 'Over there, please. In the ambulance bay.' There was some remonstration from the driver, but she continued, 'I know you're not supposed to, but you'll just have to pull up there.'

As soon as she opened the taxi door, a cluster of nurses in green scrubs whisked George from her clutches and onto a trolley.

'What's his name?' said one of them.

'It's George. George Barclay. He's a patient here. Mr Worthington is his consultant. He knows George. He'll know what to do.'

'Don't worry, Mrs Barclay.' The nurse exuded confidence and calm, but none of it was enough to reassure Sarah. All she could think of were worst case scenarios that ran back-to-back through her mind like a horror movie on repeat.

'Please don't let my brother die,' sobbed Will as he emerged from the taxi. Sarah felt awful as she looked back at her eldest son; she had almost forgotten he was there. She put her arm around his back—it had been a couple of years since she could reach to put it over his shoulders.

'Oh love, he's going to be fine. We're here now, they'll sort him out, don't you worry.' She gave him a thin smile, hoping he would take some comfort where she couldn't.

'Mum, Dad's over there, look,' said Will, pointing to his father. 'He's in the wrong bay. What's he doing? Dad, Dad, we're over here. Here!'

A small cluster of ambulances was disgorging patients and Rob stood resolute by the furthest one, hands deep in his pockets, shoulders hunched. He hadn't spotted Sarah and Will, but Sarah didn't want to leave George's side to go and fetch him.

'Can you go over, Will, tell him where we are? He's probably not expecting us to be in a taxi.'

Will ran across the ambulance bay, waving his arms to get his father's attention. 'Dad, Dad, we're over there. George is just going in. Mum's with him. Dad, we need you. Come *on*.' He couldn't seem to make his father hear him, and he jolted to a halt, watching Rob gaze trance-like at the open doors of the ambulance.

'Dad, come *on*,' said Will again, grabbing his father's arm and shaking it.

'Oh, Will, you're here already,' said Rob. It was as though his mind had suddenly re-entered his body.

'Come on, Dad, they're taking him in now. We came in a cab. Over there. Come on, Dad, we need you.'

'Yes, yes, of course,' said Rob, shaking himself down. 'Sorry, Will.'

Will couldn't understand why his father wasn't showing more urgency. Sometimes he just didn't get adults.

The taxi was still in the bay as they passed.

'Oy! You with them lot, guv?' the driver shouted to Rob. 'Before you disappear, that'll be thirty-four quid forty.'

'Oh, for Christ's sake,' sighed Rob, yanking his wallet from his pocket and shoving a pile of notes through the taxi window before running to catch up with Will.

'How's he doing?' Rob asked when they both reached

Sarah and the trolley, as it bore George down the long white corridor.

One look from Sarah was enough to tell Rob that it wasn't good news.

43

Rob left the office in plenty of time, just like Sarah had reminded him to. She knew he tended to cut things fine, would get absorbed in something and lose track of time. But he wouldn't want to miss seeing the look on Will and George's faces when Jimmy started playing.

'We'll be fine without you, boss,' Ashleigh said as Rob packed up for the day. 'It's been a quiet day. You go off and have a brilliant time, OK?'

Rob was nearing Trafalgar Square when he spotted a familiar couple ahead of him in the crowd: a man clutching a tatty guitar case and a slender young woman with hair down her back and a floor-sweeping skirt. He wondered about trying to catch up with them, which wasn't easy on the teeming London pavements, and thought better of it. He would see them soon enough when they arrived at the club, and he was sure they wouldn't want to have to make small talk with an old man.

His phone rang: Ashleigh. Given her parting words, Rob was tempted not to answer it, but the lure of duty was too strong. He stopped by one of the lion statues to take the call, a finger in one ear to block out the noise of the streets.

'Now this is just a courtesy call to keep you in the loop, guv, but I thought you'd want to know that we've had to scramble a team,' she said. 'You'd just left, but it was fine because there were enough of us here to deal with it. I didn't really want to disturb you, and we've got it covered.'

'Do you want me to come back in?' Rob said, his heart sinking.

'No, no need for that,' said Ashleigh. Rob twitched with pent-up energy as Ashleigh explained how the police had been called to an incident of a man brandishing a knife outside the Playhouse Theatre on Northumberland Avenue. He'd been apprehended very quickly, and the area had been secured, but they had sent in a team to do a post-incident report.

'They're not sure if it's terror-related at this stage,' she said. 'Most likely just a random event, but the same protocol must be followed, nonetheless.'

'OK. Sure you don't need me?' said Rob, crossing his fingers behind his back.

'It's not a threat to national security, boss, so we can manage without you.' Rob was relieved to hear the sarcastic edge to Ashleigh's voice. 'Just thought you'd want to know.'

'Thanks. Appreciate that.'

'Now, off you go. Give my love to them all. And a kiss for your gorgeous George, OK? One for Will, too, if he'll let you,' she said, laughing.

Putting the phone back in his pocket, Rob glanced down Northumberland Avenue towards the blinking blue lights in the distance. It was a wrench to move on and not involve himself, but he knew that was exactly what he had to do.

He scanned the bobbing heads in front of him, but Jimmy and his girlfriend were now long gone.

He hit a logjam of people waiting to cross Charing Cross Road. The steps up from the Tube continued to disgorge more bodies into the mêlée and he became concerned for people's safety. When an elbow hit him in the ribs he spun round, instantly on alert.

'Hey! Watch what you're doing,' he said. 'No need to push.'

The culprit, a young man in a business suit, raised his palms in apology. 'Sorry, mate,' he said, before dodging away to find a gap elsewhere.

Rob wondered if flashing his ID card might help to create some order amidst this chaos. It did come in useful now and again, as many people assumed it was police ID. He knew he probably shouldn't take advantage of their ignorance, but Security Services and Metropolitan Police ID cards did look pretty similar.

Rob spotted the man who had collided with him, now further along the street, his head bobbing up and down as he ducked through the gaps. There was still no sign of Jimmy and his girlfriend.

And then, the air split with a cry.

It was more of a howl, like an animal in pain, and the atmosphere in the crowd changed instantly. As one body, it continued to surge forward, though forward now seemed like the wrong direction. Rob's professional training kicked in once more and he cut quickly through the panicked throng.

'Call an ambulance,' a man yelled. 'And police.'

A woman was screaming. Incessant screaming. Screaming as though she couldn't stop.

'Security Services, let me through,' Rob yelled, waving his ID above his head. The sea of people parted, closing into a human amphitheatre behind him. Before him the stage was empty, apart from two people, one of whom lay on the pavement, motionless, blood pooling at his side. The other was the source of the piercing screams.

'Oh God, no,' Rob sighed, reaching for his phone.

'Ambulance and police are on their way, officer,' said an elderly woman to his left. 'I just called them.'

Rob crouched down to assess the extent of the man's injuries. There was a wide slash on his side, and Rob pushed the ball of his hand onto the wound, trying to stem the flow of blood. The elderly woman touched his shoulder.

'Here, use this,' she said, passing him a floral scarf, which he held tightly against the man's stomach.

'Hang in there,' said Rob. 'Come on, please, you have to.' He looked up at the man's companion, who was now being comforted by the same elderly lady.

Rob listened impatiently for the first signs of the emergency vehicles. 'Come on, come on,' he said. 'Hurry up. You have to hurry up.' Every second felt like an eternity. More time for this man's blood to ebb away into the gutter.

'Do you know him?' asked the woman at his side.

'Yes, I'm afraid I do,' said Rob, staring down at the familiar mess of red hair as sirens sliced through the chilling silence.

44

Eve had failed Jimmy.

She couldn't believe how it had all gone so horribly wrong. Couldn't cope with the overwhelming sense of failure that threatened to engulf her.

By the time Eve arrived on the scene, the paramedics were already strapping Jimmy onto a stretcher. She stood there, helpless, as they attached a drip and wheeled him carefully up the ramp. She wondered if that was how it had been with her. Had Luca stood beside her broken and battered body, feeling as utterly useless as she did now?

She climbed into the ambulance behind them, and stood at the end of the stretcher, ludicrously trying not to get in the way of the paramedic who was attending to him. She desperately wanted to touch Jimmy, offer some kind of comfort, so she leaned over to rest her hand on his. She expected him not to feel her, but perhaps in the semi-conscious world that he now inhabited he would take some comfort from it. He looked so white, so ghostly already; she wished she could tell if his skin was warm and vibrant, or clammy and deathly cool.

Eve hadn't even managed to warn him. Hadn't had the chance to tell him to be careful, to look out for danger, because she was so preoccupied with her own grief. She had failed him, totally and utterly. Everything was her fault.

'I'm so sorry, Jimmy,' she said to his motionless body. 'Forgive me.'

Jules stood beside him, tears rolling down her cheeks.

'Sit down please, Miss, and put your seatbelt on,'

said the paramedic. Jules looked as though she wanted to throw herself on Jimmy, to try and breathe some life back into his body. 'I know it's hard, but you really mustn't touch him until we can get him to the hospital and assess the extent of his injuries.'

'I'm so sorry I didn't keep him safe for you, Jules,' said Eve. 'So very sorry.'

It was all her fault. She had taken her eye off the ball since Luca died, and when Jimmy was attacked, she had been asleep. Asleep! How could she have slept through something so monumentally important? Why didn't some inner alarm clock wake her up in time to get to him?

After all the weeks she spent waiting for something to happen, was this now some kind of test, a judgment to see if she was worthy of re-joining her human form? If it was, then she had failed quite spectacularly. Had failed at the one thing she was destined to do in this existence, the very thing she had been brought here for.

She hated herself for it.

Eve could remember exactly what she was dreaming about as though it were real. She had been with Luca, in a world he still inhabited. For those few brief and ecstatic moments it was as if he hadn't died at all. In the dream he was there beside her. She could see him, hear him, feel him even, and he was telling her to wait for him.

Oh, if only. But to see him again would mean her dying, too, and even though she was miserable without him, she still wanted to get back to her life. She desperately wanted to see her family and friends, but she had a dreadful feeling that failing so badly had ruined her chances of ever getting back there.

She was a fallen angel; even her wings couldn't get her there in time to help Jimmy. When she had woken from the dream, she'd known right away that she needed to get to him, but she was too late. Seconds too late, but still too late. It didn't matter whether it was seconds, minutes, hours, or days. Late was late, however you looked at it.

A man had been standing at the side of the stretcher when Eve arrived. There was something about him that made him stand out from the rubberneckers. He appeared to have taken charge of the situation. Streaks of blood stained his grey business suit, and his face was ashen. He ran his hands through hair flecked with white, and now red, too. Too solid and earthly to be another angel. Eve knew that he was real enough, and not another one like her.

She had seen him before, this man, but in the panic of the moment couldn't place him. Eve heard him ask the paramedic if he could accompany him to the hospital.

'No, sir, I'm afraid it's next of kin only in the ambulance,' the paramedic said, touching the man on the arm.

As the ambulance doors closed and the sirens began to wail, Eve recalled that it was just a few feet from here, on the steps down into Charing Cross Station, that she had fallen. Was there some significance to the location, she wondered? It seemed that this bizarre episode in her life had come full circle, now that she was there with Jimmy, back almost exactly where she had started her journey. Only she had failed to do what was intended for her during her time here, so what was the point of it all?

Eve still wasn't entirely sure quite what had happened to Jimmy. Had he been stabbed? But who on earth would want to hurt someone as kind and gentle as him? There was an awful lot of blood, and some kind of surgical pack on his stomach. A silk scarf, now stained red, lay on the floor of the ambulance. Was it Jules' scarf? Had she tried to stem the flow until the ambulance arrived? Poor girl. Eve couldn't imagine the trauma she had been through.

Eve watched through the blacked-out window of the ambulance as the man who had tried to help hailed a cab. His mouth made soundless words to the cabbie as he indicated to follow the ambulance. The taxi kept close, and Eve could see him leaning forward, not daring to take his eyes from it as they sped in convoy through the London streets, defying traffic lights and jams to stop them.

When the ambulance reversed into the A&E bay at St Thomas' he was there again, dismissing the taxi driver with a hurriedly presented bundle of notes and rushing around to the rear doors as they disembarked.

Jules climbed out first and Eve followed. There were bloodstains on Jules' dress and black rivulets down her cheeks. She seemed to be carved from a solid block of grief. Eve placed one hand in the small of the girl's back and closed her eyes.

'Be brave, Jules,' she whispered. 'He's here now, and they will look after him.' She could only hope those words were true, and that some of her calm, her hope, would transfer to Jules and keep her holding faith.

Eve glanced at the man again and his eyes locked onto hers, widening in disbelief.

He had seen her. She was sure of it. Somehow, she had become visible to him, if only for a few brief seconds. And then there was a voice in the distance, calling to him, and the moment was broken. He shook his head and rubbed his eyes, as though to dispel an apparition.

'Dad, Dad, we're over there. George is just going in. Mum's with him. Dad, we need you. Come *on*.'

He was needed elsewhere now.

Eve stuck close to Jules as they followed Jimmy and his medical entourage into the hospital.

45

Jimmy's face mirrored the starkness of the corridors, his eyelids now blue blurs against the whiteness.

Eve felt a pang where her heart used to beat and hoped that fate was not about to deliver to her another fledgling angel in the form of this lovely young man. She prayed that recovery was Jimmy's destiny. But if it wasn't, then it was likely that she would be the one to take this talented young man, who had love and a life in the real world, on a journey of discovery.

Her shoulders sagged with the weight of responsibility, but she would do it again—had to do it again, because of what she had done. Or rather, what she had failed to do. She was tired, and the thought of it dragged her down, but somehow she would find the strength and rise to the occasion.

When they whisked Jimmy into the operating theatre, Eve sat nervously by Jules, her translucent hand over Jules' delicately pale one. Eve scanned the corridors constantly, half-expecting to see his spirit wandering from the operating theatre.

For four long hours they waited there, Jules quiet and still, Eve alternately pacing and sitting, unable to be in one place for too long.

No one had come to join Jules, and Eve wondered about their family situation. If they were alone in the world, she and Jimmy, who would look after Jules if the worst were to happen? Eve shuddered, not daring to contemplate a future for her without him.

Come on, Jimmy, she willed him. *Look at her, she has no one else. She needs you. You have to come back to her.*

And then finally Jules had company. A middle-aged woman in a beige suit with padded shoulders pushed open the doors at the end of the corridor and click-clacked her way towards them. The only family resemblance was the green of their eyes; in all other ways, Eve thought these women seemed poles apart.

'Mum!' yelled Jules, throwing her arms around the older woman. Eve noticed a cold pause before the mother reciprocated.

'It's OK, Julia, we're here now, my love,' she said, patting Jules' back perfunctorily before pulling away. 'We'll look after you. John's just parking, he'll be along in a mo.'

Jules bristled at the mention of this man's name.

Eve shuffled a few chairs along, leaving space for the older woman to sit down, in respect for their personal space as well as her own. As a surgeon approached, all three sprang to their feet, and once again Eve was at Jules' side, both ready to hear everything he had to say.

'Miss Fletcher? I am David Pinkerton. I operated on your partner. Please, do sit down.'

'Is he OK? He is going to be all right, isn't he?' begged Jules, her eyes darting from side to side as she tried to read the surgeon's expression.

The surgeon took a deep breath and looked down at his hands. He turned them over to examine both sides. Eve thought it was an odd gesture; presumably it gave him time to gather his thoughts.

'Well, the operation went as well as we could hope. We've done all we can, and now only time will tell. He sustained a serious penetrating abdominal trauma which pierced his pancreas. We have repaired the wound, but there is always the risk of further internal bleeding, and infection, which we will, of course, try to minimise.'

'How long will it be until he wakes up?' asked Jules. 'You must know. You've operated on him. You've seen what's happened to him.'

Jules' mother tried to pull Jules close, but Jules resisted and stepped to one side.

'There is no way of telling, I'm afraid, Miss Fletcher. I wish I could be more precise but this early on it's very hard to make an accurate prognosis. We're taking him down to ICU now, and you should be able to visit him in an hour or so.' He smiled weakly.

Jules sighed with exasperation and walked away from the surgeon, her hands in her hair.

'Thank you, Doctor,' said Jules' mother apologetically, with a sideways glare at her daughter as the surgeon retreated. 'That's good, isn't it?' she said to Jules, once he was out of earshot.

'Good? Nothing's good, Mum! How can any of this be good?' She laughed in her mother's face.

'Look, I'm just trying to see the positive side of things here, love. There's a lot to be said for positive thinking in situations like this, isn't there?'

'Mum, now isn't the time for your motivational bollocks. It might have worked when I was little, but that's my boyfriend in there, the love of *my* life, fighting for *his*. For God's sake, how can you see the positive in that?'

She paused, pulling herself up to her full height.

'I don't want you here, Mum. I didn't ask you to come. I think you should go.'

'Oh, come now, Julia, don't be like that. I just want to help you.'

'No, you don't. You don't want to help me. You just want another case study that you can talk about in your courses. An interesting little anecdote. We don't need your help, Jimmy and me, we're fine on our own. We've always been fine on our own. And don't call me Julia. I left that name behind when I left home. When I left you and that useless git you call a husband.'

She ran down the corridor and flew through the swinging doors at the end, so fast that Eve could barely keep up with her.

46

'You can go in and see him now, Miss Fletcher,' said the nurse. 'Just for a little while, though. We don't want to wear him out.'

Jules gave the nurse a puzzled look, and Eve wondered how it was possible to wear out someone who was in a coma. She knew that her own visitors had been given similar instructions, especially in the early days, when they thought there was a chance of her coming round at any moment. By now it was likely that they'd all given up hope of a sudden return to consciousness.

By sheer coincidence, Jimmy had been admitted to the room next door to Eve's, the same one that Len had occupied before his death. She couldn't believe how things had turned out. She didn't want him there; he shouldn't *be* there. Following Jules into the room, Eve felt the burden of guilt and responsibility sitting heavily upon her shoulders.

The room was just as it had been when Len was there. It was just as still, just as sterile. A familiar set of equipment attached to Jimmy. The same eerie silence was broken only by the intermittent beeping of machines.

After her earlier outburst, Jules was calm again. Eve watched as she marched up to the bed, her eyes never leaving Jimmy's face. She smoothed her long skirt under her bottom before sitting on the chair at his bedside and placing her hand over Jimmy's. Her back was as straight and strong as the words that came from her mouth:

'You can do this, my love. You can beat this. You'll win, I know you will. You're a fighter. You're so strong,

Jim.' Although she was smiling, Eve could hear the sloosh of tears behind her words.

Eve moved to stand behind Jules and enveloped her in a hug she would never feel, amazed at the strength and composure this young woman possessed in Jimmy's hour of need. Then a surge of emotion welled up inside her and she couldn't bear to be in the room any longer. It was too painful to see them like this, together but not together. She had to get out. There was little she could do for either of them right now, but some time away from them might throw some clarity on how she could possibly help them. She needed to feel fresh air—or at least the memory of it—on her face.

Eve slipped through the door as someone opened it, cursing herself for her continued lack of courage. She faced the same predicament when she reached the sliding doors at the hospital entrance, waiting until they opened for an elderly couple before gliding through to the outside world.

Two men stood near the top of the steps, their heads close together, eyes brimming with emotion. *No,* Eve thought as she looked at them more closely.

Sudden recognition hit her like a hammer-blow.

'Will!' she cried, rushing towards him as though she were still his favourite teacher. As though he would see her . . .

And then everything fell into place. A father's face recalled from school events and parents' evenings; in the café, talking to Jimmy and Jules; with Jimmy again at the scene of the accident. And now here with Will, while his younger son was presumably somewhere else in this hospital.

'He's going to die, Dad, isn't he?' The words caught in Will's throat.

'Oh, Will, no,' said Will's father, putting an arm around his son's shoulder and pulling him close. Eve then saw realisation dawn on the father's face. The time for sugar-coating the facts had passed. 'I actually don't know, Will. I really don't know what will happen. I can't bear to think that this time, he just might. He needs a kidney now, or his chances aren't good. But it's not like waiting for treatment, or an operation, or anything that the doctors can control. And the thought that someone else has to die to save our beautiful boy…' He sniffed and wiped his nose on the back of his hand. 'It's all down to luck, now. And fate.'

Of course it is, thought Eve. *I know all about fate.*

She raced back to Jimmy's room with a sickening feeling in the pit of her stomach.

Oh God, just what exactly am I caught up in the middle of here? she wondered as she ploughed through the door into Jimmy's room, hoping to goodness she wasn't too late.

47

'Drink your coffee, love,' said Rob. 'It's going cold.'

'I don't want it,' said Sarah. She pushed the cup away and flopped back in her chair with a sigh. Rob had managed to persuade her to leave George's room for a few moments while the doctor carried out some more tests. She felt that her place was at her son's bedside, but her visible anxiety was making George fretful, and the doctor had insisted she take a break.

'They're doing everything they can,' said Rob, putting an arm around his wife.

'I know they are, but they should know by now what's going on, and they don't. No one knows why he went downhill so quickly.' She jerked away from Rob and jumped to her feet. 'They thought he was stable. We *all* thought he was. He was, wasn't he? It wasn't just us, trying to be positive.'

'It seemed so, but we're not the experts, are we?' said Rob.

'Well, I just wish these *experts* would hurry up and tell us why our boy is so sick, and what they're doing about it. I can't accept that we might have reached the transplant stage and there really is nothing else they can try. What if…'

'Sarah, shh. You're no use to George if you're in this kind of state.'

'I can't help it. It's just so . . .' She sat back down, turned to face Rob, and took a deep breath in, which she let out slowly, trying to ease the tension in her body.

'Anyway, Will said you were already on your way here, earlier. Why was that?'

'Oh, love, it's Jimmy,' he said with a deflated sigh. 'The busker. Sorry, the musician. He was caught up in something and he got hurt. He's in intensive care now, far as I know. They had to operate.'

'Oh my God,' said Sarah, her hand flying to her mouth. 'What happened?'

'He was stabbed. Not just him, either. There were six knife attacks at exactly the same time at various locations around London.'

Sarah gasped. 'Another terrorist attack? He's going to be OK, though, isn't he?'

'I don't know. They won't tell me anything as I'm not a relative. I need to go and find his girlfriend at some point, find out what's happening. I spotted her earlier, but then Mum and Dad arrived to collect Will, and she'd disappeared by the time they left.'

'Oh, God, Rob. How very sad.'

'Yeah, and on my afternoon off as well. I should have been there. Should've been in the office when this happened. Ashleigh called me to tip me off about something and I should have gone back in. Turns out now that it was related.'

'You didn't know this would happen, darling.'

'But it did. I felt it. And I should have been there.'

'You are entitled to some time off now and again.'

'Yeah, but . . .'

'Yeah, but nothing,' said Sarah. 'You had a planned afternoon off. You can't be there twenty-four hours a day, and even if you had gone back, there's no guarantee you'd have been able to prevent it.'

Rob stood up and paced around the seating area.

'They caught a seventh guy,' he said. 'That was the incident Ash called me about, outside the Playhouse. Apparently, he was on his way to carry out an attack near the Eye, but he lost his nerve, drew attention to himself and they intercepted him. They couldn't get him to talk, so we didn't know he was part of the bigger plan until it was too late.'

'You shouldn't beat yourself up. It's not your fault.'

'Yes, but . . . of all the people in the world, why did one of them have to be Jimmy?'

Sarah's face was stony pale. 'Wrong place, wrong time. Your chances of being caught up in something like this are so small, but fate is cruel sometimes. Did the others pull through?'

'Three died at the scene, the other two are in hospital. It's not looking too hopeful for one of them.'

'Oh my God,' said Sarah. 'I'll never understand what compels someone to hurt another person like that.'

'I wonder about that every day. Bizarre how two separate, equally horrible things, brought us both here this afternoon, eh?' said Rob.

As Sarah sat quietly, her eyes downcast, Rob could almost hear her mind whirring. Call it intuition, but he knew exactly what she was thinking.

'Rob, you don't think—?' she said.

'Don't even say it, love. I know what you're thinking, but it's too awful for words.'

Rob realised that as soon as he told Sarah about Jimmy she would start to wonder about the potential of the situation. Jimmy was very poorly, but he was a talented young man with so much to live for. So, he left Sarah in the waiting area while he went outside to get some air. If they stayed there together any longer, he knew one of them would voice what they were both thinking.

That unspeakable thing.

Putting it into words would make it sound so wrong—and yet so right for George. Their son was also a talented young man with his whole life ahead of him. In any case, Jimmy's injuries might not turn out to be as serious as they thought, and he might make a full recovery. And if he didn't, the kidney might not even be a match. Jimmy might not even be a donor, for Christ's sake!

It felt so wrong to raise their hopes this way. But they were parents. They couldn't help it.

What Rob hadn't mentioned to Sarah was the bizarre experience he'd had when he first arrived at the hospital. He couldn't bring himself to tell his wife about the woman he had seen standing by Jimmy's girlfriend as she'd climbed from the ambulance. She had stared him right in the eye, and he knew at that moment that she wasn't a figment of his imagination.

She was real, whatever real meant.

Rob had been transfixed. He would have found it hard to describe her to someone else, because she was there and yet she wasn't. She wasn't human, wasn't *real,* in the true sense because she was kind of translucent. He knew it all sounded like utter nonsense.

But he was certain he had seen this woman. This *thing.*

A person, with wings. *Real* wings. Which made her an angel, didn't it? They were wings just like the ones you saw in religious imagery, on statues in those fancy graveyards, keeping watch over the dead.

This angel had been standing still, her wings were folded and tucked up neatly behind her back, glowing white and kind of . . . well . . . *holy* was the best word he could think of to describe them. Ethereal and other-worldly. And utterly beautiful.

'Jesus. God, what the . . .' he had said, running his fingers through his hair, his blasphemy feeling wholly inappropriate in the circumstances. He didn't understand what it all meant. It frightened him.

He couldn't tell Sarah. She was fragile enough and wouldn't know what to think. She would try to believe him, he was sure, but she didn't need any added stress right now. It would just make her concerned for his state of mind, at a time when he needed to be strong for her.

Rob had watched the angel as she tried to comfort Jimmy's girlfriend, that petite little slip of a woman with the long hair and long skirt. The angel had barely taken her eyes off the girlfriend, other than for those few brief moments when she had looked away and seen Rob. She placed her hand in the small of the girl's back, and there was a moment when Rob wondered if the girl might really have felt something.

He saw her tremble a little, like a shiver had run down her spine. It made a shiver run down Rob's own spine, now, to think about it. Was he, too, being touched by an angel's hand? Did he have one of these divine creatures standing by his side right now, trying to comfort him, hoping everything would turn out all right for him and his little family?

He shook himself down and berated himself for his foolishness.

But he knew what he had seen. Somehow or other, he had managed to break through this angel's cloak of invisibility. He had no idea how, or what it meant.

One thing he knew for certain was that he would never tell Sarah.

48

Eve rushed back up to Jimmy's room. She couldn't let him out of her sight, not now. However upset she was, none of this was about her. It should be all about them. About *him*. She had to get back inside. Jimmy was the one she was supposed to be looking after, the one who needed her support.

It had been a shock to see Will and his father so distraught, especially knowing Will as she did. That poor family; no one should have to go through what they had endured. But she had to get her priorities straight and make sure that Jimmy was properly looked after, that everything was being done to get him on the road to recovery.

She couldn't let him down again.

She was reassured by the gentle buzz of staff around Jimmy. Jules still sat beside him, her back ramrod straight, holding his hand and talking to him as though he could hear her.

'Come on, love,' she said. 'You can do this.' Her positive words contradicted her ashen face and dark, sunken eyes.

Eve was relieved not to see the shadow of Jimmy standing by his bed. She half-expected him to be there when she returned—a bemused figure trying to make sense of what was happening. She could only hope that the absence of his spirit form was a good thing, as she clutched at a vain hope that this lovely young man would get better. She searched the medics' faces for clues, but their stoic expressions gave nothing away. She slumped on the end of the bed, wishing there was something useful, something practical, that she could do to help.

And then, it was as if a bomb had gone off. A sudden cacophony of blaring machines. The room erupted into action.

'Come with me, please, Miss,' said a nurse, leading Jules towards the door.

'What's happening? What's wrong with him?' Jules shrieked, pulling away from the nurse. She dug her heels in. 'I'm not leaving him.'

'CPR can be very distressing for the relatives,' said the nurse.

'I don't care,' said Jules. 'I'm staying here.'

'You need to leave,' said the nurse. 'Please, it's for the best.' But, summoned to the bedside, the nurse sighed and was forced to desist, leaving a panicked Jules in the corner of the room.

'It's all right, Jules,' said Eve. 'I'll look after you.' The pair of them stood in shocked oblivion, and Eve hoped that Jules could sense her presence in the midst of all this chaos.

One of the doctors took charge, conducting the resuscitation team like a finely tuned orchestra. Jules and Eve watched in horror as the paddles were charged up.

'Stand clear!' the doctor yelled. Eve wished she could place her hands over Jules's eyes as Jimmy's pale torso flew off the bed and back down again with a thud.

And then again, and again.

'Save him, please!' Jules screamed. 'Help him!' she called. 'Jimmy!' Her hands flew to her mouth. She shouldn't have to see this, Eve thought. It was too much for anyone to bear.

And then Eve saw him.

There was a blurring of lines and the outline of his body seemed to shimmer. An essence emanated from him, gradual and yet sudden. A distortion of air and space, both beautiful and frightening to watch. Then he was there in his entirety, standing at the foot of his own bed, a frown of confusion furrowing his translucent brow.

'Jimmy,' Eve said, reaching out her hand. 'Jimmy, over here.'

He smiled at her as though in recognition, but she didn't understand how he could possibly recognise her. They had never met in the real world.

'Hello,' he said, his eyes wide in wonder. He turned to look at Jules and there was sorrow etched deep into his shadowy face. He extended his hand towards her, but it was too late.

He was starting to fade.

'No, Jimmy! No!' Eve yelled. 'Jimmy! Don't go!' He smiled at her and there was forgiveness in his eyes, but then his spirit form was no more.

'No!' Eve screamed again. Over his body, a puff of mist had gathered, insubstantial and fleeting. She watched as an outline rose from the bed, a silhouette of Jimmy's human form. It seemed to acknowledge the mist above it, and Eve watched, wide-eyed, as the two entities merged and then were gone.

All that remained of Jimmy was the empty shell of his body.

49

Rob found his wife sitting outside George's room. He sat down beside her and took hold of her hand.

'Jimmy didn't make it, love,' said Rob. 'He passed away a little while ago. I've just seen Jules, his girlfriend. This whole thing is a mess.'

'Oh, Rob, no,' said Sarah, tears welling in her eyes. 'That lovely young man. What a waste.'

She buried her face in her hands and Rob put his arm around her shoulders. He couldn't believe Jimmy was gone. A young man with everything to live for, struck down in an attack of pure evil. It was a sad fact that incidents like that happened every day, all around the world, and someone, somewhere, would always be in the wrong place at the wrong time.

But when that someone was a person you knew—even if not that well—then it was an entirely different feeling. He was filled with rage, but also with great sympathy for Jules. It was quite evident that they meant the world to one another.

Rob had bumped into Jules just after Jimmy died. He'd gone off to buy a sandwich for Sarah, even though he knew she was never likely to eat it. Jules came out of Jimmy's room and, recognising Rob from earlier, wrapped her arms around him and clung on for dear life. When he realised she had no one with her, Rob stayed while she sobbed on his shoulder.

'I'm so sorry,' he'd said, rubbing her back gently as she cried, not knowing what else he could say that would offer any comfort. It wasn't the time to tell her that he thought Jimmy was the most talented musician he'd ever met. Not now, when it was all gone. Blown away in the blink of an eye, in the split second of a random act of violence.

How delicately our lives hang in the balance, ready to be snatched from us at any moment.

He thought back to what he had seen by the ambulance. The—dare he say it—the *angel.*

If he'd ever given any thought to angels in his life, which wasn't often, then it was as mythical, benevolent souls, there to guide and watch over people. But if he really had seen an angel, if that apparition genuinely was one, then why had she allowed Jimmy to die? Why hadn't she tried harder to save him, or was that beyond even her supreme power? Or maybe . . . just maybe . . . there was a higher purpose, and that was why he had been able to see her.

Because that purpose involved his family?

It was all too much to think about. Rob jumped to his feet and ran his hands through his hair.

'We need to get back in there with George,' he told Sarah. 'We should be by his side. He's our boy. We can't lose him. Life is so fragile, so precious.' A tear escaped his eye and he brushed it away with the back of his hand.

Rob could see Sarah's mind working. 'Do you think . . .?' She cleared her throat nervously. 'Would it be wrong . . . Would it be really wrong to say this now, after everything that has happened?' She hoped Rob would fill in the gaps for her, but he couldn't bring himself to say those words. 'What if Jimmy's death was for a reason?'

'I know what you're thinking, but it feels so wrong. Besides, it doesn't work that way. Just because Jimmy and George are in the same hospital . . . I mean, there's protocol for these things, surely? There might be someone whose need is even greater than George's. Somewhere else, in another hospital, anywhere in the country. We don't know, do we? And besides, he might not be a match.'

Rob did know that Jimmy was a donor, though. Jules had told him, as he held her in his arms and her tears soaked his shirt, just as Jimmy's blood had earlier that day.

'They told me he was a donor,' Jules had said. 'That's just the kind of guy he was.'

Rob couldn't tell Sarah this. Couldn't raise her hopes, only to be dashed again. It would be too much of a blow. He also couldn't tell his wife that he had paid a quick visit to the chapel after seeing Jules. For the first time in his life, he had prayed in earnest, prayed for a miracle for his son, with a new and heartfelt belief. He also sought forgiveness; he couldn't help but think that, if he hadn't asked Jimmy to put on the concert for them, then he wouldn't have been caught up in the attack and he would still be alive.

Rob was sure the guilt would stay with him for the rest of his life.

If there really was someone listening to his prayers—and now he suspected there just might be—he wasn't expecting too much of a return on his very late investment. As he looked up at the images of the angels on either side of Christ on the cross, the only face he could see was the one belonging to the very real angel he had seen that afternoon.

Today was a day for keeping secrets.

Aware

Eve had heard noises from the room next door before. It was only to be expected, as the walls were paper thin. But this time it was different. She strained every nerve to try and distinguish individual voices, but above the general furore it was impossible.

A crisis was unfolding and, rather than remaining an impassive listener, Eve wanted to be a part of it. She longed to get out of that bed, to walk into the room and help. Somehow, anyhow. Something tugged at her very core, drawing her in so much that she felt as though part of her was already in that room, her heart and soul waiting for her there. She knew it was a ridiculous notion, when all she had and all she was lay helpless in this damn bed.

This compulsion to help was new to her and she didn't understand its urgency. Perhaps someone she knew was in the adjacent room. Was her conscience reaching out to them?

Enough. Enough of this constant state of blind inertia and these insane thoughts. She couldn't bear it anymore, trapped and useless, an object of pity to family and friends, a clinical conundrum to the medical staff. She should be getting better by now, that was what they all said. None of them could explain why she hadn't woken up. But then, none of them knew how active her mind had been during her coma, thoughts and feelings raging day and night, coming at her from all directions since the moment she found herself there.

Instead, they all spoke as if she were already dead, seeming to have given up hope of her ever recovering. But things were different. She had changed. She was healing, she knew she was. It was only everyone else who couldn't see Eve's progress from the early days until now.

Where once she had lain in a stupor, at the mercy of the death-darkness and barely coping with the pain, now her body was recovering and her mind raring to go. But all they saw was that body, still pinned to the bed by its insubordinate, leaden limbs.

In that moment, Eve knew the strange presence that had visited her before was in that room next door. It was that presence that drew her in, reeling her towards it. She didn't know how she knew, but an invisible magnet between her and that presence was compelling them to be together.

It wasn't something to be afraid of, like she'd first thought. It wanted her to join it.

She had to get to it. Had to join the presence, whoever or whatever it was. It was time for them to be together.

She just didn't understand why.

50

Jules staggered down the corridor like a woman lost, Eve following close behind. The young woman's shoulders were hunched and there was a lack of precision to her movements. She looked like she might topple over at any minute but didn't care, as if she had nothing now to live for.

Eve recognised the symptoms of shock and wished there was something she could do for Jules, some tangible way she could support her through her pain. But there was nothing; she had hands that wanted to comfort and arms that wanted to hold, but they had no substance to them with which to do anything useful. All that remained was to watch over Jules and hope that, somehow or other, she could sense something of Eve's essence and take comfort from it—even without knowing what it was.

It was all Eve's fault. She had failed Jimmy, and her failure had resulted in this. A wonderful young woman had been left alone in the world, deprived of the man she loved. Jimmy, so full of life, so talented, and with so much to give to the world, was gone. She could have prevented it from happening. She could have saved him. *Should* have saved him. Being his guardian was the one thing she had been brought into this strange half-life to do, and she had failed because she was too wrapped up in her own grief.

Eve didn't know how she could continue to live with what she had done. She didn't want to be there, carrying all that guilt, that disappointment, but neither did she want to die. She had no idea where the best place for her would be, now that she had failed at everything else.

Maybe it would be better for everyone if she just slipped away quietly, passed peacefully in her sleep. Then she would be no trouble to anyone anymore. They would switch off her machines and get back to their lives.

But then she thought of her parents, who still came to visit her on alternate days, and the effect her being in hospital had had on them. Being trapped in a constant state of not knowing had ravaged them, and old age was carved permanently into their faces. And so, she knew she didn't mean it when she thought she wanted to die, because that would mean wishing the worst thing imaginable on them. The loss of their beloved daughter.

Eve passed through the doors behind Jules and into the open air. Small and fragile against the vastness of the clear autumn sky, Jules stretched her arms to the heavens as though in supplication, her eyes brimming with sadness and disbelief. When her arms dropped loosely to her sides again, her whole body seemed to cave in.

Sobs wracked her slim frame as she collapsed onto a nearby bench and bent double, hugging her knees. Passers-by gazed questioningly but no one approached her. No one came to sit beside her to offer a friendly ear or a shoulder to cry on.

Eve sat down beside Jules and she, too, gave into the tears. Only her tears were dry.

'Jules, I'm so sorry,' she said. 'I wish you could know just how sorry I am, wish you could hear me now. I'm here beside you, trying to help you, but it's all too late and I'm so desperately sorry for everything.'

But her outpourings were worth nothing and wouldn't bring Jimmy back.

It was then that Eve's hands began to tingle, like she had pins and needles in the tips of her fingers. The sensation moved down her hands, little by little, and Eve held them up to examine them, but they looked just the same, still as translucent. As the tingle moved up her arms, they began to shake. She jumped up from the bench, but then her body started to shake, too, and she sat back down quickly, hugging her limbs to her torso.

Her whole body juddered now, jolting hard as though some external force had her in its grip and wanted to shake the remaining life force from her. She couldn't control it, couldn't rein it in, and then it was as though something was pulling her, an invisible force, an entity more powerful than her alone. Although she wanted to stay there with Jules more than anything, she knew it wasn't going to be possible.

The force compelled her to go back inside, dragging her towards the doors. She had to go, had to get back to her room. With a sudden feeling of impending doom, she knew she had to get there before it was too late, although for what, she had no idea.

In a brief moment of clarity, she knew that someone, somewhere had chosen this path for her. All she could do now was accept that choice, whether it led to death, or to another chance at life. For the first time since Luca died, she understood why, as he'd faded away, he was so resigned to whatever awaited him beyond this existence because she, too, had that same feeling of calm acceptance now. She glanced over her shoulder at Jules one last time, and with a silent apology for deserting her, ran back inside the hospital, her body trembling all over.

Outside her corridor, her parents were waiting for visiting time to begin. For them it was just an ordinary day, another visit to their sick daughter, another day of waiting for something to happen. Out here, away from her bedside, their expressions were laid bare and Eve saw the true extent of what her illness had done to them. Gone were the hopeful smiles that they forced for her benefit.

Eve couldn't stay and watch over them; the invisible force continued to reel her in, like a fish on a hook. Gliding past the nurses' station, and now no longer in control of her own movements, she closed her eyes tightly as the solidity of the door to her room loomed. And then she was through, on the other side, and there was her body on the bed, far beneath her now. The machines continued to churn out the same noises, only this time they were more distant. She was floating high above it all, and it was truly wonderful, the most liberating and peaceful feeling ever. She was as light as gossamer as she hovered over her body, which began to judder and shake like nothing she had ever seen.

She drifted down towards it. And then, there was nothing.

PART 5

MAKING A LIFE

51

Five Weeks After Waking Up

Buster jumped onto Eve's bed and sat down heavily on her chest. He stretched out one paw to touch her gently on the cheek, purring fit to burst.

'Morning, you,' Eve said with a sleepy giggle. Eyes still closed, she reached a hand out from under the duvet to stroke his plush back.

To say Buster was happy to have his human home was an understatement. He'd been Eve's shadow since she was discharged from the hospital, barely letting her out of his sight. He'd been perfectly content at her parents' and they had taken great care of him—although he did seem a little chubbier around his middle—but Eve thought he was probably worried she might desert him again.

She and Buster weren't properly home yet; Eve had been staying with her parents since she left the hospital. She shouldn't rush to do too much yet, they said, but she felt almost back to normal now and was desperate to get back to her own home. And return to work as soon as she could.

'One step at a time, Eve,' her mother said frequently. 'Don't run before you can walk.' That idiom had applied quite literally in the early days of Eve's recovery, and although Mary still trotted it out now that Eve was mobile again, she didn't mind. She knew it was all part of the love and care that her parents wanted to lavish on her.

That summer had been indescribably hard for all of them.

The first time she opened her eyes, Eve barely recognised the two elderly people who stood by her bed, each clutching one of her hands as though their lives depended on it. She was shocked to see how stooped her mother had become and how sallow her father's skin. Had she not noticed age catching up with them before the accident, or was this what her spell in hospital had done to them?

'Oh, Eve,' her mother said. 'Hello, my darling girl.' It was all she was able to say before collapsing into sobs of relief.

'Don't try and speak yet, love,' said Douglas, his own voice cracking as he patted Eve's hand.

Eve thought she had said in reply, 'Don't worry, Dad, I won't.' But it had come out as a series of grunts. Weeks of being intubated had played havoc on her throat, and even now she thought her voice sounded different.

More raspy, but more mature, somehow.

She knew that if she let it, today would be a day just like the other thirty or so since her release from hospital, but she was ready for a change. She scooped up Buster and the pair of them climbed out of bed. Eve slid her feet straight into the fluffy slippers her mother had left on the floor. She padded down the stairs, now no longer needing the banister for support.

'Be careful, Eve,' called her mother from the kitchen. 'Don't kill yourself on the stairs for that cat.'

'He's not just *that cat*, mother,' said Eve. 'I know you love him just as much as I do.'

'Oh, we do,' said Mary, tickling Buster under the chin as Eve set him down for his breakfast. Mary had chopped up some cold chicken for him, which he set upon eagerly.

'See,' said Eve. 'Spoiled rotten. He won't be getting that kind of treatment when we move back home. Speaking of which . . .'

Eve decided the previous evening that today would be the day she would raise the subject of moving home. They would protest, she knew, but she was almost back to her pre-accident fitness, and mentally she needed to move on. Her parents had been wonderful, and quite literally nursed her back to health once she was declared strong enough to leave the hospital, a full two weeks after waking up. She soon discovered that what the medical staff deemed strong enough wasn't actually very strong at all. Lying in a hospital bed for months on end did a lot to the human body, and none of it was good.

To begin with, Eve was so weak she could barely get up and down the stairs unaided. Several times a week she had to return to the hospital for physiotherapy, resenting the wheelchair her father always fetched to transport her from the car to the outpatients' department.

'I'm not disabled, Dad,' she'd moan. 'I don't need it.'

After the first week of treatment, she refused to use the chair any longer, determined to drag herself inside with the crutches the hospital had loaned her. She was always exhausted by the time she reached the ward.

By the end of the second week, she could pull herself along the parallel bars, supporting most of her weight on her legs.

'Will I ever run again?' she asked the physiotherapist.

'You will,' said the physio. 'You just need to learn to walk again first. And look at the progress you've made so far. You'll be walking out of here on just your dad's arm by the end of next week, I reckon.'

Douglas' face lit up at that comment, but Eve's was still steely.

'My legs weren't injured, so why are they taking so long to get back to normal?' Eve asked Miss Thompson—or Lucy, as Eve had come to know her—at her next check-up.

'Your legs weren't, but your brain was,' Lucy explained to her. 'Even though you've suffered no lasting detectable brain damage, some things are going to come harder to begin with. Walking is often one of those things. That, plus the months of lying there doing nothing, can result in a loss of muscle power. But you're young and you were fit before this, so you'll get back to your normal self, I'm quite sure of it.'

Eve had astonished the medical staff when, at the end of the fourth week of treatment, she insisted on going back to her gym and doing some gentle exercise—walking on the treadmill and lifting some light weights. 'I'm going to crack this,' she told the physio with a smile a week later.

'I think you pretty much have, Eve,' said the physio. 'One more week, then I think we'll be able to discharge you.'

Now she knew it wouldn't be long before she was running again, and with that renewed dose of energy came the feeling that she wanted to get back to work. *Needed* to get back to work. Her mother considered it way too soon, but Eve knew that once her body was fully mended, her mind would need something to occupy it.

'I know what you're going to say, love,' said Mary

now, sitting down at the kitchen table. 'I know you're ready to go, although I do wish you'd let us look after you a little longer. Maybe just until Christmas? Especially now you're on your own.'

'Thanks for the reminder, Mum,' said Eve. 'But I've told you, I'm over him. I really am. And besides, Christmas is still a few weeks off yet. There's so much I want to do before then.'

Once Eve had woken up, her parents knew she would start asking questions about Nathan's absence. They broke the news to her as gently as they could, trying not to cloud it with their own judgement of him, but Eve could still hear the implicit *he wasn't good enough for you* in her mother's tone of voice.

'We're so sorry,' Douglas said. Eve had turned her head away so that they couldn't see the tears pouring down her face. Learning she had been dumped in the early days of her coma had come as a huge shock, which quickly turned to anger.

'We thought you'd heard us when you were still unconscious,' Mary said a few days later, once Eve had time to digest the news. 'We made the mistake of talking about the break-up while we were standing by your bed, and tears began to roll down your face. We felt dreadful. I mean, what a way to learn that your boyfriend has done something so awful.'

'I don't remember that,' said Eve. 'Don't remember it at all. It must just have been a coincidence, I suppose.'

'Anyway,' said Mary. 'Anyone who abandons their loved one in an hour of need is ill-suited for that role.' She folded her arms firmly over her chest and harrumphed.

Despite the ignominious way she had been dumped, Eve surprised herself to find that, over the coming week or so, while still in hospital—though no longer in ICU—she began to draw the same conclusions. She waited for a gaping great hole in her heart to open up but it didn't, and the heartbreak was soon overshadowed by the sheer joy of being awake and alive with no major, life-changing injuries.

There was no benefit in staying angry with Nathan because the loss of him was miniscule compared to what she had gained—her *life*.

'So, when were you thinking of going?' asked Mary.

'This weekend, I think,' said Eve.

'You want to get back to your life,' said Mary, 'and that's understandable. Just don't rush it on the work front, though, will you? Don't do too much too soon.'

'I won't, Mum. Anyway, the physio's finished now. I haven't got any more appointments, so that frees me up a lot.'

It amused Eve how she had become a source of fascination to many people, from friends and family to colleagues. Everyone wanted to know what being in a coma was like. An ambitious young journalist from the local newspaper had even wanted to do an article on Eve, though she'd declined. And that was because to Eve, being in a coma was like nothing at all.

She couldn't remember anything between her accident and waking up with a bunch of doctors and nurses smiling down at her, as though she had done something incredible.

'Could you hear us talking to you at all?' her parents asked her on many occasions, almost as though her initial negative answer might change as time progressed and she remembered more. 'Could you feel pain? Were you frustrated? Did you feel trapped in your body?' She wasn't frustrated and she didn't feel trapped. She didn't feel anything. But she understood what drove their questions; they would have liked to believe that their constant visits and the hours spent at her bedside had counted for something.

But for Eve, they honestly hadn't.

'Sorry, no, I didn't,' she said every time. It sounded harsh, but while she was in the coma, she simply wasn't there. She wasn't listening. She couldn't hear them. It was a shame for them, but that was how it was. Being in a coma was simply a state of nothingness, almost as though someone had switched off her brain the entire time; in fact, she was quite shocked to learn that she had been absent for so long. It could have been a day, or a month, or a year. It would all have felt the same.

'As long as you're sure,' her mother said now. 'It's been a long recovery. But you do look a lot better, really you do.'

'I'm glad you can see that, Mum,' said Eve. 'I've been very lucky. And lucky to have you two to look after me, as well. Thank you so much. I love you both very much.'

Mary pulled her daughter into a hug, and Eve heard the slosh of tears on her shoulder. She really did feel lucky. Things could just as easily have gone the other way—Lucy had told her at a recent check-up that there had been no guarantee she would ever wake up, as she'd been in a coma for so long and her body seemed to have settled into some kind of plateau state. Not one of the doctors could explain why she had chosen that particular day to come back to them.

'There was no obvious medical reason for it,' Lucy said. 'But luckily for us, you did come back.'

'And I'll be thankful for that every day for the rest of my life,' said Eve.

She knew she genuinely would be.

52

Six Weeks After Waking Up

Eve sat in her classroom, loosely supervising her A-Level students as they buzzed about the studio. It was her first full week back at school and she felt truly blessed to be there. She rested her chin on her hands and smiled.

'It's so good to have you back, Eve,' Cali said that morning, as Eve fetched them both a coffee from the machine in the staffroom. 'No one's missed you more than I have.'

'But you only saw me on Saturday,' Eve joked, tucking her feet up under her on the sofa.

'You know what I mean,' said Cali. 'I missed this. Us. Here. Being partners in crime.'

'Yeah, it's good to be back. Back to normal. Well, not quite normal, but as normal as I'll ever be.'

'There is something different about you, though,' said Cali. 'Am I allowed to say that?'

'I suppose you mean this gammy leg of mine, which still doesn't want to work properly, despite all the effort I've made?'

Eve tried hard to mask the slight limp she had been left with, more self-conscious about it than she needed to be. Her head had taken the brunt of the impact and no bones had been broken, so she couldn't understand why she had this bizarre new gait, especially after all the physiotherapy. She was as strong as she'd ever been, and probably fitter than before; she just couldn't walk the same way she used to. It hadn't stopped her getting back into her running though, and she loved the fact that when she ran, her limp vanished.

'No, not that, you daft thing. It's hardly a limp at all, anyway. I don't know what you're so worried about. No, it's just that you're always so happy, so positive. You never really were a morning person before, were you, and now . . .'

'I'm just too happy? I can't help it, sorry,' said Eve. 'Are you saying I was grumpy before, then?'

'No, I'm not. But you know what I mean. There's a new purpose to you, and it's wonderful to see. It's like you've discovered a new joy in life, and given all that you've gone through, I think that's fantastic.'

'That is exactly how I feel. I know I was out of it for most of the time and didn't understand what I'd been through until everyone told me about it afterwards, but I feel so lucky to have been given a second chance. I'm going to live this new life to the fullest. Every day, even the crap ones. I'll try not to be too annoying about it, though.'

'You are funny. And an inspiration to us all, you really are,' said Cali.

Other than the limp and a barely noticeable scar on her left cheek, there was another side-effect Eve hadn't told anyone about. It was the strange feeling she had sometimes of not quite being properly inside her body. It had happened a handful of times now, including one afternoon in school the previous week.

She'd been sitting at her desk, talking to one of her pupils, when she felt as though she was hovering over herself and the child, looking down on them from on high. It only lasted a few seconds and then she was back on the ground, but it was the strangest feeling, and so hard to explain. She was able to watch the scene as well as be in it, almost as though there were two parts to her, one inside her body and the other on the outside.

Even though it was odd, she felt she didn't need to be unduly concerned about it, although she would mention it to Lucy at her next check-up, if it persisted.

Will came past her desk now, clutching a piece of work he had just finished.

'How's it going, Will?' Eve asked, smiling up at him. She had been thrilled to learn that he'd decided to take art through to A Level. He was a talented boy, and there was something quite admirable about how he'd handled himself through all the hard times with his brother's illness. Eve could swear he had grown a few more inches, but thought it probably had something to do with the weight of the world being lifted from his young shoulders.

'Good, thanks,' said Will. 'We're all really glad you're back, by the way.'

'It's very kind of you to say so,' said Eve. 'I'm glad to be here. And how's George? I hear he came back to school last week, too. That's fantastic news.'

'Yeah, it's great having him back to his old, annoying self,' said Will. He rolled his eyes, but Eve could see the love in them. 'It's gonna be a good Christmas, I reckon.'

'So, what are you doing for Christmas?' Eve asked. She'd already heard a rumour in the staffroom, but wanted Will to tell her about it, too.

'Well, all the usual stuff, but then on Christmas Eve we're going back to the hospital where George was. He's giving a little guitar concert to the kids who don't get to go home for Christmas. He started teaching himself after the transplant, when he had all that recovery time at home, and he's pretty good now.'

'Oh, that's a lovely idea. How kind of him.'

Will hesitated before continuing. 'He thinks he got his new kidney from this guy we knew who played the guitar, you see.'

'Oh, really?' said Eve. 'That's interesting.'

'Yeah, Mum says we'll never know who the donor was, that you're not allowed to know because of their family and stuff. But he's convinced it's this guy, Jimmy. He died on the same day George had his transplant, in the same hospital, and it was so weird, because we were meant to have gone to see him play that afternoon. That's where we were going when George got sick. The whole thing is totally freaky, but George likes to think he has a part of Jimmy inside him. That's what made him want to learn the guitar.'

A shiver ran down Eve's spine, and she wrapped her jacket tighter.

'Well, I've always been a great believer in fate, and in things happening for a reason. And whatever happened, whoever's kidney he has, it's brilliant news that he's better now. And how lovely that he wants to do this concert for the children. I think you're all going to have a wonderful Christmas.'

'The best ever,' said Will, picking up his work and heading for the drying rack.

The door to the corridor swung closed as Will walked past; Eve rose, ready to prop it open again.

'It's all right, Miss, I'll do it,' said Will.

Sometimes Eve couldn't bear to be behind too many

closed doors, even though she'd never suffered from claustrophobia before the accident. It was different with the front door to her home—that was her security—but when she was away from home, she liked open space around her as much as possible.

There had been other door-related incidents, too. The previous weekend she had gone on a Christmas shopping trip with her mother to a huge complex on the edge of town. They parked in the outdoor car park and headed towards the centre, but Eve had frozen in front of the sliding doors, unable to go forward.

'Wait, Mum,' she said. 'Just give me a minute.'

'What's up?' said her mother.

'I don't think I can go in there. It's those doors.'

Her mother laughed, then became concerned when she realised her daughter was serious.

'Come on, hold my hand,' said Mary. 'Close your eyes if it makes it easier.'

'Are we through yet?' Eve asked.

'Yes,' said Mary. 'You can open your eyes, now. What was that all about, Eve?'

'I don't know, really,' said Eve.

She couldn't explain the irrational fear she had of the doors not opening properly, and of her becoming stuck between them, trapped like a butterfly on a pin. She could only assume it was a side-effect of her injuries.

When they stopped for a coffee an hour later, Mary raised the subject again.

'Well, if that's the only scar that accident left you with, life can't be too bad,' said Mary. 'I'm sure you'll get over it.'

Eve wasn't so convinced.

The December sky was darkening as the students began to pack away their work. Eve couldn't wait to be home, snug in her little house with the curtains drawn and the fire lit. Buster would be waiting for her on the doorstep as he always was, winding himself around her legs, almost tripping her up with affection.

By the time she pushed open her squeaky gate and walked up the garden path, it had begun to rain hard. Instead of hurrying indoors as she would have done in the old days, Eve paused on the doorstep, looking up at the sky and letting the rain soak her hair and lick her cheeks.

She could almost feel the neighbours' eyes on her, peering out from behind their curtains, wondering if the accident had addled her brain. But she loved being outside in the elements these days, more so than ever before. People spent far too much time rushing around, taking for granted the wonders of nature all around them, even in the middle of busy London. When she saw people walking through the rain with their heads bent, looking down at the pavement, she wanted to tell them to look up at the sky instead. Look up and see what the rain was doing to the trees, how they were revelling in the water, drinking it up.

The forecast called for a bitterly cold Christmas, and Eve really hoped they would have some snow—that would make everything just perfect. She couldn't wait to lie down in it and make a snow angel, like she used to as a small child, flapping her arms and legs to form the heavenly shapes in the virgin whiteness.

Buster's mewing brought her back to the moment, obviously wanting to get into the warm and dry. She scooped him into her arms and tucked him inside her coat. All the poor creature wanted to do was go indoors and have his tea, but she resisted for as long as she could, until he started to wriggle, and she suspected his claws might do some damage.

'You're not enjoying this amazing weather like Mummy is, are you?' she said, as they finally headed inside. 'I've got you some chicken tonight. Just don't tell Granny I'm spoiling you.'

53

The following evening, it was pitch black by the time Eve left school, though she didn't mind.

Christmas lights glittered on every building, their colours dancing in the puddles. The rain had stopped, but everywhere glistened with moisture. As Eve walked through the park towards the hospital, she found the smell intoxicating, the heady mix of damp grass and foliage transporting her to the countryside.

Eve negotiated the sliding doors at the hospital entrance with no trouble, headed upstairs to the familiar waiting room, and sat down in one of the many identical plastic chairs bolted to the floor in rows. She'd requested a late appointment so that she could come after school; there were only four other people in the waiting room and the whiteboard read that there were two consultants on duty.

When Lucy called her through, Eve looked up and caught the eye of a man sitting in the opposite row of chairs.

He smiled at her and, slightly taken aback, she smiled in return.

She noticed how blue his eyes were.

'You're doing very well indeed, Eve,' Lucy pronounced. 'We can reduce you to a yearly MRI and check-up now. But please do get in touch if you're ever worried about anything.'

Eve hadn't been able to bring herself to tell Lucy about the strange out-of-body sensations she had experienced. A quick search online led her to believe it was the territory of eccentrics and not a medical condition, and certainly not something she should raise with her surgeon. It would probably pass in time, anyway, as she recovered further.

Desperate for a sugar hit after her appointment, Eve headed to the newsagents' shop in the foyer and grabbed a chocolate bar and a drink from the shelves. As she queued to pay, someone touched her on the shoulder.

A strange tingle shot through her arm, and she turned round.

'Hello,' said the man behind her. The same man who had smiled at her in the waiting room.

'Hi,' she said, not wishing to appear rude. On closer inspection, Eve was sure she knew him from somewhere—other than the waiting room—but couldn't think who he was or where she had seen him before. His face bore a similar expression of bewilderment as hers. Their eyes remained locked and there was an uncomfortable pause when neither knew quite why they were looking so intently at the other. Finally, the cashier called to Eve that it was her turn, and the spell was broken.

Once she had paid, Eve dawdled from the shop, hoping the stranger might catch her up. When he did, he said, 'I'm really sorry, and this sounds like a terrible chat-up line, but I'm sure I know you. At least, I think we've met before.'

'I think we might have,' she agreed, cheeks turning pink. His piercing blue eyes were mesmerising, and she loved the way they crinkled at the corners as he spoke.

'Listen,' the man said. He put his hand gently on her arm, and there was that tingle again. Like pins and needles, only lighter and more fleeting. 'This might be a bit presumptuous, but are you in a hurry? I'd really like to buy you a coffee. Not here, though. I'm sure both of us have spent far too much time in this place.'

It suddenly seemed the most important thing in the world that she say yes to this total stranger, who for some reason wasn't a stranger at all.

'Yes, no, I mean, yes,' stuttered Eve, and they both laughed. 'Well, that came out wrong, didn't it? Yes, I'd love to have coffee with you, thank you.'

'Come on then, let's go. I know a good little place just along the South Bank,' he said. 'It should still be open.'

They didn't speak much as they headed down the steps of the hospital and along Lambeth Palace Road. Eve glanced sideways at the handsome stranger, surprised to feel something happening to her insides that she hadn't felt in a long time.

Riverside Café read the sign over the door. They both reached for the handle at the same time. 'Sorry,' said Eve.

'Allow me,' said the man, opening the door wide and leading her into a warm and cosy interior, with wonderful views of the wintry Thames, lights shimmering on the black surface.

The café was empty apart from a woman in biker's leathers, with a mane of long, dark hair. She finished her drink and returned her empty cup to the counter. 'Bye, Antonio,' she called to the owner.

'Careful on that bike, Nadia. The roads are wet,' he called back.

Eve and the man stood at the counter, eyeing the pasties and sausage rolls behind the glass. Eve still had a lot of weight to put back on—although that probably wouldn't be an issue once she spent the festive season back at her parents' house—but she didn't think the butterflies in her stomach would allow her to eat anything at the moment.

The stranger unwrapped a striped scarf from his neck and freed his blond hair to hang just over the collar of his smart woollen coat. Eve couldn't help wondering how it would feel to run her fingers through that hair. She cleared her throat, feeling suddenly self-conscious.

'Why don't you go and grab a seat over there,' he said, pointing to a cosy booth on the far side of the room. 'I'll order. Skinny latte with an extra shot for you, isn't it?'

'Er, yes. But how . . .' Eve trailed off, amazed he had guessed her regular coffee order. The man looked just as surprised as she was, his eyes quizzical and brow furrowed in confusion.

Eve stared at his back as he ordered, taking in the broad shoulders and that blond hair, so fair and fine. She noticed that his left arm remained by his side most of the time—maybe he had suffered an injury to it and that was his reason for being at the hospital.

He must have said something amusing to the sad-eyed barista as he ordered. Eve saw her eyes dart upwards and she flicked a long ponytail over one shoulder.

'Jules is going to bring them over,' he said, sliding along the leather banquette opposite Eve. 'Special treatment. I'm a bit of a regular here.'

There was an awkward silence before he spoke again.

'So, here we are, having coffee together for the first time, and I don't even know your name.'

'I'm Eve. Eve Chapman. Pleased to make your acquaintance.'

He put out a hand and reached to shake Eve's over the table. They both smiled at the formality as another tingle shot up Eve's arm. From the look in his eyes, Eve suspected the feeling was mutual.

'I'm Luca. Luca Diaz. Delighted to meet you, too, Eve.'

Acknowledgements

This novel takes places largely in the Intensive Care Unit of a fictional version of St Thomas' hospital in Lambeth, South London. I have tweaked the layout and geography of the area very slightly, in order to give Eve and Luca some glass doors in which to catch sight of their wings which, I hope you will agree, is necessary artistic licence and crucial to the plot! Apologies to any London purists, to whom this does not quite read as the Lambeth that they know and love.

I am full of admiration for anyone who works for our incredible NHS and I know that, after the two years we have just lived through, I am far from alone in this sentiment. I live next door to two NHS workers, one of whom, Richard Lovegrove MD FRCS, was instrumental in helping me 'keep things real' in terms of hospital procedure, vocabulary, and how medics speak to one another. Thank you, Richard—anything I still have wrong is of my own doing.

During the summer of 2019, while working on an early draft of this book, my mother was taken into the ICU of another hospital, where sadly she passed away a few days later. Many of the minor details I added into the book afterwards, I'm sad to say, are from first-hand experience of seeing the amazing medical teams in action as we gathered by her bedside. They looked after her with such compassion, and we owe them huge thanks.

Thank you to the many friends I made on the CBC Edit and Pitch Your Novel course for their inspiration and advice—and continued friendship. Thank you also to Jericho Writers for their support and amazing events, both in person (back in the good old days pre-COVID) and online.

I really enjoyed reading *Do No Harm* by Henry Marsh, a real-life brain surgeon. Nothing too technical from his book ended up in mine, however it did inspire the scene with Ms Ormandie and Dr Shah and the 'right middle cerebral artery aneurysm.' I certainly learned a lot of new words in reading it, most of which I have since forgotten.

My friends are a continued source of support. Thank you Sarah Davies, Alli Neal, and Ginny Getting for reading early chunks of this book and offering encouragement. My family, too, are always behind me; thank you especially to Wadham for your constant faith and support, and to Jack, Harry, and Emilia for being the best kids ever.

And finally, thank you to Tom Corson-Knowles, Nicholas Holloway, and the rest of the team at TCK Publishing/Quilla Books for your unbridled enthusiasm for this book, and for taking it through to publication.

Thank you for reading and stay safe.

Sara x

ABOUT THE AUTHOR

Sara Downing is the author of the popular *Head Over Heels* contemporary romance series, plus a further romance, *Stage Fright*, and historical and supernatural novels, *Urban Venus* and *The Lost Boy*.

She began writing in 2009, after giving up a career as a Chartered Accountant to raise her family. She lives near Worcester, UK, with her husband, three almost grown-up children, a dog, and a cat. She has no plans to return to accountancy anytime soon.

Sara's other pastimes include reading, playing the piano, and drinking wine.

ALSO BY SARA DOWNING

Head Over Heels
Hand On Heart
A Head Over Heels Christmas
Stage Fright
Urban Venus
The Lost Boy
The White Angel

CONNECT WITH SARA DOWNING

Sign up for Sara's newsletter at
saradowningwriter.co.uk/newsletter

To find out more information visit her website:
www.saradowningwriter.co.uk

Social Media
@SaraDowningWriter
@sarawritesbooks

BOOK DISCOUNTS AND SPECIAL DEALS

Sign up for free to get discounts and special deals on our bestselling books at

www.TCKpublishing.com/bookdeals

Made in the USA
Columbia, SC
04 September 2022

66591997R00202